COBWEB

Margaret Duffy titles available from Severn House Large Print

Tainted Ground

COBWEB

Margaret Duffy

Severn House Large Print
London & New York

This first large print edition published 2008
in Great Britain and the USA by
SEVERN HOUSE PUBLISHERS of
9-15 High Street, Sutton, Surrey, SM1 1DF.
First world regular print edition published 2007 by
Severn House Publishers, London and New York.

British Library Cataloguing in Publication Data

Duffy, Margaret
  Cobweb. - Large print ed.
  1. Gillard, Patrick (Fictitious character) - Fiction
  2. Langley, Ingrid (Fictitious character) - Fiction
  3. Murder - Investigation - Fiction 4. Detective and
  mystery stories 5. Large type books
  I. Title
  823.9'14[F]

  ISBN-13: 978-0-7278-7711-6

Printed and bound in Great Britain by
MPG Books Ltd, Bodmin, Cornwall.

Epitaph

If DCI Derek Harmsworth could have known that, in a couple of months' time, he himself would be the subject of an exhumation order, he might have handled things a little differently. As it was, he let himself out of his home on that Sunday morning leaving his wife Vera – she of the baggy cardigans and slightly wobbly dentures – asleep in bed.

There had been a heavy dew and Harmsworth swore under his breath as the overgrown privet hedge that bordered the path unloaded what seemed to be a pint of water down the sleeve of his jacket as he brushed against it. Not for the first time he told himself that the hedge would have to be trimmed. Or grubbed out. That would sort the bloody thing, he thought balefully. Harmsworth hated gardening.

He did not mind working at weekends – hell, he'd done enough of it in his time – and was bearing firmly in mind that his retirement loomed ever closer. Not long now, just another four months. He was aware that as far as this date was concerned he was a bit like a sailing ship of old journeying towards the horizon, the crew having no idea what might happen when they actually arrived. He had made no plans, he never seemed to have the time or energy to sit down and think it through. A little bungalow in Seaford – Vera's ambition? It gave him the cold shivers even to contemplate that kind of full stop to his life.

No, no time. Just get in the car, drive to the nick and head the investigation into who, just over thirty-six hours previously, had jumped a Member of Parliament in an East End park, knifed him in amazing fashion and *then* cut his head off for good measure and tossed it into a nearby rubbish bin. Even Harmsworth, who thought he had seen everything and plumbed the depths of the criminal mind, had thrown up in the blood-spattered bushes.

With the occurrence of such a serious crime Harmsworth would have worked on a Sunday anyway but now had the prospect of Special Branch breathing down his neck. Either that or a specialist unit headed up by one Commander John Brinkley. So far, though, no designer macs had materialized, not even at the briefing that had been held the previous day. Harmsworth was not sure whether this reflected the fact that the murder victim had been a low-profile back-bencher or had more to do with under-manning. He rather thought that Monday morning would be crunch time and there would be a 'visitation', as the Super, Fred Knightly, had put it, and had absolutely no intention of being caught on the hop.

According to the pathologist, the deceased, Jason Giddings, had been drinking but could not have been described as drunk even though he would have been over the limit as far as driving was concerned. Seemingly, though, he had had no intention of driving, as his car had been left at home in the village of Beech Hanger on the edge of Epping Forest and the MP had gone to the city by taxi and train. Although having apparently been expected home fairly early that evening, as they were giving a dinner party, he had failed to appear and nothing had been heard of him until an off-duty policeman taking his dog for a walk – thank God children had not found the body, Harmsworth thought – had come across the remains.

Predictably, media interest had been enormous, the police station at Woodhill Old Street having been inundated as soon as the news had broken. Giddings's watch, wallet and credit cards had been missing but the wallet had been recovered from another litter bin several hundred yards away, minus the money but, unusually, still enclosing his credit cards and driving licence. So they had been able to put a name to the bloodbath almost immediately, which, Harmsworth supposed wearily, was something.

The Super, not a man to be an awful lot of

use for most of the time, did at least come in handy in a situation like this: he had a huge flair for dealing with press conferences and enjoyed being in the public eye, appearing, surreptitiously combing the last surviving strands of mousey hair across his balding pate, as soon as the cameras were rolled out. Harmsworth only had to make sure that he was properly briefed.

As Harmsworth arrived there were a few reporters and the like hanging about outside the nick, which was a muddled complex of concrete and glass box-shaped buildings in various shades of dirty grey. He dodged the media by driving down a narrow side street, bumped across a slightly raised area with large plant tubs that, strictly speaking, was for pedestrians only, squeezed his small Ford between two bollards at the entrance to another lane that descended gently to the rear of terraced houses, ghosted down it and emerged through a gap in a chain-link fence at the far corner of the nick's car park. Permitting himself a little smile of satisfaction, he parked and went in through one of the two rear entrances of the building.

There did not seem to be many people around, not even in the canteen, where he quickly drank a cup of coffee – it didn't do to savour the stuff – before making for his office. They were probably all out preparing to do house-to-house calls in the area surrounding the park with DI John Gray behind them cracking his whip. Younger than Harmsworth by at least fifteen years, he could be hot-headed and impulsive but got the job done.

The DCI met DS Erin Melrose on the staircase, which afforded him another small twinge of pleasure, as, unlike just about everyone else in the place, men and women, she was a delight to behold. This was not to say that he thought women ought to be mere objects of beauty, for although he was old-fashioned in some respects this was not one of them. In a drab, grey world Derek Harmsworth was always on the lookout for things that would gladden his heart, whether they were a sunset, birds in a park, sunlight shining through leaves – tiny moments that made up for some of the rest.

DS Melrose had only just been promoted and was John Gray's assistant. Gray had reservations about women in the job, in senior positions in particular, but even he had to admit that the girl worked hard and had a good head on her shoulders. She was also a vast improvement on his previous sergeant, a morose individual who had munched on an untidy moustache, probably the cause of his chronic indigestion. But Harmsworth, giving Erin a brief nod as they passed, was glad she did not work directly for him, as he would not have been able to tolerate literally looking up to her all day long – she was at least five feet ten inches tall in her silky black tights. And that mane of red hair made her stand out like a beacon. No hanging around trying to merge into the background watching local yobs with that one.

Harmsworth had interviewed Honor Giddings, the murder victim's wife – who, interestingly to him, was a forensic scientist by profession – the previous afternoon after giving her a few hours to recover from her appalling shock. He intended to talk to her again, and very soon, but first of all wanted to grill, at some length, her son by her first marriage, one Theodore du Norde, whom she had said was an interior designer. Mrs Giddings had been unable to conceal from Harmsworth that there had been tension between du Norde and his stepfather, especially since her husband had stopped paying an allowance to him. Reluctantly, and after he had persevered in questioning her along these lines, she had gone on to say that she had been worried about her son for some time on account of what she described, with a toss of her head, as 'his rubbish friends'. The DCI had pricked up his ears at this for, in his experience, rubbish all tended to end up in the same pile.

Harmsworth grumpily rummaged amongst the muddle on his desk for a pen that would write. It looked as though he would have to go and see Theodore du Norde, who had been in the north of England on business, on his own, DS Boles having gone home the previous day with a toothache. Boles, who at least could have driven the car, giving Harmsworth a chance to think, was not much more help than someone with toothache normally. Harmsworth could not but wonder if du Norde had had a hand in the killing and done a runner until things had died down a bit.

Collecting the new case file from where a note on his desk in John Gray's handwriting indicated that it had been left – down the corridor in Fred Knightly's virginally tidy office – Harmsworth went out, reviewing what he knew already. It was understandable that a large part of the widow's shock would have stemmed from the ghastly circumstances of her husband's death, not least because the park was a well-known meeting place for homosexuals. But she had been adamant that he had never had any inclinations in that direction and could think of no reason why he should have gone there. The post mortem had not revealed evidence of sexual activity of any kind, so Harmsworth was nudging his thoughts in the direction of a killer half-crazed with drink and drugs – a mugging that had turned into butchery. That was if du Norde was proved to be in the clear. But what the hell had Giddings been doing in the park?

Retracing his steps to his car – it was going to be another unseasonally roasting day

11

despite the overnight thundery rain and the vehicle was still hot from the day before – Harmsworth removed his jacket, opened all the windows and sat still for a couple of minutes, deep in thought. No, first of all, he would go and take another look at the scene of the crime. He had turned the key in the ignition when he spotted DS Boles driving into the car park. When he had locked up and was about to walk in the direction of the building Harmsworth tooted his horn and got out of the car.

There was no doubt about it: the man's pallid, normally round face was now like a one-sided balloon.

'I'm on painkillers and antibiotics, sir,' was his response to the question.

'They used to yank 'em out,' Harmsworth observed. 'Solves the problem straight away.'

Boles winced. 'It's actually a gold crown – they do sometimes play up after a while.' He dropped his gaze. 'I know I drove here but I'm not really supposed to while I'm on these pills, sir.'

Harmsworth sighed and got back behind the wheel.

The park was not a large one – more like a recreation ground, about fifteen acres in size – and had the usual grassy open spaces, tennis courts, a bowling green and also a Victorian fountain, defunct, its basin full of litter, at the end of a short avenue of rather

12

weary-looking lime trees. Near the bowling green, seemingly disused, the grass long, was a shrubbery with wide linking paths which curved between the planted areas, finally merging at a circular flower bed in the middle, from which most of the plants were missing. Police incident tape was still affixed to the metal railings that surrounded the planted areas, cordoning off one section.

Harmsworth pulled up to the rear of a police van parked on one of the paths and got out. 'This place still stinks of death,' he muttered, ducking under the tape, Boles following on.

It did, even after the rain, the tall laurels, hollies and viburnums preventing any breath of breeze cleansing the air. At some time during this day, when every search, test and examination had been completed, a team would be permitted to move in to eradicate all traces of violent crime. Harmsworth acknowledged with a brief wave the presence of a uniformed constable keeping an eye on things from the driving seat of the van, reckoning that quite a lot of soil would have to be removed as well as some of the smaller bushes.

'The initial PM findings weren't in before you left yesterday,' he reminded Boles briskly. 'And if we're not talking about a psycho who's been let out and hasn't taken his pills, then it's a maniac who should be inside and has taken far too many. Judson, the pathologist, couldn't pinpoint which of the twenty or so stab wounds had been the cause of death but finally narrowed it down to five. He could not say whether he had been disembowelled before or after death. As you know, the guts were trailing from the body but that could mean that either Giddings was still alive and moved, or the body was shifted after he was dead. Or, of course, the killer pulled the innards out himself. Judson's fairly convinced the head was cut off after Giddings was dead and that wasn't the actual cause of death.'

Boles nodded unhappily.

'Before all that happened to him,' Harmsworth continued, 'Giddings was fairly healthy for a man of forty-five, but there were early signs of cirrhosis of the liver so we can assume he had a history of drinking too much. Goes with the job for some, perhaps. What we've got to find out is why he came here instead of going home for the dinner party.'

They had reached their destination, a little dell with mangled vegetation and stained beaten earth. Above was a small tree of some kind. All was now protected from the elements by a special awning – a tent had been impractical in the circumstances. Although the forensic team had removed as much of the aftermath of violent murder as possible, even shovelling up bagsful of blood-soaked earth for testing, body fluids that had not escaped into the ground had dried to a dull brown colour. There were clouds of flies.

Harmsworth was trying to banish from his memory the way the victim's intestines had been draped over some low branches. 'Any problems?' he asked the constable, who had left the van and followed them.

'No, sir.'

'Have SOCO finished?'

'They were here early, sir. They've been gone about twenty minutes.'

'They found nothing else interesting, I suppose?' the DCI asked hopefully.

'Nothing they told me about, sir.'

Harmsworth grinned. 'Never mind, lad. You ought to know by now that Scenes of Crime officers were oysters in their previous lives.'

The man did not smile.

'It's vital that we trace Giddings's movements on Friday,' Harmsworth said to Boles as they walked away a few minutes later. He wanted to discover, if possible, what course the murder victim might have taken on this last part of his journey to a meeting with death. Also, as was the DCI's habit, he needed to get the feel of the place.

They negotiated the tape and walked across the park heading east. 'We've discovered that he was at the House of Commons in the morning and was seen on the terrace having coffee and a doughnut at around ten fifteen,' Harmsworth went on. 'He'd left his car at home and used public transport, which apparently wasn't unusual. The PM revealed that he ate scampi and chips at around five hours before death, so was that a late lunch or an early tea?'

'People like that usually have something like sandwiches and cake for tea,' Boles pointed out in his somewhat lugubrious fashion.

Harmsworth, originally from Birmingham, had never got used to southern habits. 'But he'd got a long time to go, hadn't he?– before he could have a decent bite to eat, I mean. There was a dinner party planned and likely as not he'd have had to wait until around eight thirty or nine that night. Well, I know that Vera and I don't have folk around very often, but she'd kill me if I forgot all about it. What was Giddings up to? There wasn't much alcohol in his blood, so he didn't get half plastered and it slipped his mind. Had he and his wife had a row and he was paying her back by not turning up? She's insisting he wasn't homosexual, so what the hell was he doing coming *here*?'

'Would she admit it if he had been?' Boles offered.

Harmsworth grunted, hearing church bells over the sound of traffic. He was not a religious man, but the contrast between that and what they had just seen and been talking about made the crime appear even more obscene.

Theodore du Norde remained elusive and over the next couple of days, with extensive house-to-house enquiries ongoing, Harmsworth concentrated on trying to trace Jason Giddings's final movements. Then, on the Tuesday of that week DS Erin Melrose tracked down the taxi driver who had picked up the MP at the nearest tube station. He had dropped Giddings off at a pub, the Green Man, which was about five minutes walk from the park, at around five forty-five. Giddings had been alone, his demeanour 'normal'; he had not appeared to be in any kind of stressed state nor in his manner hinted at any concerns.

In the very early hours of the following Wednesday morning a car went through temporary barriers on a road bridge over the M25 near Woodhill, crashing on to the motorway beneath. It was the site of a similar accident two days previously involving an articulated lorry, when several people had been killed in the resulting pile-up. This time, probably owing to the time of night, no other vehicles were passing beneath at the time, though several drivers had to take avoiding action. The emergency services were at the scene almost immediately.

DCI Harmsworth had died instantly.

One

I wrote that brief reconstruction of the last
few days of Derek Harmsworth's life quite a
while afterwards from several sources:
personal experience, accounts given to me
by colleagues, his wife and from things he
had jotted down in his own notebook and in
the case file. I also used my imagination, for
I am a writer by trade. I use my maiden
name – Ingrid Langley – but normally stick
to fiction, and this was anything but that.
Neither I nor Patrick, my husband, would
have been involved at all but for other occur-
rences in connection with the Jason Giddings murder inquiry.

Patrick had resigned his army commission
some months previously then been 'volunteered' for a pilot scheme allowing one-time
officers in the services and similar professionals to join the police at fairly senior level.
During a probationary period he had tackled
the assignment he had been given with his
usual aplomb, meaning that he broke most
of the rules, and those in charge had become
exceedingly nervous. But he had finally been
offered a job, as an investigator in a section

that was, to quote Commander John Brinkley, 'a sort of a branch of a branch'. Patrick, late of D12, a fairly high-flown department in MI5, had surmised that this was the equivalent of a twig, had taken a dislike to Brinkley and co.'s somewhat devious methods – they had deliberately been obstructive to see how he would react, thereby risking the outcome of the case – and none too politely declined.

Matters had not stopped there, however, and shortly afterwards a letter had arrived from the Home Office asking if Lieutenant-Colonel Patrick Gillard would consider being an 'independent advisor' for the newly formed Serious and Organized Crime Agency on a contract basis. His pay grade would be that of superintendent even though all SOCA personnel working directly with the police are nominally constables. If his wife wished – I had been his working partner in the MI5 days – she could act as a 'consultant'. Not surprisingly, Patrick had written straight back asking for more information.

The reply was not exactly enlightening, emphasizing that Patrick's MI5 experience was what was needed and quoting a statement by the PM when he had said 'We will have to do things differently' owing to the level of brutality used by organized crime and 'The law has been too weak in recent times and the criminal too strong.'

'But there still have to be official ground rules,' Patrick commented, rereading the letter. He grimaced. 'Shall I go for it? Four young mouths to feed and all that.'

We have two children of our own, Justin and Victoria, and adopted Patrick's brother Larry's two, Matthew and Katie, when he was killed a couple of years ago.

I said, 'It mustn't be just thought of from that point of view. What do *you* want to do?' What did he now want from life? come to think of it; but perhaps this was not the right time for an in-depth discussion on the subject.

'I'm not sure really. It sounds interesting though. And I can't just stay at home and be your toy boy' – this with a mad grin; he's three years older than me.

'Go and ask George,' I suggested. George is Patrick's horse.

So Patrick went for a ride on George up on Dartmoor and when he returned wrote to accept the job, provided what he referred to as 'certain conditions' were met. The distaff side of the family, having done some thinking of her own, agreed to assist as well. Surely, I thought, two heads were always better than one. The letter posted, we were not to know that within a couple of weeks we would receive a phone call and be on the job.

We were not called in because DCI Derek Harmsworth's mutilated body had high levels of alcohol in it, nor even because his colleague DI John Gray was adamant that Harmsworth hardly ever drank when working on a case, and at other times only in moderation. Nor was it because Gray was making rather a nuisance of himself, raging at anyone who would listen to him that what had happened to Harmsworth was not an accident and there ought to be another PM. Then, somehow, the local press got to hear of his misgivings, which were duly plastered all over the front pages and the DI was carpeted.

No, we were called in because Gray was then murdered, at home, knifed in similar fashion to Jason Giddings.

There was no question, however, of loss of nerve among Harmsworth's colleagues even though we found out later that the DCI's sergeant, Paul Boles, had gone on long-term sick leave having suffered some kind of 'breakdown'. I had an idea that an outsider's presence would be resented, even a rookie member of SOCA, and Patrick would have a difficult job on his hands. First, though, he would have to be fully briefed by SOCA officers on the workings of the new organization and, on the morning following the phone call, duly caught the train to London.

I did not hear anything from him for a couple of days and reasoned that there was no need to bother him. Then, very early on the third morning, the phone rang.

'I'm starting work for real in an hour or so,' he began. 'It would appear that someone put a word in for me, saying I was indispensable – heaven knows who – plus what another bod described as "your ability to get the opposition shit-scared". Someone's insisting I use my old army rank and I shall be permitted to carry a weapon on assignments if I think it necessary.'

'But you're not under the same kind of *carte blanche* status as in the old days surely.' I was hoping that this did not mean he was going to be given the most dangerous jobs.

'No, but no one's actually saying a lot with regard to that.'

'Patrick, I really feel you ought to establish exactly what's what before you begin this,' I argued.

He chuckled. 'I've always enjoyed surprises. Do you still want in?'

I thought his reply typical of a man and highly unsatisfactory, but said, 'Having agreed to do so, have I a choice?'

'Yes, you do. I insisted that the family and your writing come first. You can just be on the end of a phone and ready to help me with ideas if you want to.'

Perhaps I was getting more cautious as I got older. 'What would you want me to do right now *should* I decide to saddle up?' I enquired.

'Undertake, or rather pretend, to research for a new novel set in Essex. Snoop a little on the Giddings widow and see what you can find out about her and the family. I'll fix you up with the address, which is in the poshest part of posh Woodhill. You could hang around in the locality where Giddings was murdered – that's in fairly neck-end Wood-hill – and get the feel of the place.'

'Where will you be?'

'I don't know yet so I can't tell you. I'd prefer it not to be known at the nick that you're with me – not yet anyway. If you see me we don't know one another unless I give you a kiss. Look, I must go. Give my love to the gang.'

'I really could do with more information before I do anything.'

'I know. I'll meet up with you somehow, or give you a ring. Keep your mobile switched on.'

He rang off before I could say any more.

'Expenses?' I said out loud. 'Train tickets? Conditions of employment? Or am I just on Patrick's expense account under sundries like petrol, dry cleaning and stationery?'

I did a swift mental recce around my writing plans. I had just completed reworking the screenplay for a novel I had written some years previously, *A Man Called Celeste*, and sent it off to the States. I actually had no concrete ideas for what I was going to do next, other than that it would be a crime novel set in Devon with echoes of Holmes, Dartmoor and all things dark, wild and bog-ridden. But, hey, Woodhill was probably a wild sort of place in its own way and wasn't there a thundering great forest right on the doorstep?

A few minutes later the phone rang again.

'I've just had a call on my mobile from our Richard,' Patrick said, as though there had been no break in our conversation.

Colonel Richard Daws had been our boss in MI5 days. 'He's found out about your new venture?' I hazarded.

'It's better than that. He's one of those with his hands on the reins at SOCA – on the intelligence side of things. It was he who wanted me in. I should have guessed he'd be involved in a set-up like this.'

'I thought he'd retired.'

'I expect growing roses and writing letters to *The Times* gets tedious after a while. And, as you know, SOCA did recruit a lot of senior service people due for retirement to get the structure right.'

I also knew that this new agency was essentially an amalgamation of four others: the National Crime Squad, the National Criminal Intelligence Service and the investigations divisions of HM Customs and the Immigration Service.

'So you'll be working for Daws?'

'Indirectly and as long, as he put it, "as everything works out satisfactorily". Presumably that means as long as I still have balls in the right places. It was he who insisted I call myself Lieutenant-Colonel – as he put it, "or some jack-in-office might treat you like one of the cleaners".'

'We didn't arrange a place where we could bump into one another.'

'There's a pub near the park where Giddings was murdered called the Green Man. I'll be in there between eight and nine for the next few evenings.'

'I probably won't be there tomorrow.'

'OK.'

'How d'you want me to be?'

'Yourself, for the present.'

Good. I did not want to be bothered with assuming a disguise if I was to undertake research, genuinely or not, for a new novel. This was not to say that I would necessarily have to refrain from using a change of appearance at all, as Patrick had intimated. It is amazing the transformation a temporary colour-rinse and change of hairstyle, different make-up and weird and wonderful clothes can make, the latter often freely available in charity shops. With this in mind I planned to travel light.

When, after a pause, the door of my friend Maggie's flat opened and the most beautiful man I had ever clapped eyes on in my life gazed at me sleepily, I thought I had come to the wrong address.

'You're Ingrid,' he said with a smile that turned my knees to jelly.

I prayed that I had gawped neither at him nor at his deep-violet-coloured pyjamas.

'Maggie told me you were coming,' he went on, opening the door wide. 'She's out right now, seeing a client, but told me to wait on you hand and foot until she comes back. I'm Julian, by the way, the lodger.'

I endeavoured to slay any suspicion of another arrangement he and my old friend might have, telling myself sternly that Maggie was in her early fifties. Sadly, I failed. Unless this gorgeous mortal before me was gay.

As I already knew, her homes always reflected Maggie's chosen career – that of interior designer – although I was also aware that she never invited her clients to where she lived, at least not since she had had a bad experience with a slightly dodgy character who had tried to steal a small but valuable item when her back was turned.

I went in. My friend had only lived in this particular apartment for a few months and had certainly had the place redecorated: the smell of paint still lingered. I do not have time to pore over home and garden magazines, but here, surely, were the latest trends imbued with her personal taste. In the living room were the 'signature' silk-covered and hand-embroidered cushions and lamp-shades as well as the woven wall hangings and antique furniture that I recognized, remembering that she had inherited them

26

from an aunt.

Julian had taken my travel bag from me without my noticing and was bearing it away, presumably in the direction of the spare bedroom. 'Tea? Coffee?' he asked over his shoulder. 'Or are you one of those writers who like whisky at any time of day?' – this with the kind of grin that told me two things; well, one really: he wasn't gay and was flirting with me for his own amusement.

'Coffee, please,' I answered, adding, 'I hope I didn't get you out of bed.'

'You did, but I'm glad. I hadn't meant to sleep in. Rehearsals at noon.'

'You're involved with the theatre?'

'Dance. I'm with the Royal Ballet.'

Maggie had been saying for a while, during our periodic telephone conversations, that I must come and stay with her and see the new flat. She lived quite a way from what was to be my zone of operations, in West Hampstead, but I did not intend to inflict myself on her for very long nor return to her home every night, and would be out for most of the day.

'I understand you're in London to research a book,' Julian said over coffee. He had changed, ready to go out, into black jeans and black roll-neck cotton top and looked good enough to eat. 'What's it about?'

'Murder.'

'Don't tell Maggie – that kind of thing makes her nervous.'

27

It suddenly occurred to me that if our activities stirred up trouble right from the start – in other words, if Patrick and I stirred up a nest of criminal hornets – I would have to be very, very careful that I was not followed back here.

The next morning, with a slight hangover, Maggie and I having drunk far too much wine as we had yarned into the small hours, I set off for Woodhill, using the tube. This mode of travel did nothing to improve my headache and it was a decidedly grumpy novelist who arrived and headed straight into a chemist's for some kind of cure and then into Starbucks for something with which to wash it down. Part of my irritation was caused by the realization that I had behaved stupidly in not staying clear-headed, and it was unfair to blame Maggie even though she does have a bad effect on me. A general 'What the hell?' attitude seems to rule her life. Without it I think she would be far more successful in what she does.

No more wine and late nights, then.

And no, I was none the wiser about the true status of the delectable Julian.

Slightly restored, I found the public library and read everything I could lay my hands on in back numbers of the local papers about the Giddings murder, DCI Derek Harmsworth's death, DI John Gray's misgivings about it, and then his own violent end in his own home the previous week. I made detail-ed notes, which took me around one and a half hours. Though I was aware that Patrick would eventually brief me with details that would not reach the press, it was at least useful to have a framework upon which to make a start.

Even knowing as little as I did, it seemed odd that Harmsworth's car had gone through the parapet of a bridge over a motorway in exactly the same spot as had a heavy goods vehicle two days previously. The damaged and missing railings had been temporarily replaced by orange tape and plastic netting by the Highways Agency. Locals, according to the letters in the papers, thought the place an accident black spot – something to do with a bend in the road just before the bridge. I decided to bring the car the next day and have a look for myself.

One had also to take into consideration that, according to Gray, Harmsworth had not been an excessive drinker – in fact had been known to hardly touch alcohol at all while working on a case. He had been a very careful driver. Another point was that he had been due to retire soon and although Gray had known his chief had been looking forward to this he had made no plans with regard to what he would do with the rest of his life. This had bothered him slightly but not depressed him. Questioned further, the DI had said he was convinced that Harmsworth really was looking forward to leaving the job and not pretending. Besides which, he had always had a very dim view of people who took their own lives.

I decided that I wanted to leave the police to investigate the murders and try to find out what had happened to Harmsworth, as that matter now appeared to be regarded as closed. Someone from officialdom, preferably someone with clout – Patrick, for example – could grill Honor Giddings and lurk near the park where her husband had died. Bitchily, perhaps, I had already cast her in the shape of a differently named lookalike – tall, thin-lipped, haughty, violent even, as she had assaulted a press photographer who had come too close – as the number one crone in my new novel.

Even more bitchily, as a stinking red herring.

The Green Man was situated at a crossroads at the western, Woodhill end of Epping Forest (the entire area being far greener than I had imagined it would be) and I had an idea it was one of those very old hostelries that had recently been modernized out of all recognition. The children's play area had one of those plastic trees that my two boys sneered at as pathetic – even Justin, who once had to be rescued by the Fire Brigade from a real one, bigger, at the age of three. This and the brightly coloured swings were bereft of little ones, though, as it was term time.

It seemed a good idea to have a look at the place, besides which it was lunch time. Julian had still been in bed and Maggie had disappeared while I was in the shower and her hospitality had not run to breakfast. I had had a tentative rummage in the kitchen, found lots of things like fresh anchovies, fillet steak, wildly expensive olive oil and kumquats, but no bread or cereal.

For some reason I could not get Derek Harmsworth out of my mind, possibly because of Gray's obvious loyalty and high regard for him. 'One of the old school,'the DI had said. 'As honest as the day is long. Right on the line,' clichés that somehow made the homespun integrity of both men more poignant and their deaths pure tragedy. I found myself wondering if investigating them would answer quite a lot of other questions. Gray had been killed in the same ghastly way as Giddings, but was this a copycat killing by someone hoping to draw suspicion away from themselves?

The car park at the pub was practically full and even though it was a chilly day after the unseasonably hot start to spring, some hardened souls were sitting outside at the rustic tables. From the blue smoke emanating from the chimneys I knew that inside was what I was really after: log fires. There was one at each end of the huge bar area in which I found myself and I bought myself an orange juice and gravitated to the nearest one, where there was a group of armchairs, all vacant. In so doing I walked past someone I knew, Patrick, who was leaning on the bar talking to a tall and rather beautiful redhead.

Having seated myself still within sight of him, but not her unless she moved, I studied the menu I had picked up, giving the pair an occasional glance over the top of it. My cat's whiskers had already told me that Patrick had seen me, was not chatting her up, even though in charm mode, and that they were probably talking business. She was Bill, then, and I amused myself Holmes-style by judging that she was either Scots or Irish with that hair and superb complexion, was neat, tidy and efficient. Had she worked for either Harmsworth or Gray? The annoying thing was that it did not seem I was about to find out, as himself was making no move to recognize me and in the circumstances it was out of the question for me to go over and speak to him. No matter how professional I try to become at this game I always fall at this particular fence and right now wanted to upend his pint of Old Fart – or whatever the hell he was drinking – all over him in revenge for the smile on his face. I toyed with the idea of treating Julian to dinner this evening instead.

I wandered over to a separate counter where one ordered food, again passing quite close to the pair – just to get him all of a twitch – and organized some lunch for myself. A mobile rang; it was the redhead's, and she went outside to answer it. Patrick then finished his beer, gave me a leery wink and headed off in the opposite direction to where I was standing in a short queue, and I did not see him again just then.

So be it. I would come back later.

I decided to walk around the district in order to get the lie of the land, although for the time being I intended, as requested, to stay right away from the nick. I was really regretting having left the car behind as, although one tends to notice more while on foot, a vehicle can be used as a base where one can consult maps, have a rest or even a nap. It was going to be a very long day.

The business of researching a novel had gone right out of the window; it seemed wiser to concentrate solely on the job in hand, although I intended to use it as an excuse if challenged while snooping perhaps where I should not be. Thundering great forest or no, for some reason this area held no mystery for me and if somewhere does not immediately set your imagination alight, then forget it.

As seems to be my fate, unanswered questions about some aspects of the three killings with which I had promised myself I would not get involved kept niggling away in my mind. What had Jason Giddings been doing in this area and, in particular, in the park?

The local paper had been at pains to report that the park was infamous after dark as a place frequented by homosexuals. His widow had apparently been appalled when asked about this, insisting that there was no question of anything like that. However, I was recollecting a fuss generated several years previously by a gossip columnist in a tabloid rag – somehow avoiding being sued for libel – suggesting that Giddings was bisexual and had married for respectability reasons upon entering politics.

Another thing that was bothering me was that no one had appeared to take DI John Gray's concerns seriously – about which, strictly speaking, he should not have gone public. A Superintendent Fred Knightly's name had been mentioned in the papers and I seemed to remember seeing among the many others a photograph of a balding man with a heavily lined face holding a press conference.

It occurred to me after I had finished my lunch that fishing for possible insider knowledge from my old friend DCI James Carrick of Bath CID might be a good idea.

Unusually, Carrick, now fully recovered from a near-fatal shooting just under six months previously, had a little time on his hands, probably on account of having recently been given more personnel. After the usual pleasantries I brought him up to date with our news.

'SOCA!' he exclaimed.

'Our old MI5 boss wanted Patrick,' I explained. 'Anything on the grapevine about this affair in Woodhill?'

'I've met Richard Daws,' he recollected. 'So you're in on it too?'

'In a strictly advisory role.'

He chuckled.

'Well?' I asked bullishly.

At this he laughed outright. 'Were you in an advisory capacity when you dealt with half a dozen drug-squad blokes who'd been ordered to rough up that man of yours in the Gents' of a Bristol pub? What did Patrick say about it at the time? "Ingrid's really evil with a bog brush."' He hooted with laughter again.

'Women get very angry when their menfolk are attacked,' I said, on reflection, primly.

'Most run like hell,' he told me soberly, adding, 'The boys in Bristol have never lived it down.'

'Woodhill?' I prompted gently.

'I honestly don't think I can help you. I'd never met either of the men who died even when I was in the Met.'

'What about the Super, though – Knightly ?'

'Nope.'

'There's a tall redhead I've just seen Patrick with who may or may not be involved.'

'That fits the description of DS Erin Melrose. I know because there was a bit about her in the *Bath Evening Chronicle*. Her parents have retired to Gurney Slade and are worried about her. I can't say I blame them after what's happened.'

'Did she work for Harmsworth? No, come to think of it, that was Bowles.'

'She was Gray's assistant. Tell Patrick to keep an eye on the girl. I reckon there's a nutter in that neck of the woods who hates cops.'

Two

'Well, he would be concerned about her, wouldn't he?' Patrick said. 'She's a compatriot of his, from Crieff. And, yes, the loud smell of smouldering coming from your direction at lunch time was noted.'

'I'm hoping for all insider and official information about these cases,' I told him.

'Of course. I'll copy all the important stuff for you.'

'To be honest, I'd much rather find out what really happened to Derek Harmsworth first – if he was involved in a genuine accident or not. Otherwise I'll be replicating police work and, frankly, it'll be a waste of my time.'

Patrick looked thoughtful. 'I wasn't planning on your working in an independent way at all, actually,' he said quietly.

I took a sip of wine, good intentions regarding abstaining having, predictably, vanished. Very hungry, I had waited for almost an hour for him in the Green Man and it was now seven fifty.

'I've given this a lot of thought today and come to a couple of decisions,' I said. 'I'm not dogsbodying. I'd rather go home and be your oracle, adviser and Devon landlady. I have no intention of undertaking work that bona fide cops should be doing and probably already have done. And I'm certainly not hanging around in that park – it's not a good place to be.'

'I wasn't suggesting that you should go there after dark.'

'I'm not talking to the Giddings widow either. She's a poisonous bag. Besides which, I've no real authority.'

His face was now wearing its stubborn look. 'I thought you already had good cover – the author researching a new book and all that.'

'The woman isn't stupid. She'll smell a rat. And that's the whole point: I *am* an author and I don't want my name in the papers because she's had me arrested and I'm associated with that kind of crappy falsehood. She would too – she's already thumped a press photographer. No, sorry.'

He was staring at me in most unfriendly fashion.

I stared back and then said, 'Delete that last word and substitute "balls".'

Patrick sighed. 'Dinner. Hot nosh cures all, even wives.'

I snatched up two menus from a holder on the bar and slapped one down in front of him.

He was quite correct in one respect,

though: we both needed a hot meal.

'Right, then,' Patrick said when we had eaten, and having drained his coffee cup. 'You want a rethink.'

I said, 'Sorry, but I'm of the opinion that the thinking wasn't all that sound in the first place.'

'OK, tell me what you want.'

'Firstly, we owe it to DI Gray to investigate his suspicions. Actually, it's a basic requirement – everything else might hang on it.'

'Look, there *was* a PM. Harmsworth had sufficient alcohol in his blood for it to have impaired his driving ability. His body actually smelt of booze. He suffered multiple injuries when the vehicle crashed down on to the motorway below the bridge. Death must have been instantaneous. Who knows? Perhaps he was celebrating something or other and for once broke all his own rules about drinking. Perhaps another car was involved that nobody knows about and it was that driver's fault. The police appealed for witnesses to the accident but no one's come forward.'

'We could sit here and suppose all night,' I commented waspishly. 'What have you been asked to do?'

'Work independently of other police personnel. Find out if there's any connection between Giddings's and Gray's deaths, given the ghastly way they both died, and, most important of all, discover if there's a further risk to police officers.'

'And who do you take orders from?'

'SOCA, of course. A bloke called Michael Greenway. He's ex-MI5 too. Daws is his boss.'

'Carrick may be right and DS Melrose could be at risk. Has she been working with you?'

'No. I really am independent. But, obviously, she's been briefing me and that's what I've been working on: building up a picture of events. No, Erin's deliberately been given other things to work on. I have to say, though, she's not at all happy about it.'

There was a short silence, which I broke by saying, 'I think you know how I feel now.'

'You're saying that if I want you to stay and help me you'll need bona fides – in other words, some kind of warrant card or written authority. And you don't fancy going down into the Essex woods alone. Ingrid, the whole time you worked for MI5 you didn't have an ID card because it was decided you were safer without it.'

'Sort of. But this is different – it's the police. What I'm really asking for is those same working conditions. I'm quite happy for you to refer to me as your assistant. Besides, we'd get far better results working undercover.'

There was a longer silence while he thought about it.

'OK,' he said slowly at last. 'You do have a

good point – several actually. I agree, but on condition that we go in openly until we've exhausted possibilities in that fashion and then change tactics if necessary. We'll hold hands in the park and you can man – nay woman, the cannon loaded with grapeshot while I interview the grieving widow. How's that?'

Despite the coffee cups, a cream jug, a tea light in a glass holder and a small vase of flowers, I leaned over and kissed him.

I had, of course, well and truly scuppered Patrick's plan of action. Later that evening, though, when he had obviously had a re-think, we discussed it again and agreed that, for a short while longer, perhaps a couple of days, he would go his own way, at the same time soaking up as much information as possible. With my concerns in mind, he would question DS Melrose again about Gray and try to discover what the DI had been doing immediately prior to his death, especially any investigations he had made with regard to Harmsworth's death that had been on an unofficial basis.

I, meanwhile, in exchange for a sympathe-tic reception to my ideas, would undertake a little research into Theodore du Norde, who was, like Maggie, an interior designer, and Jason Giddings's stepson. Patrick gave me his address. There was a possibility, he thought, that Maggie might have heard of him and she *was* a terrible old gossip, wasn't she? Fair enough, I thought, and that was quite enough time spent in Woodhill for one day.

'Never heard of him,' Maggie declared for the second time that night. 'I've already said so, haven't I?'

I had caught the note of scorn in her voice at the first time of asking. 'No?' I queried.

'No. Don't you believe me? Look, duckie, there are thousands of us in London.'

I had not said where he lived and she only called me that when she was annoyed with me. Regrettably, it was very late and we were on the wine again, but this time it was a deliberate ploy on my part. 'Lying cow,' I said with a big grin on my face.

'Why do you ask, anyway?'

'Patrick wondered if you knew him.'

She sprawled back in her chair, crossed her long legs and took a big swig from her glass. 'You know, I never thought you'd stay married to that man – it being the second time around for you and all that.'

'Divorced people do remarry,' I pointed out, determined not to be sidetracked.

'Yeah, they do, but not usually to the same folk all over again. Mind you, he's got something going for him. Is he good in bed?'

'Mind-blowingly so,' I answered smugly. 'And you do know something about Theodore du Norde. I can tell.'

After a pause Maggie said, 'OK, he's a complete shit. He once rubbished me to a client and I lost a big commission.' When I did not comment, she snapped, 'I just didn't want to be reminded of him, that's all. What's he done?'

'Nothing, probably. Patrick's just making enquiries about a case.'

'Oh, he'll be involved in there somewhere, honey. I tell you, slime drips from the tips of his fingers.'

'How did he get to know about your possible commission?'

'The woman lived in the same block of apartments as he does; they met in the lift and she gushed all over him, bragging about how much money she intended spending. She didn't know then that he was into design too. Thick as cold glue, mind.'

'And...?'

Shrugging lightly, Maggie said, 'And what? Nothing. That was it. He got the job.'

'Look, I simply can't believe that she dropped you there and then just because of what some bloke said to her in a lift.'

'As I said: thick.'

I sat there, gazing at her fixedly, waiting.

'All right!' Maggie said furiously after a few seconds. 'He took her to see someone he knew who hadn't been too pleased with what I'd done for him – a real geek who'd upset just about everyone who'd worked on his house-restoration in Richmond. Naturally, he didn't mention that bit.'

I was sure there was more to tell, but this wasn't the Spanish Inquisition.

'I'm not the only one who's had him stick his nose in my business either,' Maggie added.

Did that mean he was completely ruthless or merely highly professional? Had he actually threatened her to back off? 'Is he any good?' I asked.

'Mediocre. That's why he has to poach.'

'But, bragging thickos in lifts apart, how does he find out what's going on?'

'God knows,' Maggie drawled. 'Bloody, isn't it?'

'How can I contact him?'

'My advice is don't, Ingrid.'

You never get anywhere by taking advice from the nervous.

This was a genuine opportunity to wear my writer's hat and undertake some research into interior design that could be filed away both in my head and on the computer. You learn more from talking to people than from books and I had tried several times to get Maggie to tell me about her work, but she never wants to talk shop and hasn't the patience to sit down and explain even the basics.

The number Maggie had reluctantly given me rang for quite a long time, but no answering machine cut in. Then it was picked up.

'Du Norde.'

I introduced myself, explained what I wanted and asked for an interview.

'Who put you on to me?' he enquired, the voice patronizing, bored-sounding.

'A friend of a friend who had a house-conversion done in Richmond,' I replied. 'I'm afraid I can't remember his name.'

There was a short silence and then he said, 'I'm a busy man and expect a fee from other professionals. I take it you are a professional writer – I can't say I've heard of you.'

My hide can rival that of a fossilized elephant if necessary. We agreed a quite ridiculous amount of money – promising myself grimly I would put half on Patrick's expenses – and he informed me that he had one vacant slot that afternoon between two and three or it would have to be put off until the following week. Deciding that he was a liar as well as probably quite a few other unsavoury things, I said that would be fine.

He then had the bloody cheek to tell me not to be late.

Mediocre or no he was either rich or clever enough to have an address in Holland Park, a stone's throw from the park itself. It was one of those places where there are copper artworks that double as water-features set on emerald-green lawns on both sides of the curving drive that no child or pet cat or dog has ever stepped on for the simple reason

45

that, here, both are banned.

I rode up to the sixth floor in one of the four lifts. Utter silence prevailed: I could have been in a museum. There were stairs, too, in white Italian marble, tasteful pictures on the walls, discreet light fittings, very expensive plants in even more pricy containers on each landing – one of those places where, regrettably, I yearn to lean over the balustrade and shriek 'Yeee-haaa!'

A plumply well-groomed individual opened the door – after leaving me waiting for a good half-minute or so – and I was ushered within and into the living room. I recognized one of the latest fragrances for men which, when lavishly sprayed upon Patrick recently in Harrods by a languid beautician, successfully ambushing him for possibly the first time in his life, had driven him straight into the Gents' to wash it off. A printable and politically correct translation of what he said afterwards would be utterly impossible.

'Coffee, Miss Langley?' du Norde enquired, his tone suggesting he would rather I refused.

'Oh, yes please,' I replied chummily, sitting down without being invited to and getting a notebook and pen from my bag.

'Oh, yes, and write me out a cheque while I get it, will you? Otherwise we might forget.'

He disappeared, giving me a chance to examine my surroundings, which I was staggered to see were what I can only describe as resembling a set for a Miss Marple film, an overwrought chintz nightmare. I almost expected a corpse to appear, drawbridge-style, from one of the gloomy alcoves on each side of the phoney fireplace. Well, his mother couldn't have designed it for him and he hadn't dared change it: that steel-cold Rhinemaiden was almost certainly into minimalist chrome and white-painted concrete toilet-roll holders. I wrote out the cheque.

'Sorry it's instant,' said du Norde when he reappeared with a single mug and handed it to me. 'I've run out of the real stuff.'

It looked like the bathwater of a Ten Tors competitor who had fallen into Fox Tor Mire.

I sized him up, literally: probably measuring more around the equator than he did from pole to pole; light-brown receding hair, large blue eyes, a pale complexion with slightly coarse features – he oozed self-satisfaction in a floppy, running-to-seed kind of way. Something warned me, though, that, if crossed, he might turn very nasty indeed. Murder, though?

Fishing for reactions, I said, 'I was very sorry to hear about your stepfather.'

He sort of congealed and then said poisonously, 'It's not public knowledge that Giddings was a relation of mine. Who told you?'

'A policeman friend.'

Overplaying being affronted, he grated, 'I

47

hope whoever it was didn't send you along to ask questions!'

'Of course not,' I replied with a big smile, adding in pure revenge, 'but no doubt he will be shortly.'

'I've already been questioned at length.' He seemed keen to impress this on me. 'But I was away the night it happened, in Birmingham on business.'

'But *surely* the police can't suspect you,' I gushed, after taking a sip of the sludge-coloured coffee. He must have had it in the cupboard for years.

'There was a rather public difference of opinion,' du Norde went on, 'between me and Giddings, at their house one evening recently. He'd had too much to drink and picked a row. You know how it is, how people get. Others overheard and someone must have mentioned it to the police.' As he spoke, his podgy fingers wove together like sausages fighting.

'Did he have a drink problem?' I asked innocently.

'Not to my knowledge,' du Norde said. 'He was just a loudmouth' – and then changed the subject abruptly, wanting to know how he could help me.

Ten minutes later I realized that I was wasting my time all round, learning nothing that couldn't be garnered from *The ABC Book of Interior Design for the Under Tens*. I was wondering how I could escape gracefully – even when with graceless folk you still have to behave yourself – when my mobile rang. I apologized and rose to walk over to the window, which overlooked the garden at the front, to answer it.

'Not been nobbled by a troll yet then?' said Patrick's voice.

I ignored the implied criticism of my courage. 'Where are you?'

'Parked right outside where you are,' he answered in a Neddy Seagoon voice.

So he was.

'Do you want reinforcements?' he went on to ask.

'Well, since you've come all this way...' Without putting a hand over the phone I said to du Norde, 'It's my policeman friend. Is it convenient for him to ask you a few questions?'

'No,' said the designer. 'It isn't.'

'Oh, good. Only I want to explore with you in some depth how the surrealists have affected design, artists like Magritte and Ithell Colquhoun. And then perhaps we could go on to talk about abstract impressionism. I mean, have you seen Mark Rothko's Seagram Murals at Tate Modern and not wanted to surround yourself with such stunning ideas? Not only that—'

Du Norde had held up an imperious hand. 'No. Wait. Perhaps I ought to talk to this officer after all. If I don't, he'll only return when it's even more inconvenient.'

A couple of minutes later I celebrated my stratagem by consuming another teaspoonful of coffee while he answered the door. All I had to do now was work out how I was going to avoid having to politely leave. I need not have worried.

It immediately became apparent that the visitor was in a very bad mood. Worse, it seemed that only wringing the nearest person's neck would restore him to a sunny disposition. I am Patrick's wife and knew he was only play-acting, but when he is like this he is too big, too close and too damned dangerous. He gave me a tight smile and proceeded to stalk the room like a Balrog on an over-long leash.

I gathered up my bits and pieces and moved to leave.

'You could stay, if he doesn't mind,' du Norde said hopefully to me, one eye on the new arrival. 'I – I mean, he's a friend of yours, isn't he? You'd like to chat with him afterwards...?' His voice ran down as though it needed rewinding.

'We could have lunch,' I said to Patrick winningly.

He appeared to consider. 'OK,' he said, going on to bark, 'But what passes between du Norde and me is absolutely confidential. Understand?'

'Of course,' I murmured, and settled myself down again.

'How did you get to hear of your stepfather's death?' was Patrick's first question. He had remained standing, obviously a man of little education, picking his teeth. Put simply: rough as rats.

The other cleared his throat, his discomfort having duly gone up a couple of notches. 'My mother rang to tell me.'

'When you were in Birmingham?'

'No, when I got back. She was furious with me as she'd left several messages when I wasn't here that I hadn't yet accessed as I'd got home very late. She ended up phoning at five thirty the next morning.'

'Don't you have a mobile?'

'Yes, but I've never given her the number.' Du Norde smiled in sickly fashion. 'She'd ring me all the time if I did.'

'Don't you get on well with her?'

'I don't see what that has to—'

'Please answer the question.'

After a short pause du Norde replied, 'It's all right between us for most of the time. She's always been a somewhat domineering woman. I was an only child and I'm afraid that, sometimes, she still treats me like one.'

'And your father?'

'Sir Cedric du Norde. He was – is – an architect. My mother divorced him when it became obvious there was another woman in his life.'

'What was your reaction when she said she was marrying Giddings?'

'That's none of your confounded business!'

Even I jumped when Patrick moved with horrible speed to lean over du Norde in his chair, a hand resting on either arm of it. 'My business is murder!' he shouted. 'I want to know if the person who disembowelled a man before or after cutting off his head then went on to be responsible for the deaths of two police officers who were working on the case. Answer my questions or I'll take you straight down to the nick.'

I felt that du Norde would either burst into tears of self-pity or lose his temper. Amazingly, it was the latter.

'All right, I told her she was raving mad!' he yelled, struggling to his feet and thereby forcing Patrick to step back. 'He was an ineffectual, strutting, ten-a-penny idiot who behaved as though he was God's gift to the party and actually took pride in retaining a safe seat in a by-election after the death of a man whose name will go down as one of the best back-bench politicians in recent history!' Du Norde strode over to the window and smashed a hand on to the small moth that had been fluttering against it, brushing the resultant silvery mess from his fingers. Turning and speaking in a furious whisper, he went on, 'He was a perverted, disgusting little *shit* to get himself killed in those revolting circumstances.'

'So it's true then, he was homosexual?'

The other bit his lip. 'Well, it stands to reason, doesn't it? Why else would he be there – in that park?'

Eyebrows raised, Patrick said in amazement, 'The man might have merely been taking a short cut.'

'No, all right, I had heard gossip about him. Apparently the place is notorious after dark. I understand he drank in the pub nearby, so it was impossible he didn't know of the area's reputation.'

'The Green Man – is that the pub you mean?'

'I think that's what it's called. I don't really know. I don't go into pubs. My mother might have mentioned it.'

'So you think the sole reason for his being in Woodhill itself that night was to pick up a man?'

'Yes, that is what I think. And probably not for the first time either.'

'You had a quarrel with him shortly before he died,' Patrick said. 'What was that about?'

'It was my mother's – Honor's – fault. If she hadn't been so heavy-handed with the booze that night, having drunk a bit too much herself until she didn't know how much neat gin she was actually pouring into everyone's glasses, it wouldn't have happened. Everyone was sloshed. If whoever it was who blabbed to the police had used their sense, they'd have known it was only the drink talking.'

'What did you row *about*?'

There was quite a long silence before du Norde said, 'Money. He'd been paying me an allowance as business wasn't good – told me it would have to stop, as his funds weren't too healthy. He was lying.'

'Oh?'

'They'd just come back from a month's trip to New Zealand, for God's sake.'

'That might have been why he was broke,' Patrick observed drily.

'No, my mother's loaded – and she gets a huge salary.'

'She's a pathologist, I understand.'

'Lectures most of the time now.'

'And obviously doesn't give you a handout now and then.'

I thought du Norde would start shouting again, but he merely muttered, 'He wouldn't let her.'

Or perhaps the lady now famous for her right hook was furious with herself for not having drowned her offspring at birth.

'Word has it you threatened him,' Patrick said silkily.

'As I said just now, it was the drink talking.'

'You told him he'd be sorry – to make sure he locked his door at night.'

Du Norde swallowed hard and said, 'Look, I didn't kill him. I couldn't do anything like that.'

'You could have paid someone else to.'

'No.' He was shivering now. 'For one thing

54

I couldn't afford to. I'm practically broke. That's why I got so upset with him over the allowance.'

With a horrid smile Patrick said, 'He despised you.'

'Yes.' This was uttered in a whisper. 'But I didn't kill him. I swear I didn't.'

'I want full details of your trip up north,' Patrick said briskly. 'Now. All the hard evidence you can lay your hands on. Did you go by train?'

'Yes, I did.'

'OK. Tickets, credit-card slips and hotel receipts, as you must keep that kind of thing for your tax returns. Car hire, restaurants – everything. I'll wait while you trot off and find it all.' Seemingly happy at last, he turn-ed to me and said, 'Your place or mine?'

On the way out I picked up my cheque from a side table and said to du Norde, 'What a pity we were interrupted when we'd hardly started. Perhaps we'll make it another time.'

Three

'Did you *have* to make me look like your bit of totty on the side?' I said ten minutes later, but aware that it was revenge for my huffiness the previous day.

Patrick grinned, then said, 'What did you make of him?'

'He's dodgy, hated Giddings, is a bit of a creep and kills insects with his bare hands but probably wouldn't have the bottle to commit that kind of murder.'

'Unless he drank too much again and was with someone who had the nerve and who owed him a favour.'

We had found a sandwich bar not far away, near Olympia, Patrick making rapid inroads into a 'house special', a triple-decker creation that looked as though it had half the contents of the establishment's fridge and most of the garden inside it.

I said, 'It doesn't quite fit, somehow. But you could have asked him for a list of all his past clients.'

He grunted, mid-munch.

'Do wealthy crooks employ someone to tell them which wallpaper and curtains to buy?'

I wondered aloud. 'They must do. Anyway, why did you really come over here this morning?'

'I spoke to Erin Melrose first thing – asked her everything she could remember about working with Gray on the Giddings case. He interviewed du Norde first time round and Erin went with him. They both thought him, as you say, dodgy, but it didn't appear that he'd ever actually got into trouble with the law. I thought I'd come over and see for myself.'

I told him what Maggie had said about him.

'It sounds as though he might have threatened her,' Patrick commented. 'Told her not to make any waves after pinching her client. And who's this character she mentioned who was restoring the house in Richmond and got up everyone's nose?'

'One must resist seeing the Mafia behind every bus stop,' I countered. 'I can't see that it's important.'

'I agree. But I think I'll ask him all the same.' Patrick reached for his phone.

Du Norde made the expected bleats about client confidentiality and so forth, and it was only after Patrick had again warned him that he would be taken to a police station for further questioning that he came up with the information.

'Possibly not our man,' he said after mentioning the name of a controversy-ridden

57

nobleman. 'I'll get our Richard on to that one.'

As well as tending all grapevines Richard Daws is the fourteenth Earl of Hartwood.

'Did you remember to ask Erin about DI Gray looking into the circumstances of Derek Harmsworth's death?' I said when we were walking back to where we had left the vehicles. 'You said you would.'

'No, but I will. One thing at a time.'

Somehow, I curbed my impatience. 'I was going to have a look at where Harmsworth's car went over the bridge today.'

'It hardly seems worth your while to drive all the way back to Woodhill,' Patrick said. 'I know what we decided yesterday, but I'm still concerned that tackling these three deaths as a whole will end up by making everything very confusing.'

'And as I said yesterday, I'm sure everything hinges on discovering if Harmsworth died as a result of an accident or not. When that is established one way or the other, all the investigations can be properly addressed.'

Patrick thought about it for a few moments. 'I have my brief and don't know how much I dare get sidetracked. Even if Harmsworth *was* killed as a result of some criminal action, there might not be any connection with the Giddings case.'

'I just think it ought to be sorted out first, that's all.'

He gazed upon me with a kind of blank expression in his eyes and I realized with a shock that, despite appearing to have come to an understanding the previous evening, the pair of us were actually heading for a very large difference of opinion. I said, 'As I understand it, my role is to be your adviser, the one you phone up when you're stuck and want a few ideas.' We had actually stopped walking and people were having to go round us on the pavement.

'Yes. But I'm not stuck. I know exactly what I must do.'

Desperately, I said, 'Look, you're bloody wonderful at whichever job you tackle, but what happens when I want to give you advice and you don't think you need it?'

'I probably have to be the judge of that.'

Trying, and probably failing, to make light of the situation I said, 'There's no override button, then?'

He shook his head and there was a short silence. Then Patrick said, 'This is stupid. Suppose we go to Woodhill, I take your car and park it at the nick and then you come with me to interview Honor Giddings. We can stop and look at the site of Harmsworth's accident on the way.'

'Fine.'

'I also suggest we leave your motor at the nick and I'll drive us both back and spend the night at Maggie's. She might recollect a bit more about du Norde – with a little prompting.'

I accepted this suggestion gratefully but nevertheless wondered if we were only postponing the inevitable. Just because you are married it does not mean there is a marriage of minds, but I was hanged if this new job was going to threaten our relationship. Oh, I could go home to Devon and be on the end of a phone, but my greatest dread when we worked for MI5 had been that one day Patrick would go out of the door and I would never see him again because I hadn't been there to watch his back. It had almost happened once, when I had shot and killed a man gunning for him. We used to be, and almost certainly still are, on several terrorist organizations' hit-lists.

I had expected the bridge over the motorway to carry a main road, but it turned out to be a very minor one that led from Woodhill along a ridge of low hills into the countryside, necessitating us making a detour. Villages could be glimpsed through the trees in the pretty valleys on either side, signposts pointing to Little Mossly, Kingsbrook and others. The road then descended slightly, in a series of hairpin bends, a ruined tower on the left-hand side set on a hillock. Then suddenly it straightened where, obviously, it had been reconstructed on the approach to the bridge.

'Ah, the place where everyone tries to overtake,' Patrick said, accelerating slightly. 'But actually, looking ahead, there's a pretty tight bend after you've crossed the bridge, so anyone coming the other way could be faced with several idiots all going like blazes. Badly designed, isn't it?'

'The local paper said something about a bad bend,' I recollected, gazing as we passed at the replaced tape and netting that was still strung across the gap in the railings. 'But in which direction was Harmsworth travelling? The report didn't say.'

'And what about the lorry that went through the railings a couple of days beforehand?' Patrick stopped the car in a lay-by after we had rounded the bend and got out. 'Shall we walk back?'

This did not prove to be at all hazardous, as there was hardly any traffic. The opposite was true on the motorway, of course, and we stood in silence for a few moments, watching the unceasing rivers of vehicles roaring beneath us.

'This isn't what I expected,' Patrick said. 'I thought we'd have a situation where there was an accident black spot on a very busy road, a place where prangs were taking place on a regular basis. Even though there's a warning sign, I'm sure the bend *is* dangerous if people drive too fast and accidents have happened; but for two vehicles to leave the bridge in exactly the same place in the space of forty-eight hours...' He leaned over

61

slightly and looked down. 'You can still see the marks where they hit the road.'

'You've changed your mind a bit then?' I said lightly.

He gazed at me and said, 'It would have been a very handy little gap to shove someone through, wouldn't it? Worth trying to find out if Harmsworth regularly drove this way. Where did he live, in Woodhill itself?'

'Yes, so he wouldn't have had to come this way home from work. The accident, or whatever it was, happened in the very early hours of the morning. Did he need to work that late or was he on to something important connected with the Giddings case?'

Patrick had a quick look around, examining the ground, but hundreds of cars had passed this way since the DCI's death. Then he said, 'I wonder if Gray did a lot more investigation into this than he let on and got too close to someone for his own safety?'

We walked back, in silence.

'Part of my brief is to find out if any more police officers are in danger,' Patrick reminded himself when we were sitting in the car. 'The rest is involved with discovering any connection between the murders of Giddings and Gray. No, you were right all along: first we must find out about Harmsworth. And while I'm not at all convinced that his death was anything to do with that of Jason Giddings, I don't like the way Gray was done to death as soon as he took over sole charge

of the case, having doubted the inquest findings on Harmsworth.'

'What about Fred Knightly, the Super?'

'I don't think there'll be much input of a
constructive nature from him with regards to
any investigation into Harmsworth's death –
he's far too busy with having to do most of
the work of heading up the Giddings inquiry. There's another individual lurking
around who's reputed to be from Special
Branch, but they don't even know his name
yet. Going back to Knightly: he gets wheeled
out and well briefed when there's a press
conference and that's about it. He's good at
PR. Erin was quite clear on that. Normally
spends most of his time filling in risk-assess-
ment forms and attending every government
law-and-order-initiative conference he can
to get himself out of the building. He definitely thinks Harmsworth ought to be laid to
rest.'

Due for retirement? Over the hill? Dead?
Did it matter to no one but us?

The village of Beech Hanger, some two miles
from Woodhill, was select, as I had expected
it to be: crisply clipped hedges, glimpses of
very large gabled houses down gated drives,
paddocks and rows of loose boxes. The
Giddings residence, The Chantry, was at one
end of the village street, just past a pretty
church.

'Have you made an appointment to see

her?' I asked as we turned into the drive.

'Yes.'

'Just as well, as she takes lumps out of people.'

'You've really got your knife into this woman, haven't you?' Patrick said with a chuckle.

The drive wove through a rather contrived but very beautiful planting of *Betula utilis jacquemontii*, white-barked Himalayan birch, and then straightened on the approach to the house, which, surprisingly, appeared to be very old. Perhaps it incorporated a real chantry, I thought, a chapel where monks had prayed for the souls of the dead.

A woman who was not Honor Giddings answered the door and without introducing herself led us through a hallway to a large, low-ceilinged room on the left. I thought for a moment that the room was unoccupied, but as the door was closed almost silently behind us the widow rose suddenly from a winged armchair that had its back to us facing the fireplace.

'Patrick Gillard,' she said – a statement of fact, not a question.

Patrick inclined his head slightly by way of response and then said, 'This is my assistant, Miss Langley, who, if you have no objection, will take notes.'

'Your sergeant?' queried Mrs Giddings, giving me a hard look.

'No. SOCA personnel don't necessarily

have police rank. Miss Langley is a civilian.'

She smiled coolly. 'That's fine. I just like to know exactly who is in my house. Do sit down.'

We all sat, Honor Giddings perching herself on the edge of a sofa, and I took out my notebook and without staring at her wrote a short description of her, in shorthand in case anyone tried to read over my shoulder, in other words to enable me to be as rude as I wished. But I had to be honest and admit that she did not fit the mental image I had built up. Even keeping in mind that she had just lost her husband in ghastly circumstances, here was not the gaunt and tight-lipped harpy staring from the pages of the newspapers. Perhaps she just came out very badly in photographs. Wearing a very well-tailored black trouser suit with a white blouse relieved at the neck by a pale-pink silk scarf she looked every inch the professional woman, her dark shoulder-length hair glossy, her complexion fine and clear.

Patrick offered her our condolences and she thanked him.

'I do realize that you've been interviewed already,' he continued.

'This is the third time, actually,' Honor Giddings drawled. 'First by someone by the name of Harmsworth, then I think by an Inspector White – or was it Gray? – who arrived with a girl with red hair, and now you. No, there was someone else – a man who said he was from a department of Special Branch whom I found rather objectionable. It's been a real circus, actually.' The reproof was there.

'I'm only here because, tragically, the first two officers you mentioned are no longer with us,' Patrick said quietly. 'But, obviously, you've had other things on your mind.'

'You mean they're *dead*?'

He nodded slowly. 'It would *appear* that Detective Chief Inspector Harmsworth was involved in an accident, but Detective Inspector Gray was murdered last week in similar fashion to your husband. My job is to discover if there's a connection and ensure that no other police officers' lives are at risk.'

'But that's awful. Surely—'

Patrick interrupted her with, 'Had your husband ever met either of them, do you know? Had he – and I'm sorry to have to ask this – been in any kind of trouble with the law that might have resulted in a visit from the local police? A traffic offence, perhaps?'

I found myself impressed that the lady did not get on her high horse. She reflected for a few moments and then said, 'I think he had a few points on his licence, but everyone does these days, don't they? There's nothing else that I can think of.'

'Could he have met them socially? Was he a Mason?'

Patrick told me afterwards that Gray had been, Harmsworth not.

66

'No. But he belonged to the local Round Table. And it's perfectly possible that he could have met them at a constituency do. But I must point out that he had very little time for that kind of thing, what with being on committees and so forth. I simply can't believe that there was any kind of real *connection* between my husband and these men.'

'I understand he was due home quite early that night as you were giving a dinner party.'

'That's right. Just us and a few friends.'

'At what time were you expecting him?'

'Somewhere between six thirty and seven, but it was just an informal affair. There were no important debates that night. Our entertaining has – had – to be on the impromptu side, as I never knew when he would have to stay late.'

'Was he coming straight home, do you know? Had you asked him to pick up anything for you on the way here? Something to do with the dinner party, for example?'

'Oh no. Hilary sees to all that. He never went shopping.'

Patrick ignored her snooty implication that the MP had been far too grand to pop into an off-licence, saying, 'I understand she's your housekeeper.'

'Yes, but she doesn't clean – someone else does that. And there's other help in the garden.'

'They've all been interviewed. Do you have any theories as to why your husband was in the park?'

'Everyone's asked me that!' the woman snapped. 'No, I don't, not one.'

'A taxi driver has come forward who picked him up at the station and dropped him at the Green Man at around five forty-five. Did he make a habit of going there for a drink on the way home?'

I made a note to check whether enquiries had been made there.

'I've no idea. I suppose he could have done.'

'Surely you must know if that was his habit.'

She was beginning to lose patience. 'Well, I don't. Wives shouldn't expect to know absolutely every last detail of their husbands' routines.' Gazing on his wedding ring she added, 'I'm sure your wife doesn't grill you about all your movements.'

'No, I tell her what I've been up to,' was the swift response. 'It's too far to walk home from the pub, though, isn't it? He'd have had to get another cab.'

An irrritable shrug was all that was forthcoming on this.

'Your son reckons he went there to pick up men.'

A real fan of bombshells; I drew a five-pointed star on my notepad and a load of sparks.

'I can't remember how many times I've told you people that my husband wasn't gay!' Honor Giddings raged. 'Besides which, Theo has absolutely nothing to do with this.'

'No, he just threatened to get even with his stepfather for having his allowance stopped. Is he so prone to making drunken threats that you get used to them and they're safely ignored?'

'No, of course not.' She rose wearily to her feet and went over to stand by the window. 'I'm sorry but I've had enough of your questions. When can I have Jason's body so I can arrange his funeral?'

'That's not in my jurisdiction, but I don't think it will be just yet.'

There was a short, tense silence and then she turned abruptly to face us. 'No, Theo isn't in the habit of making threats. He'd just had a little too much to drink that evening. But Jason and he had never really got on. I suppose some sons find it difficult when their mother remarries and Theo did – very much so. He's rather a possessive person.'

Patrick leaned back in his chair and stretched his legs, scrutinizing her closely. 'It suggests there's a huge difficulty – hatred, something much more than just about money – when people make those kind of accusations. The park where your husband was found has a very bad reputation after dark. If he wasn't there for nefarious purposes – and arguably it wasn't yet quite dark then although a very overcast evening when he arrived at the pub – then he must have been killed somewhere else and taken there, where his body was mutilated. Again, that speaks of the deepest hatred.'

There was another silence broken by Patrick asking, 'Is your son capable of that?'

'No,' Honor Giddings replied in a low voice. 'Not at all. But I have to tell you that he is reputed to have some very unpleasant friends.'

'Criminals?'

'I wouldn't go as far as to say that. All we had to go on was something a colleague of Jason's said about seeing Theo in a club with people he thought were undesirables. Jason told me he was going to have some checks done. There was the chance, you see, that someone might have tried to get at him through Theo. There are some terrible people about – not that I need to tell you that.'

'Who was this person who told your husband about it?'

'I don't know – Jason didn't say.'

'Did the Special Branch officer who came to see you mention it?'

'No. And I was too distraught to think of asking him.'

'Do you know the name of the club?'

'I think it's called Jo-Jo's. But I don't know where it is.'

'Was your husband involved with anything controversial? Supporting hunting or animal testing, for example?'

'Not that I'm aware of. He didn't have wildly strong views on anything, really.'

'When he didn't come home at the time you expected him, what did you do?'

'Just carried on as normal for a while. It wasn't unusual, you see; the trains are late all the time.'

'And then?'

'I made sure there were drinks and nibbles organized, as our friends were due to arrive, and drove to the station – in case he hadn't been able to find a cab. There was no sign of him.'

'Was it usual for him not to take his car?'

'Oh, yes, quite usual. He got sick of getting stuck in traffic jams. And it meant he could have a drink with colleagues before he set off for home.'

'Then what did you do when you couldn't find him?'

Honor Giddings was getting really fed up with her inquisitor now. 'Why came home, of course! There was nothing I could do but chat for a while with guests and then ask Hilary to serve the meal, as she was worried about it getting spoilt and everyone was hungry. I'd already tried to reach Jason several times on his mobile to no avail. By nine thirty I was getting really worried and rang the police. I felt a real fool as it wasn't as though he'd been missing for all that long. Then I heard nothing until the phone call the next day. I hadn't slept – I had a feeling

71

something horrible had happened.'

'I understand you couldn't get hold of your son until early on the following Monday.'

'That's right, he'd been up north. God knows why. I was furious with him for not being around when I needed a bit of support for once.'

'Would he have been any use?' Patrick asked baldly.

'No, probably not,' she answered through her teeth. 'Is that all you need to know? It's not just you I've had to put up with since this happened, but the whole damned world. I've had the media camped on the doorstep, not to mention my sister Fiona being a thorough nuisance.'

'She's no help either then?' Patrick said with the ghost of a smile.

Fists clenched, the resentment boiling out, Honor Giddings said, 'That first morning she was here not half an hour after I'd phoned her husband Quentin with the news. Floods of hysterical tears, but only to get her picture in the papers and hoover up the attention and sympathy. And here was I, having to give it to *her*. We've never really got on, even as children. She was lazy and greedy – still is; and now it's beginning to tell. I've told her several times to lose weight or she'll be ripe for cardiovascular hypertension or atherosclerosis, not to mention thrombosis. For God's sake, the woman's already prone to breathlessness and has varicose veins. She didn't speak to me for a whole year once when I told her that she reminded me of a woman I'd done a PM on who'd been lying dead in her flat for over a week. She'd died of a burst atheromatous aneurysm of the abdominal aorta. Perhaps I shouldn't have emphasized how I'd had to cut through layers of rancid fat before I discovered the massive internal bleeding.'

Really quite impressed with this outpouring I said, 'Returning to your husband again, there was a newspaper article a couple of years ago, at the time of your wedding, suggesting that your husband was actually bisexual and had married for professional respectability purposes before entering politics. Is there any truth in the allegation?'

'All kinds of filth are printed in the gutter press,' Honor Giddings said heavily. 'Are you just brought along to ask that kind of question?'

'Answer it,' Patrick requested softly. 'And for the record, no, she isn't.'

The woman paced back and forth before the window a few times, chewing her lip. Then she said, 'I understood from Jason that when he was in his early twenties he did have an ... infatuation ... for another man. They were barely out of their teens and both had girlfriends. It was just a growing-up thing and happens all the time. That was all! Now please go away and leave me alone!'

★ ★ ★

'It didn't happen to me,' Patrick said sadly. We were on our way back to Maggie's. 'I obviously dipped out there.'

'I always had crushes on much older men when I was a teenager,' I admitted.

'We're freaks.' Patrick chuckled and then blew a raspberry in my direction.

'She loathes her sister – really boiled over.'

'In quite poisonous fashion too.'

'I think she suspects du Norde might have had something to do with her husband's death but didn't really want to say so. And to be fair, Giddings doesn't seem to have been the complete waste of space that du Norde tried to make out. I mean, if he belonged to the local Round Table he must have been interested in the community in which he lived.'

'And this old cynic says that might have been just a pose.' Patrick patted the briefcase that was on the seat between us, heavy with copies of the case files. 'I'll go through this lot again, but I can't remember anything about Giddings requesting his stepson be kept an eye on with regard to whom he was knocking around with. I shall have to ask the man from Special Branch.'

The unusual diffidence in his tone made me say, 'You are using your army rank.'

'Not from choice. And this isn't the army. Everyone knows I'm a rookie. It's not in my interest to throw my weight about and the only way I'll get their respect is to earn it. So

I'll ask him nicely. What might get up his nose is the business of being allowed to carry a firearm.'

'Your old friend a Smith and Wesson?'

'No, I've gone for a Glock 17, lighter and better able to knock an armed man off his feet. Also virtually impossible to jam.'

'So I won't need to buy hefty handbags in future for when you don't want to actually have it on you.'

'Oh, I don't know,' he said with a grin, waving at a motorist who had given him a two-finger salute for daring to overtake after flashing him out of dawdling in the fast lane. 'A few hundred clips of ammo should keep your muscles in trim.'

'What evidence would we need to ask for a second PM on Derek Harmsworth?'

'Something pretty substantial.'

'I'd like to find out where that club Jo-Jo's is.'

'I was just thinking the same.'

'If you keep driving at this speed you'll get points on *your* licence.'

'You don't look a day older,' Maggie said, not having clapped eyes on Patrick for about five years.

'It's the whisky,' he told her. 'I'm pickled in it.'

'Would you like a dram now?'

He made a play of looking out of the nearest window. 'Sun's over the yard-arm. Why not?'

'The price is not grilling me about any of your bloody suspects I might have heard of,' she informed him grimly.

He threw himself into one of the large squashy armchairs and gave her an unsettling grin. 'I have only one question along those lines and it can wait.'

'If you absolutely must I'd rather you asked it now, if you don't mind. Then I can relax.'

'OK. Do you know any of Theodore du Norde's friends or acquaintances?'

'Not him again! I didn't know he had any friends,' she retorted.

Patrick just sat there gazing at her like an owl.

'I understand he has associates,' she continued after a pause. 'A sort of network of creeps who fix things for him.'

'What sort of things?'

'You said one question. God knows. This is all from the grapevine so it might just be gossip. I believe it, though – from what I've been told, whatever he wants du Norde gets.'

Four

DI John Gray had been unmarried, living on his own in a ground-floor flat situated in a quiet suburb of Woodhill. He had been very ambitious and good at his job and everyone at the nick had assumed that he would be promoted and would take over when Derek Harmsworth retired. Working long hours and expecting his staff to do the same, he had earned a reputation as a bit of a slave-driver but nevertheless had been popular, not passing the buck if things went wrong and often taking his team out for a drink, sometimes to the Green Man but usually to a nearer, 'unimproved' and much more down-to-earth establishment called the Railway, where the beer was reckoned to be better. Besides being involved with his local Masonic lodge, Gray had been a member of Woodhill Gilbert and Sullivan Operatic Society, not as a performer but on the production side, mostly lighting. A practically life-long vegetarian, he had just acquired an allotment, which had resulted in a little good-natured ribbing from his colleagues.

I gathered all this information the following morning from the files and from Patrick, who had attached notes he had made from what Erin Melrose had already told him. He had added that she was still deeply upset by her boss's death. Interestingly, Patrick had elaborated on something he had mentioned to me already, on a Post-it note to be removed and destroyed, for my eyes only: that he not only knew she very much resented being ordered not to involve herself with either Gray's or Harmsworth's deaths now that SOCA and Special Branch were on the scene, but in his opinion might do a little investigating privately.

There having been no further discussion as to what I should next turn my attention to – other than an arrangement that I would meet Patrick for lunch in the Green Man – I had decided to devote the next morning to this studying of all the case files, which Patrick wanted back when we met at midday. He did not have the time, he had said – nor patience, it must be admitted – to copy them all off for me. I set to, just after he left Maggie's – she soon also went out – gleaning everything remotely useful from my own particular angle, again making notes.

It was a bright, sunny day, I saw, when my gaze strayed to the window a couple of times. To hell with it, the flat was cold and airless, the windows all locked with no keys in sight: I would go to Woodhill early and find somewhere to work in the open air.

I found myself wondering whether Gray had left behind any written evidence connected with investigations he had been conducting, officially or otherwise, into Harmsworth's so-called accident. Nothing was mentioned in the files. Not having got as far as the one on Gray's murder, I postponed going out for a little while longer and turned to it now.

What I read posed questions immediately. No one had so far mentioned the fact that the DI's flat had been ransacked. He had been found knifed, his throat cut, eviscerated, in the living room on a Sunday morning by the woman who lived in the flat directly above him. She had been returning from buying a newspaper when she'd noticed his front door was wide open and there were bloodstains on the step. Tentatively investigating, she had subsequently had to be treated for severe shock.

As the man had lived on his own and no one could be traced who had visited him or knew him well enough to be able to say if anything had been stolen, it was impossible to discover if any of his possessions were missing other than the obvious; a new television, the receipt for which was discovered in a home file, and his computer. The case was being treated as a burglary that had gone wrong and, in the words of corny crime novels, the trail had gone cold.

I went out, mulling all this over. Then I

found myself thinking about the allotment. Allotments nearly always have sheds and from what I know about men their shed is often a refuge, a place to escape from the world and especially any womenfolk – in short, a holy of holies. I might as well go and have a look at the DI's allotment on the grounds that probably no one else had thought to. Anyway, temporarily or not, I seemed to be condemned to tinkering and poking about on the edges of these investigations.

It took several phone calls, as I sat in the car, to find out that Gray's allotment was one of two dozen or so situated almost right in the centre of Woodhill. The land had apparently originally been part of an estate owned by an eccentric eighteenth-century industrialist with no family, who had left it in his will to be run as a charitable trust, the house as an education centre, the gardens open to the public and the meadow, walled vegetable garden and paddocks turned into allotments for artisans and their families. I was told that at one time the waiting list had been long, one had literally had to wait for people to die or move away from the district to get one, but now local people had apparently lost interest and quite a few of the plots were vacant, although plans were afoot to remedy this. The actual gardens were closed to the general public at the moment as they were being restored, but I could go and view the allotment area if I so wished.

Eventually, I found them, the directions having been somewhat vague. Now completely hemmed in by houses, the entrance was no more than a horse-drawn-carriage-width lane with a very small signboard directing the visitor to the Benfleet Centre, presumably referring to the house. I soon discovered there was a resident warden who kept a close and severe eye on things from a lodge just inside the gate. He was waiting for me.

'I understand you're here on behalf of Woodhill CID,' said this custodian of the cabbages ponderously. 'I was called just now by the council's allotment officer – whose responsibility this place isn't, of course, as it belongs to the Trust.'

I introduced myself, regretting the white lie, but if I had started explaining about SOCA it would have taken all morning.

'I don't think poor Mr Gray had had a chance to do more than start to prepare the ground. So tragic. You'll have to leave your car here, I'm afraid, as there isn't room to park farther in. All available space is taken up by earth-moving machinery, as they're working on the gardens. You'll need the keys – just as well I have spares. You might ask for Inspector Gray's to be returned, by the way.'

Keys?

Wending my way between parked diggers in the narrow lane, I soon discovered why.

These were very, very special allotments. Each was walled or fenced and had a gate, just like a private garden. Standing on tiptoe and peeping over the tops of a couple of the gates as I walked by, I saw that they had small summer houses painted in shades that are sometimes referred to as 'heritage' colours: grey-blue and the palest of greens. Pretty tables and chairs were set outside these and there were spring flowers everywhere. Number 16 was right down at the end. The large key turned easily in the lock and I went in.

This, then, had been John Gray's little bit of private heaven. He had done more work than the warden had thought, the neat beds raked smoothly, not a stone in sight, lavender newly planted to border the paths. My eyes misted as I beheld the brand new canes erected to support runner beans that he would never sow, rows of peas and broad beans that he would never taste just emerging from the soil. A watering can stood full, ready to water them. I watered them.

There was no summer house, just an ordinary small shed in a far corner that was well maintained and had a large barrel on one side to collect rainwater. As I got closer I could see that repairs had been carried out to part of it and the roof had recently been refelted. The window had been replaced at some stage with an old leaded-glass one, the kind that was used in front doors during the thirties and forties, giving the whole structure a strange kind of charm. I unlocked the door with the other key on the ring and entered.

As neat as a new pin, the interior had shelves fitted to the rear wall that held plant pots, washed, a few seed trays, ditto, packets of seeds, small tools and gardening magazines, the other walls being devoted to a potting bench beneath the window and clips that held the shafts of larger tools. Just inside the door on the right-hand side was a metal cupboard, the sort that might have seen service in an office. This was secured by a sturdy padlock.

I reached for my mobile.

Twenty minutes later I met Patrick at the main entrance and it was obvious that he was not pleased with me.

'I know, I know, you can't be expected to come rushing over at my every whim,' I said.

I got a long-suffering look.

'I haven't whimmed in your direction for ages,' I pointed out.

'What do I have to do?'

'Open a padlock.'

He sighed and retraced the few paces he had walked from the car to rummage in the cubby box. I do possess a set of keys that will open some locks, but they're no match for modern padlocks. I don't know where Patrick acquired his – probably from a thoroughly modern safe-breaker.

The padlock surrendered after a couple of minutes of careful work, which was gratifying, as we are always reluctant to use bolt cutters and it would have meant finding some. The door seemed slightly ill-fitting but grated open.

A stainless-steel spade, fork and edging tool, a brush cutter, and a pair of new green wellington boots were arrayed before us. That was all.

'Why on earth did he keep his wellies locked up in a cupboard?' I said to cover my disappointment and, it must be admitted, embarrassment.

Patrick shrugged. 'They're incredibly posh and expensive ones, that's why. Can I go now?'

I lifted them out and looked at them. There was something rolled up in the right-hand one: papers. I pulled them out, uncoiled them and saw that it was several pages of handwritten notes stapled together.

'It seems to be about cases that Derek Harmsworth had worked on,' I reported after quickly reading part of the top sheet. 'Cases that resulted in trials and people being sent to prison.' I handed the bundle to Patrick. 'Gray *must* have thought Harmsworth was murdered – by someone he'd put in jail, by the look of it.'

'One must assume it is his work,' Patrick murmured. 'It shouldn't be too difficult to find a sample of his handwriting at the nick.'

He shot me a sideways glance. 'This is a real stroke of luck. Sorry for being such a pain in the neck.'

'What will you do with this?'

'That's a good question. It doesn't actually have anything to do with Special Branch, as I've discovered this morning they're only officially interested in the Gidding's case. But this joker apparently relishes sticking his nose into everything. So I'll ignore him and mention it to my boss, Mike Greenway, before it goes to Knightly.'

Over lunch, seated in a quiet corner of the Green Man, we read through the notes. Gray's anger was imprinted on every word, literally, the ballpoint pen he had used having been pressed hard into the paper. The handwriting was small but easy to read, the work concise but giving every impression of having been done in a hurry. As I had already guessed, he had listed all of Derek Harmsworth's cases of a serious nature that had resulted in convictions, right through his police career. There were quite a few of them. The final page was devoted to his own thoughts and investigations. Obviously, he had only just started on the latter, having written a mere three or four paragraphs before he was killed.

'He can't have wanted any of this on computer,' Patrick commented. 'Possibly not even on his own at home. Which, as we know, was stolen. Was it taken because of information it might hold or did he merely disturb a thief and was killed because he recognized a local thug? And why was he so secretive about this anyway?'

'He'd been carpeted for stirring things up,' I said. 'Anything else apart, I do wonder if pressure of work caused those in charge to be quite happy to call Harmsworth's death an accident. I mean, there's been a PM, so let's get on with life, guys, and not worry about an old stager who was due to ride off into the sunset soon anyway.'

Patrick glanced up at me. 'You're really angry about this, aren't you?'

'So are you, really.'

He nodded. 'Yes, but like you I can't think there's any *sinister* reason for his senior colleagues failing to follow up Gray's theories. He was, Erin admitted, rather prone sometimes to having wild ideas and had to be brought back down to earth.' He tapped the pages of notes. 'We haven't the time to read all of this now, but it's well worth looking into. I'll check up on some of these characters on the database before I hand it over.'

A shadow fell across the table as someone came between us and the nearby window. In the same instant Patrick slapped his hand down on the paperwork between us, forestalling an attempt at its removal. Then he was on his feet.

'Relax,' drawled a dark-haired man in dire need of a shave. He went on, 'I thought I'd find you here.' Gaze drifting down to me, he said in offhand fashion, 'Who's she?'

'My wife,' Patrick said evenly.

'You know who I am?'

'You might just be the prat from Special Branch who hasn't actually bothered to introduce himself to anyone at Woodhill nick.'

Patrick had not used the word 'prat', but a more vivid, much ruder, noun.

'Just because you were MI5's blue-eyed boy it doesn't mean you can lord it over everyone now,' the other countered.

'I'd like to see your warrant card.'

There were a few seconds' tense silence in which I thought we were only a few more from Patrick tossing our visitor through the aforementioned window and then he reached inside his jacket and produced what had been asked for. Patrick gave it a glance and handed it back.

'So what can I do for you, Detective Chief Inspector Colin Robert Hicks?'

'What's that?' Hicks wanted to know, gesturing towards the papers.

'I think I'm safe in saying that it has nothing to do with Jason Giddings's murder – which is *your* brief.'

'Why don't you both sit down before I get a crick in my neck?' I suggested into the leaden atmosphere.

This they did, but the change of level made

no difference to the eyeball-to-eyeball state of affairs or the mood of the newcomer as, grimly, he continued, 'The department I work for doesn't come under Special Branch, actually, but it saves explaining to these hicks in the sticks. I deal directly with Commander John Brinkley. The section's unique, independent. We troubleshoot.'

Patrick tut-tutted. 'He's got above himself, has John. You might be interested to know that he offered me the job and I turned it down.'

'So I understand. He asked me to keep an eye on you.'

'That sounds to me as if our John's throwing his toys out of the pram over my refusal and wants you to rat up my new career.'

'You'll save me the job and screw it up yourself from what he told me. You're a loose cannon. Just be aware that you're being watched. People have been told of your methods, how MI5 hushed up how many you killed and maimed in the course of your so-called duty.'

Patrick laughed. 'It's bloody strange, then, how badly Brinkley wanted me.'

There was another short, brittle silence and then Hicks stood up and stalked away.

'Funny eyes,' I said. 'Like something alien and a bit bonkers in *Doctor Who*.'

We giggled in juvenile fashion.

It was a mistake not to have taken Hicks more seriously.

Patrick was staying at a bed and breakfast in a quiet close in Woodhill. Having been invited, nay lured, to accompany him back there that evening, seen the immaculate state of the house, his huge double room, and been told about the cooked breakfasts that were being lavished upon him, I decided to leave Maggie with her bare fridge and loaded wine rack and move in the next day. I did not actually mention this to Patrick until the next morning but went along with his plot and stayed the night, borrowing his toothbrush. In all fairness, I did not need any encouragement, nor nightwear, for that matter.

Still mostly ploughing through paperwork at the nick, Patrick left a message on my mobile when I was driving back from Maggie's late the following morning, having collected my things and left her a note, to tell me he had found out where Jo-Jo's, the nightclub, was and, together with making a couple of other calls, intended to give the place the once-over that evening. He was sorry but had to be vague over timings and I might have to make my own arrangements for an evening meal. He would see me 'somewhen'.

OK, I would go and talk to Vera Harmsworth.

A very tired woman opened the door of the

shabby-looking semi-detached house, shockingly looking much older than I had expected.

I introduced myself and requested an interview, explaining that SOCA had been brought in to investigate the recent deaths in the Woodhill area and that I was working on behalf of one of their operatives, naming him. I was expecting her to ask to see some kind of ID card, but she did not, inviting me in. Her mood seemed to change to something a little brighter and I wondered if she was glad of the chance to talk to another woman.

'I was just going to put the kettle on,' said Mrs Harmsworth. 'Tea?'

'Lovely,' I said.

'Derek always said that only barbarians drank coffee in the afternoon,' she recollected fondly. 'But he was terribly old-fashioned. Do sit down, Miss Langley, I won't be a minute.'

The room was old-fashioned as well but immaculately clean. There were framed photographs of babies and toddlers on the mantlepiece, presumably grandchildren, and several of various policemen in uniform, including old black-and-white ones where the subjects were stiffly at attention and had very short haircuts.

'That's Derek's father, the one on the horse,' Mrs Harmsworth said, coming back into the room with a small table and seeing where I was looking. 'He was in the Mounted Division. The others are his two brothers and their grandad – they all made the Met their career but Derek was the only one to go in the CID.'

I waited until we were drinking our tea, served with Marks and Spencer's fondant fancies – I find these almost impossibly sweet but dutifully ate one – before I asked any questions.

'I understand Inspector Gray didn't go along with the accident findings,' I said quietly.

'John? No, and I don't either. But wringing my hands and making a fuss isn't going to bring Derek back, is it?'

'No, but if his death wasn't an accident, then whoever was responsible might have killed John Gray too and other police personnel's lives might be in danger. That's what my – Patrick Gillard's concentrating on.'

She was silent for a few moments, pensively stirring her tea. Then she said, 'There was no earthly reason for Derek to have been driving along that particular road in the small hours of the morning. He might have worked late some evenings and even at weekends, but he always came home before ten. If something cropped up – and it would have had to be something serious like a new murder case or his car breaking down – then he'd phone me. I hadn't heard from him and was really worried.'

'And he'd said nothing to you at all before he went to work that day that might explain a change of routine?'

'No, not a word.'

'Could he have been on a private errand of some kind? On his way back from seeing a friend or from buying something? – as a surprise for you, perhaps?'

'He'd still have told me he was going to be late. Believe me, he could be a grumpy old devil sometimes, but he was very considerate about his comings and goings, as he knew I was a worrying kind of person.'

'Are you sure that any errand he was on couldn't have been in connection with his retirement plans? Could he have been looking at property?'

Vera Harmsworth shook her head emphatically. 'No, not a chance. Derek would never do that. Things like deciding to buy houses would have been discussed at length between us and he always left paying bills to me, perhaps because I used to be an accountant. I think he would have lived in a tent if he could. He hated decorating, doing repairs and so forth, and I can't remember the last time he did anything in the garden. I shall have to get a man in to...' Her voice trailed away and she fought back tears as she remembered, yet again, that he would never do those things now.

'Did your husband ever discuss his work

with you?' I asked.

Dabbing at her eyes, she said, 'No, not really. Only funny things that happened to him. He knew I didn't like to hear about murders and shootings.'

'He didn't mention the names of people he regarded as particularly dangerous?'

'Only if he'd managed to put them behind bars and it was all in the papers. He was really happy then. There were quite a lot of them over the years. Terrible people, Miss Langley, really terrible. Look what happened to poor John Gray.'

'But there's no one you can remember by name?'

'No, sorry. I suppose I deliberately put them out of my mind.'

'Did John Gray come to see you after your husband died?'

'Oh, yes, several times. He was a lovely man. He was quite like Derek in some ways and loved the countryside and watching wildlife. It made life worth living after the nature of their jobs. What Derek used to call "small, fine things".'

I placed my cup and saucer back on the table. 'Mrs Harmsworth, did he tell you about anything he was investigating regarding Derek's death?'

'Yes, he told me he was going back through old cases to see if he could make any connections. He thought Derek had met someone who'd somehow overpowered him and pushed his car off the bridge on to the motorway. I mean, we both knew that Derek hardly drank at all – just the odd pint of bitter; but they said he was full of whisky. It was on his clothes. Derek *hated* spirits.'

'And yet those in authority didn't go along with that.'

'No, well, John had a bit of a reputation for wild theories and had got into trouble before for airing them. He was told that if he could find some real evidence then something might be done. And then the poor man was killed by a burglar – or that's what was said in the papers.'

'What will you do?' I asked after a reflective silence.

'I always fancied a little bungalow on the coast – Seaford, perhaps; but I've gone off the idea now. I mean, when you've got each other it doesn't matter if you don't know people for a while in a new place. I'm really not sure what to do, but I must pull myself together – you just can't sit at home and brood.'

'What about your family?'

'Both our son and daughter are married and live abroad – David's in New Zealand, Anne in South Africa – but I have to confess that I don't really see eye to eye with either of their spouses, so there would be no question of going to live with them. Not that I want to live the rest of my life abroad.' And then she really did wring her hands. 'I do so wish I could help you, my dear, but I probably wasn't a very good policeman's wife.'

'I'm quite sure you were,' I told her, really meaning it. 'The best, in fact.'

It was when I rose to go that I saw the card, half tucked behind one of the framed photographs.

'Jo-Jo's?' I queried.

Vera Harmsworth smiled. 'Oh, Derek took me in there for a meal one night. It's a nice little place with a restaurant at the back and some kind of club in the basement. I think there was method in his madness, as he went off for a few minutes to talk to someone who worked there. I guessed that it might be some kind of informer – but that is only a guess. I kept the card they gave us with the bill as it had a calendar on the back. But it's last year's – I must throw it away.'

'May I have it?'

She presented it to me with a flourish. 'I can recommend the food.'

After, believe it or not, asking a policeman the whereabouts of Shire's Yard, I found myself walking down a narrow cobbled lane, actually little more than an alleyway, in the oldest part of the centre of Woodhill. This was not to say that the place was a slum: I passed several upmarket boutiques and a hairdresser's en route to where I could see a neon sign above the entrance to my destination.

It was quite late. I had returned to our lodgings – the landlady, a retired doctor who hated having an empty home, had given us both a key – showered, written up a few notes of my interview with Mrs Harmsworth and then phoned home. All was well in Devon although George was in the doghouse for getting out of the field and munching his way through someone's vegetable garden. (We later discovered that the only casualties had been some grass and the tops of a few old Brussels sprout plants.)

The bar one immediately entered was fairly quiet, possibly, I soon discovered, on account of the prices. I ordered a glass of wine, large, telling myself that I was not driving, and settled on a stool at one end of the counter. From where I was sitting I could not see a lot, mainly because of carefully placed oriental screens and the way the place was laid out with the bar a sort of island in the centre and tables set in alcoves and off in various other nooks and crannies. It was a wonderful venue for clandestine meetings of every kind.

The Ladies' was through the restaurant, I was told, and deliberately went the long way round, establishing that Patrick was nowhere to be seen unless he was in one of the gloomy seemingly dead-ends where it would be intrusive of me to probe. He wasn't in the restaurant either.

'Do you have a table for one available?' I

enquired on my return journey.

They did, and someone fetched my glass from the bar for me while I studied the menu.

'Well, well,' said a voice I recognized from somewhere on the other side of the ornate Chinese-style pierced screen. There was the sound of movement and, moments later, he came into view.

'Hello, Detective Chief Inspector Colin Robert Hicks,' I said.

Five

He sat down in a gust of stale sweat. 'I thought I'd seen your face before today somewhere. Brinkley tells me you're the writer Ingrid Langley.'

'Police intelligence really has hit the fast lane,' I said. 'How is it progressing with finding out who killed Jason Giddings?' His untidy hair could do with a wash as well.

Smirking in superior fashion, Hicks said, 'A scumbag killed him for his cash. Then, ten to one, other scumbags knocked *him* off, ditto, and chucked his body in a river. It had to be people like that or they'd have taken the credit cards as well.'

'MPs shouldn't go for walks in the park after dark?'

Another smirk. 'I knew you were a clever girl. Got it in one.'

I decided on mozzarella with tomato-and-herb salad and some garlic bread, with possibly a dessert to follow. 'I'm disappointed. I thought you'd be following the same lead as Patrick and checking up on Theordore du Norde, Giddings's stepson, who was overheard making threats to him and apparently

98

used to meet dodgy types in here. Giddings was given the info by a friend and, according to his wife, informed Special Branch. There's word that Derek Harmsworth knew a snout who worked here. Is that a coincidence, or not?'

'Forget Harmsworth. He's out of it. The old fool got rat-arsed on whisky one night and drove off a bridge.'

'According to his wife, he never touched spirits.'

Shaking his head dismissively Hicks said, 'She's a daft old biddy, probably in the first stages of dementia. Fred Knightly should know: he met her at some police bash. He said she didn't have an idea in her head and kept asking Harmsworth when they could go home. As I said, Harmsworth's out of it.'

'I'm not surprised she wanted to go home if Knightly's anything like you.'

Deaf to this remark he gazed about. 'Where's that man of yours?'

'Goodness knows. I've only come in here for something to eat.'

'He's been working late using Gray's office – or did until you showed up. Take a look at this. Hard at it, eh?'

I gazed at the photo that had been thrust at me. It was of poor definition, taken from the rear and side, and showed a man and woman having sex. She was sitting on the edge of the desk, feet on chairs set wide apart, he between them, his trousers and underpants around his ankles. Her head was on his shoulder and you could see neither of their faces.

A waiter had appeared hopefully nearby and I gave him my order, also requesting a jug of iced water. 'It's not Patrick,' I said to Hicks when he had gone. 'And probably not Erin either but another woman wearing a red wig. Did someone in the Vice Squad owe you a favour?'

'Who else could it be? You can see it's Gray's office all right as there are the pictures of his allotment – or some bloody garden or other he had – on the wall behind the bloke's head. No one else has been working in there – it's well known in the nick that the pair of them were as snug as a bug in there for days.'

'It's not Patrick,' I said again, ignoring the blatant lie.

'I've the guy who set up the hidden camera who'll swear under oath if necessary that it is.' He tucked the photograph back in his wallet. 'This is going to Mike Greenway tomorrow. It's a pity hubby's backside's covered by his shirt or he might have had to drop his pants to try to prove it's not him.' He guffawed.

I said, 'Patrick was the second-youngest major in the British Army when he was sent out to the Falklands. They were undercover in the hills above Port Stanley when there was an accident with a grenade and he was badly injured. His right leg below the knee is now of exceedingly expensive construction and definitely not the one with which he was born. Now thank me for preventing you from making a complete silly-billy of yourself.'

I thought for a moment that he would actually lay hands on me, but he called me something highly uncomplimentary instead as he got to his feet. And then, with exquisite timing, the jug of water was placed before me and I shot its contents in the direction of his midriff as he did so. It landed in highly satisfactory fashion on the front of his overtight cotton trousers and for the second time in so many days he raged off, only this time leaving a trail of drips.

I had barely started on my meal when the chair opposite was again occupied.

'As I was a police officer already on the premises,' Patrick said in a very rural PC Plod voice, getting out a notebook, 'I said I'd investigate the management's complaint that a female member of the public has assaulted a customer. Would you care to give me your version of events, madam?'

'Hicks,' I said, 'showed me a photo of you bonking Erin in Gray's office that he's going to send to your boss tomorrow.'

Patrick's jaw dropped.

'Phoney, obviously, and I proved to him it was. I was really tempted to let him go ahead, but we don't have time for that kind of self-indulgence. He's out for your blood all right.'

Patrick took a cherry tomato from my plate and ate it, thoughts obviously elsewhere but pulling a face as he doesn't really like them. I called over the waiter and ordered calamari with garlic on fusilli for him before I lost the lot. Having to watch him eat squid was better than going hungry.

'I really hope it wasn't Erin,' he said quietly. This latest development had obviously come as a real shock.

'Not a chance,' I said. 'Come to think of it, the woman had lumpy legs. The guy had two whole ones, spindly, geekish.'

He gazed at me and the sparks of humour were back in the wonderful grey eyes. 'I don't have geekish one-and-a-half ones then?'

'You know you don't. They were the kind of thing you see on blokes who wear very short shorts with a longer anorak and are all hung about with tatty knapsacks, binoculars and OS maps in plastic bags.'

'Smelling of mildew.' He took a sip of my wine and snitched another tomato.

'Absolutely.'

His mood changed. 'I think I'll give Brinkley a ring tomorrow.'

'Please be careful.'

'No, sorry, I have no intention of being careful.'

I went to the bar and got a glass of red wine

for him. I never argue when he speaks like that.

'What next then?' I asked when he had taken the edge off his appetite.

'I think it would be a good idea to shelve du Norde for the present unless his name immediately pops up in other lines of enquiry. As you've probably realized, I asked a few questions here just now and mentioned his name but was given to understand by the manager that the boss is the one who answers those kind of queries and he's not here tonight. Shall we follow your suggestion – concentrate on Harmsworth and talk to his sergeant, whom I understand is still on sick leave? It could well be a waste of time, but who knows?'

We discovered the following morning that Paul Boles and his wife Mandy had taken an early holiday and gone to Sussex, where they were staying at an hotel in Lancing. Boles had had to have hospital treatment for a jaw infection and was still not fully recovered. The neighbour who told us this also informed us that the sergeant had been very shaken by the death of his boss, made worse by the fact that he had been one of the first on the scene of the accident.

'Reading between the lines, the man might be suffering from some kind of post-traumatic stress,' I commented as we returned to the car. 'You will treat him gently, won't you?'

'You're assuming that we're going to drive down to the south coast right now,' Patrick said. 'Should it have priority?'

'Yes, and we can work on Gray's list tonight at wherever we're staying. I mean, you won't want to come straight back and hit the rush hour, will you?'

Giving me an I-see-through-your-cunning-ruse-to-go-on-a-trip-to-the-seaside smile, Patrick turned the ignition key. 'I won't be able to claim it on expenses.'

'OK, I'll pay.'

The hotel where the couple were staying turned out to be on the sea front – in other words, overlooking the busy coastal main road, one's choice of view being either houses to the north or, in the opposite direction, a grey-looking English Channel flip-flopping tiredly on to a narrow pebbly beach. We had already decided that it would not be tactful for us to book into the same place – hardly, in the circumstances, a wrench.

The Boleses were not on the premises so we had a very late lunch and then found somewhere to stay in the north of the town, a little thatched pub at the foot of the Downs. When we returned, the tide had gone out, leaving miles of sand, in the direction of which I enthusiastically towed the man in my life.

104

'Shall I go and buy you a bucket and spade?' Patrick enquired heavily.

'Don't be such an old fogey,' I chided and we duly went for a walk on the damp, rippled sand, Patrick in a world of his own. He had not yet phoned Brinkley and I had an idea that he was drafting what he would say together with brewing up some kind of hideous and spectacular revenge on Hicks.

It was a little before six when we got back to the hotel. Patrick spoke to Mrs Boles courtesy of the receptionist's phone – they were in their room – explaining the reason for our presence and inviting them to join us in the bar for a drink and a chat.

'Not at all pleased, but she said they'd come down,' he reported.

I immediately came to the conclusion, when they came into view and over to where we were seated by the window in the practically deserted lounge bar, that Mandy was the stronger of the two and it was possible that without her Boles would have refused to see us. His nervous state was manifest even though Patrick, who had made sure beforehand that he knew what the man looked like, had got to his feet with a welcoming smile and waved them over.

'It's a day off for us,' Patrick began, having introduced me to them as his wife and asked what they would like to drink. 'So nothing official and for goodness' sake don't call me sir,' he added to Boles.

'But you are here on business really,' Mandy said to me when Patrick had gone over to the bar. 'And I have to say I rather resent being hounded when we're on holiday.'

'They're not hounding us,' Boles said to her quietly. 'If SOCA was doing that, I'd have been recalled to Woodhill.' He was in his mid-forties, I supposed, and was of medium height, a little overweight and had brown, thinning hair and brown eyes. Not a remarkable face, not a man to stand out in a crowd. He turned to me. 'Is this about the Giddings case?'

'Not really,' I replied. 'But I'll leave the questions to Patrick, he's the one who's had his head in all the files. It's not about anything you might or might not have done, though,' I hastened to assure him.

The man did not look any less tense and miserable.

My point was immediately repeated by Patrick when he returned with a tray. 'I don't want you to think we're checking up on you, because we aren't. SOCA's been called in to investigate the death of two police officers at Woodhill following the murder of an MP. I'm sure you know who these people are, or rather, were.'

'He can't talk about it,' Mandy interposed quickly. 'Anything but that. Please. He'd rather he was in trouble, and that's the truth.'

Patrick took an appreciative draught from

his beer and placed the tankard back on the table. 'Have you received threats?' he enquired of Boles in an undertone.

Boles shook his head. 'No, nothing like that.'

'Sure?' Patrick whispered.

'No. It's just that I was there ... when the DCI...' He broke off, realized his hands were shaking and put them out of sight beneath the table.

'Please leave him alone,' Amanda pleaded. 'I'm terrified he'll have some kind of breakdown.'

'Nightmares?' Patrick asked, still addressing the DS, his voice a mere breath now. 'Flashbacks?'

'He's going to resign,' Amanda declared. 'He can't live with it.'

'That won't make the horrors go away.' Patrick told her. 'And it'll be a huge waste of a valuable officer – *another* valuable officer.' Attention back on her husband, he continued, 'If Derek Harmsworth's death wasn't an accident and he was killed by the same hand that murdered DI Gray and their deaths were as a result of investigations they were undertaking...' He too broke off, with a shrug and a regretful smile. Then he said, 'Didn't you question the circumstances? A car going off a bridge in exactly the same place as another vehicle had two days previously?'

'Yes, I did but—'

Wisely or not, Patrick butted in with, 'But everyone expressed sadness and said life's a real bitch sometimes but he was getting on a bit and perhaps prone to senior moments and a second's inattention when you're driving...' An eyebrow quirked.

'Yes,' Boles said in a choked voice.

'And Knightly called you all together and said there'd be a collection for the widow and he was sure everyone would be very generous but meantime, chaps, the workload's worse than ever and even though he'd asked for extra personnel everyone should get on with it. Am I right?'

'I – I really did intend to speak to him,' Boles stuttered miserably after nodding. 'But he's never had much time for me and sort of steamrollers people he feels like that about out of his way. I knew Inspector Gray didn't believe the DCI's death was an accident, so I suppose I decided to leave it up to him. We were both well aware that the boss didn't drink spirits and questioned why he was on that road in the early hours of the morning. I should have grabbed Knightly when I had the chance and told him what I thought I'd seen. But I didn't, and then my tooth really flared up and I had to go into hospital. I – I feel so terribly guilty now.'

It seemed that he might burst into tears.

'I'm here to help you,' Patrick said, still speaking very quietly. 'Please try and relax. Enjoy your pint and we'll talk again in a minute.'

Mandy sat there hating us both, not realizing that her husband had begun to turn a mental and emotional corner.

'What you thought you saw...' Patrick continued a short while later after fetching small dishes of olives and nuts from the bar. 'Did you mention whatever it was to Gray?'

The DS had not really recovered his composure. 'No, because he had a habit of getting in a real lather about things. He was very upset and I thought that if I wasn't careful he'd be in real trouble, as he was getting ready to accuse Knightly of sweeping Harmsworth's death under the carpet. But he still hit the roof, the papers got to hear of it and he was carpeted. I was really anxious that if I added more fuel to the flames, kind of thing, with something I wasn't at all sure about, he'd end up by being the subject of an investigation and chucked out.'

Patrick frowned. 'Is there any suspicion in your mind, any gut feeling, that somewhere out there is a man, or men, who Harmsworth, and even Gray for that matter, were getting too close to in connection with the Giddings murder?'

After considering for a moment or two Boles said, 'No, not really. We weren't close to anyone. We hadn't pulled in any suspects for further questioning – in truth the trail had gone a bit cold. I don't think this is anything to do with Giddings at all. But that's only my opinion, of course.'

'Are you ready to tell me what you saw?'

Boles swallowed hard and stared down at his hands, which were tightly clasped in his lap. Then he shook his head mutely, closing his eyes.

'Please leave him alone,' Mandy begged.

'If you don't talk out the nightmares, they try to destroy you,' Patrick said. 'And if this all comes to a court case, would you be able to testify against any bastard who might have killed your boss?'

There was a long silence broken by Boles, the tears squeezing from beneath his still-closed eyelids, whispering, 'He – he wasn't quite dead when I got to him. The ambulance was right behind me. There was ... a lot of blood ... and I shall never forget the horrible way the car was sort of folded around him ... as though it was *devouring* him. But, God knows how, he saw me and moved an arm and pointed to the side of his neck, making a sort of jabbing movement with one finger. Then he went limp ... died right in front of my eyes.' After another long pause he continued, 'I think he was trying to tell me that he'd been stabbed.' His eyes flew open. 'You've no idea what I feel like ... filth, that's what I am. For pushing all this to the back of my mind. I've betrayed him!'

Patrick extended his right hand and Boles, bewildered, took it, only to have it clasped by another and shaken warmly.

'That's hardly true,' he was informed gently, 'because you've just told me and I've been on this job for only slightly more than a week. Nothing's lost and telling Knightly would have probably got you nowhere. Thank you. Come, man, and have dinner with us and over coffee you might recollect a bit more.'

He did: that it was Harmsworth's left arm he had seen and that his watch was missing.

'Oh, they said it must have got lost in the crash,' said Vera Harmsworth. 'You know, the strap broke or something like that. I didn't worry about it – I mean, it wasn't valuable.' She added sadly, 'Not that I wouldn't have liked to have it.'

It was the following morning and we had called on her straight after arriving back in Woodhill. She seemed a bit overwhelmed by Patrick's presence, forcing him to continue with the softly-softly approach. Truly, I was beginning to fear for Colin Hicks's personal safety when everything finally got unbottled.

'Can you remember the make?' Patrick asked her.

Mrs Harmsworth gave us the coffee she had made and sat down. 'I can remember everything about it, as I bought it for him, years ago. I got it from an RAC motoring magazine – it had the logo on it – and had an alarm. That was my little joke, really, as Derek kept sleeping through the alarm

111

clock. Yes, I can see it now – it was silver-coloured, had a blue face and an expanding bracelet kind of strap. Very chunky-looking and robust. You had to wind it up, though – it was in the days before battery ones.'

'So it must have been quite old,' I said.

'Gosh, yes, it was at least twenty years ago that I got it for him.'

Patrick said, 'Mrs Harmsworth, would you have any objection if I requested an exhumation and second post mortem on your husband?'

She went pale. 'On what grounds?'

'There's evidence, very tenuous, I'm afraid, that another agency might have been at work in the circumstances of his death.'

'You mean there's really something to point towards it not having been an accident?'

'There is, but, as I said, the evidence is very flimsy and I'm really sticking my neck out. I only wish I had something better to go on.'

'I personally would have no objection, because, as this lady's probably told you, I've had a suspicion right from the start that something wasn't right. But I can imagine my son and daughter being distressed by the prospect of an exhumation order. Still, it's not up to them, is it? They decided to go and live in far-away countries and cut themselves off. They both flew home the day after the funeral, you know, and didn't even ask if I needed help with anything. Yes, please go

112

ahead.'

'There will be paperwork for you to sign if I'm successful,' Patrick informed her. He took the list of cases and names we had found in the allotment shed from his document case. 'While I'm here, I'd be very grateful if you'd cast your gaze over this. All I'd like to know is if your husband ever mentioned any of these cases to you or the people involved with them.'

Dubiously she took it from him. 'This looks like John Gray's handwriting.'

'It is.'

'He did mention to me that he was digging around in the past, quietly, not officially, so I wasn't to say a word to anyone.'

'Was Erin Melrose in the know?' I asked in offhand fashion.

'Yes, I think he said he'd given her a copy of a list of names or something – perhaps it was this.'

Patrick looked at me and his eyes blazed.

'No, sorry, none of this means anything to me,' Mrs Harmsworth was saying, shaking her head. 'As I said the other day, Derek didn't really talk about his work, as he knew I didn't like the awful details, and if he did say anything I didn't retain it unless it was something funny that had happened to him.' She smiled broadly, the first time I had seen her do so. 'Like the occasion years ago when Derek was only a sergeant and they were chasing someone across a factory roof. The man stopped and danced about, taunting and swearing at them – he was a horrible character, apparently – only to slip and go right through a skylight. I know it's not really funny, because he was quite badly injured, but Derek and his colleagues thought it a real hoot. Being a policeman is a terrible tough life when you think about it.'

We had just left Mrs Harmsworth when Patrick's mobile rang and it was Michael Greenway, his boss in SOCA, asking him to make himself available for a briefing at eleven thirty. Relating this message to me afterwards, Patrick's face was sober: had Hicks sent the photo off after all?

This question was immediately answered when Greenway threw the offending item down on the table between us – we had met him at an hotel for a late coffee as he was 'just passing through' – and sat back staring at Patrick in not-amused fashion.

'You know all about me,' Patrick reminded him quietly. 'That's phoney.'

'I'm aware that it's a put-up job,' Greenway replied. 'What I really want to know is why police resources are being squandered on such crap.'

Patrick told him about Hicks's apparent role as Brinkley's hit man and, as he spoke, Greenway's anger grew.

'I seem to have been left in the dark with regard to your issues with the commander,' he said when Patrick had finished speaking.

Patrick said, 'I can only apologize and say in mitigation that until two days ago I wasn't aware that I *had* any issues with Brinkley.'

Greenway's manner did not change. 'I don't like it when my staff have excess baggage.'

Except for a curt nod, he had so far ignored me. The author was frankly finding this flawlessly dressed individual fascinating, tucking away on her own personal hard drive his massive height – at least six feet five – broad build and mane of sandy-coloured hair. A somewhat battered, albeit good-looking, countenance suggested time spent on the rugby field. He was, I guessed, between forty and fifty years of age.

There was nothing Patrick could really say in response to this comment and duly remained silent, just politely waiting for the other to proceed.

'I'm in rather a hurry, so a verbal report will do,' Greenway said, finally.

Without referring to any notes Patrick said, 'The brief you gave me was to discover whether there were any connections between the Giddings case and the death of DI John Gray. Well, as you know the only *obvious* similarities are the manner of their deaths and the fact that Gray was involved with the Giddings inquiry. Post-mortem findings have thrown up a couple of interesting points in that Giddings was dealt with in much more surgical fashion, if that's the correct description, while Gray was merely butchered. It appears that the weapons were probably different. That alone casts doubt on the murderer being one and the same person. Tentatively, I think Gray's was a copycat killing for reasons unknown or because Gray was close to the perpetrator of another, serious, crime. Gray might even have questioned Giddings's killer without knowing how close he was.'

'Other than the latter, why Gray, for God's sake?'

'Quite. Other than being somewhat impulsive and hot-headed the man appears to have been blameless in both his public and private life, although there might be things that no one knows about. So until anything else comes to light it might have to be tackled from the point of view of revenge on the part of someone he shoved in the slammer – or helped to. And if you were about to ask me if I think any more police personnel might be at risk, the answer has to be yes, possibly.'

'Evidence?' Greenway snapped.

'Nothing concrete. But you could authorize a request for the exhumation of DCI Derek Harmsworth and then I might have some.'

Greenway's face screwed up into a ball of incredulity. 'Harmsworth? But he drove himself off a bridge.'

Patrick shook his head. 'No. His car went through a hole in a bridge on a quiet road that had been made by a heavy lorry two days before. In my view that's too much of a coincidence and his vehicle was too lightweight to have done the same thing if it had hit somewhere else nearby. It would have merely bounced off, admittedly doing serious damage to everything. The railings are designed like that. Harmsworth's body reeked of whisky, he didn't drink spirits, he always rang his wife if there was a change of plan, and he hadn't. Besides which—'

Greenway butted in with, 'It's got to be dead in the water. Leave it.'

'May I finish what I was going to say?' Patrick requested.

'If you think it's important.'

Patrick told him what Boles had said and Greenway became annoyed again.

'So why didn't this pin-brained sergeant open his mouth before?'

Patrick shrugged, Gallic-style. 'Naturally timid? Hospitalized recently after half his face became infected with a huge abscess? Bullied by higher authority? Post-traumatic stress disorder brought on by his boss dying horribly right in front of his eyes? Take your pick – they're all true.'

Six

'What about Harmsworth's family?' Greenway asked, looking a little sheepish. 'What are their views?'

'His wife's never thought his death an accident.'

This appeared to remind Greenway that there were three of us. Turning to me, he said, 'What do you think about this?'

'It was Ingrid who pointed me in Harmsworth's direction,' Patrick informed him before indicating that the stage was mine.

I said, 'I'd like to mention something else first and that is that you both seem to be forgetting that Hicks's shabby little scam involved DS Erin Melrose as well. Her career could so easily have been ruined.'

Greenway had another look at the photo. 'Is that who it's supposed to be? God, I thought it was made to look as though Patrick had hauled a hooker off the street. Thank you, Ingrid. I shall bear that in mind.'

I thought this response pretty feeble but said, to Patrick, 'Do you have that list?'

With the air of a man who has forgotten something important Patrick took the sheet of A4 from his inside jacket pocket and placed it on the table.

'In answer to your question,' I said to Greenway, 'I think that a verdict of accidental death on Derek Harmsworth is shaky. That is a list of his most serious and important cases that was compiled by John Gray. He didn't think Harmsworth's death was an accident either. Of the twenty-six names seven are dead, ten still in prison and the remaining nine have been released. Of those one is in a home suffering from dementia, another in Australia, where he's living with his daughter, and the rest are at large. Out of those seven, three have been released fairly recently – in other words, could be burning for revenge and in time to have killed Harmsworth. They include a man who once fell though a skylight when being chased across a factory roof by Harmsworth and his team and who prior to his fall had taunted and sworn at them. All keepers of the peace thought his untimely exit a huge joke and laughed like drains. I suggest we check up on this character without delay.'

Greenway looked at me and I looked at him. Then he dropped his gaze with a soft chuckle. 'Richard Daws did warn me that you didn't just decorate your husband's arm. OK, but I suggest that you check up on all seven. I have an idea it'll be a waste of time, but it needs to be done to clear it out of the way. I'll have to think long and hard about the exhumation and get back to you. But look' – and here his manner hardened as his attention re-focused on Patrick – 'stay away from Hicks. I don't want to hear that he's had any run-ins with a member of SOCA, not even an exchange of opinions. Is that understood?'

'And if he really does shove a spy camera up my arse?' Patrick enquired like something exceedingly holy depicted on a Michelangelo ceiling.

'Tell me. I don't want you even to breathe too hard on him.'

'Tell teacher,' Patrick muttered a little later when Greenway had gone.

'It's mostly your own fault,' I countered. 'In other words, your reputation.' Before he could say anything else I went on, 'It might be what Brinkley's banking on. Hicks is too stupid to see he's being used as cannon fodder and Brinkley's hoping you'll lose your temper and do him real harm.' Here I bent a frown in his direction. 'As you have been known to do sometimes. And that'll be it – OUT!'

'I simply can't explain why he took my turning down the offer of the job so badly.'

'I can. I realize that you were furious with him about something else at the time, but among other remarks, which I won't repeat, you commented on his rather well-groomed person by saying he smelt like an Albanian knocking-shop. That might have offended him just the smidgiest bit.'

Patrick sort of grunted. 'Well, he did.'

'I hope you're not speaking from experience,' I commented archly.

He gave me a filthy wink. 'OK. Frinton' – and ducked as I aimed a pretend cuff at his ear.

I had no worries about Patrick's working relationship with Greenway. At the conclusion of the meeting both had risen, the latter a good two inches taller and one and a half times as wide, and there had been the smallest of smiles exchanged. But genuine smiles; an understanding. Neither would waste time in trying to score points off the other.

The man who had fallen through the skylight was now calling himself Kevin Beardshaw – possibly the latest in a series of aliases he had used during a long and distasteful criminal career – and the last address police records had for him was in north Woodhill. Our luck really was in that afternoon, for not only did he still live there but he was in and actually opened the front door of the small terraced house himself.

'Serious and Organized Crime Agency,' Patrick said, holding up his ID card. 'We'd like to ask you a few questions.'

Beardshaw, thin to the point of emaciation, pallid of hue and a little stooped even though his records intimated that he was only fifty-one years of age, shrugged, not meeting our gaze, and turned to shuffle off down a narrow hallway, leaving us to follow. One did not have to be very clever to realize that he was ill.

'As you do, once in a while,' said Beardshaw in a weak, hoarse voice when everyone was standing in a dingy living room, 'if there's a crime you think I might have had a hand in. I've only been outside for a few weeks but it's easy pickings, isn't it, calling on me? I keep telling you I'm not the man I was, but no one believes me.'

'They must do,' Patrick said, 'or you'd never have been let out at all.'

The other threw up his arms in a gesture of defeat and half-sat, half-fell into an armchair. 'All right. What is it this time?'

We also seated ourselves and a faint cloud of dust arose as we did so, setting Beardshaw coughing, a horrible rasping sound.

'Tell me about the time you fell through a factory roof,' Patrick requested.

The man tried to laugh but coughed again instead. Then, recovering, he said, 'Days of glory those. Young and fit and running rings round you lot. What a laugh.'

'But it wasn't funny when you fell though the skylight,' I said.

'Not at the time,' Beardshaw conceded. 'A broken leg and arm hurts a hell of a lot, I can tell you. Don't ever try it, lady. The cops what had been chasing me all stood round that bloody roof window looking down at me with grins all over their faces. I'd been giving them a load of lip, mind. But when they saw I'd really hurt myself they called an ambulance and then broke into the factory to find where I was and made me as comfortable as they could. A real surprise that was after the treatment I'd had from cops before. But I was only a kid then, I suppose.'

'It didn't put you off breaking the law, though,' Patrick said dryly.

'Nah. What else was there to do in them days if you'd bunked off school and the army told you you were too weedy to join up? So why d'you want to know about that then?'

Patrick said, 'The sergeant in charge was a bloke called Derek Harmsworth. You and he have bumped into one another quite a few times since and, as you must well know, he ended up as DCI at Woodhill. You were responsible for countless burglaries, robbery with violence, supplying muscle and driving getaway cars for East End gangs, receiving stolen property, conning old ladies out of money by pretending to be homeless, social-security fraud – quite a long list, eh? Ever carried weapons?'

Beardshaw shook his head emphatically. 'No.' And when Patrick continued to stare at him, 'Well...'

'Something like this?'

Patrick had taken the knife from his pocket and now sprang the blade. How could I ever forget that ghastly slicing click?

'No!' Beardshaw was staring at the weapon in horror. 'No! I was going to say I'd used a pickaxe handle once or twice when we did over a mobster and his oppos, or something like that, but no, nothing like that, ever. I swear it!'

The knife went back out of sight. 'OK.' Patrick stood up to leave.

'So what's it all about then?' Beardshaw asked. 'Is that it?'

By the doorway Patrick turned. 'Harmsworth's dead. It was in all the local papers. But now it looks as though someone might have knifed him and then made his death look like an accident by shoving him and his car off a bridge.'

'I didn't know he was dead,' Beardshaw said. 'I've been in hospital. Lung cancer. There's nothing else they can do for me.'

'I'm sorry. You wouldn't happen to know who hated Harmsworth that much, would you?'

'Everyone I know hates the Bill.' Then, avoiding our gaze, he muttered, 'I don't personally hold with killing coppers. I mean, who else would catch the shits who mess with little kids? You could try a bloke who sometimes works behind the bar at Jo-Jo's. By all accounts he knows everything what goes on.'

'What's his name?'

'No one asks – you don't.'

'It would be helpful to know whom to approach – I'm new on this patch.'

After a short silence Beardshaw said, 'Word is that he is Jo-Jo, the owner of the place, and likes to keep his hand in. An oldish bloke, Italian-looking, eyes like one of them snakes what swaller things.'

'I take it you didn't mention the possibility of a police snout being on the premises at Jo-Jo's when you were in there,' I said to Patrick when we were sitting in the car perusing the list of names.

'Not to the bloke who said he was the manager, no,' he replied. 'Just as well after what we've just been told. He did seem to be rather nervous, though.'

The saying about being caught between a rock and a hard place crossed my mind. I said, 'What did you make of Beardshaw?'

'He's a devious so-and-so and I haven't completely ruled him out of being a possible suspect. But I do have to say he genuinely didn't seem to bear any grudges against the police.'

'I'm wondering if he's as ill as he says he is.'

'Obviously, neither of us is happy about writing him out of the picture.'

'It's funny how Jo-Jo's seems to keep being mentioned. The barman who was in there the other night was quite young. We could eat there this evening, see if the owner's on the premises and and watch out for boa constrictors.'

Patrick glanced at his watch. 'Good idea. But there's plenty of time yet to call on a man called Peter Forbes. He's the only one on this list with an address in the immediate locality.'

But the terrace of houses where the house had been located – the whole road, for that matter – had been demolished and, according to a large notice board, was part of an 'urban improvement scheme'.

We seemed to be getting nowhere.

I sensed, when we entered Jo-Jo's that evening, that things were about to improve – that is, if the man standing behind the bar was indeed our quarry. Beardshaw had had a point: there was something distinctly reptilian about him, although I would have said more lizard than snake. I went to the bar with Patrick and perched on a stool because I wanted to hear what was being said.

'I know who you are,' said lizard-face, Jo-Jo, whoever, with a strong Italian accent as he fixed two glasses of wine for us. 'You were asking questions in here the other day.'

'It's my job,' Patrick replied sadly.

'And you,' he said to me, pointing with a gnarled forefinger, 'threw water over one of my customers.'

'He's a cop too,' I said, 'and out to rubbish this man in my life.'

The slit eyes momentarily opened wider. 'I like loyalty in a woman.'

Patrick said, 'We're trying to discover whether another cop, who died, was murdered.'

'The one called Gray?' said the man in surprise. 'I thought everyone knew he was murdered.'

'No, DCI Derek Harmsworth. His car went off a bridge before Gray was killed.' Patrick added, after a short silence, 'Were you his snout?'

'Such a horrible word,' retorted the other, seeming to be really offended.

'My apologies,' said Patrick gracefully. 'English idiom can be cruel. Let me say, then, that whoever it was gave him certain information. You were offended, so I'm guessing that it was you.'

'It might have been,' the other conceded.

'In return he might have turned a blind eye to some of your staff being illegal immigrants and the club you run being a bit – well – iffy.'

'I will have no criminals here!'

'I'll give you the benefit of the doubt. Now, do you know anything about Harmsworth's death?'

The old man seemed to wither a little into himself. 'It was bad, very bad,' he muttered. 'I saw him that night, you know. He came in here, just popped in, as you say. He sometimes did, not for any reason, just to say hello, Jo-Jo, how are you? We had a good understanding.'

'What time was this?' Patrick asked.

'At just before seven, I think. He was on his way home.'

'Was there any particular reason why he came here that evening?'

'He asked me if I knew anything about the Giddings man. But no, nothing. I know nothing about politicians.'

'And he made no comment about any other calls he planned to make on the way home?'

'Nothing that I can remember. We were very busy.'

'I hear what you say about no criminals being permitted here, but did you notice anyone who might have been a stranger standing near to you when you were talking? Was anyone taking a furtive interest in Harmsworth?'

Jo-Jo now appeared to go into a state of suspended animation, presumably thinking. It occurred to me that he more closely resembled one of those unfortunates who had been ritually murdered back in the mists of time and whose remarkably preserved remains are sometimes found in peat bogs. For some reason I then shivered: there was something very unnerving about this man and I would have hated to get on the wrong side of him.

At last, Jo-Jo said, 'As I said, we were busy.

I cannot remember anyone of the sort you are after. The place was full of businessmen, bank people, professional types. Most of my customers are like that – the rough ones are not welcome here. But' – and here his thin shoulders rose in an elaborate shrug – 'this person might be like – what is it called? – a creature that changes colour?'

'A chameleon,' I said.

The wizened features split into a ghastly smile. 'On the menu tonight, perhaps? You want some?' And he wheezed with laughter.

Patrick was not to be diverted. 'I'm also interested in a man by the name of Theodore du Norde. I understand he belongs to your club.'

'The club is not part of the restaurant.'

'I'm aware of that.'

'And none of the business of the police.'

'So it was a no-go area with Harmsworth, was it? OK, we'll forget it's actual set-up for now – just tell me about du Norde.'

'It's confidential,' said Jo-Jo. 'Now, that is enough. I'm busy.'

He went from sight through a door marked 'PRIVATE'.

We stayed to eat, a smiling waiter appearing as abruptly as his boss had disappeared to show us to a table. I took this to mean that there was no real enmity towards us, which I suppose was a relief, as I had a strong suspicion that Jo-Jo might be behind a lot of illegal goings-on in the Woodhill area.

'The local godfather?' I whispered to Patrick when we had placed our order.

'I reckon he must be. But who knows? The DCI might have tolerated him and those who work for him because his presence, and muscle, keep out far worse hoodlums from, say, central Europe. As he said, he and Harmsworth had an understanding – but that isn't going to prevent me from having a rummage around in his club.'

'How, though?'

'I'll think of something.'

We left the restaurant at a little after nine thirty and, not having brought the car set off to walk back to our lodgings. It was a murky night, drizzling lightly but eventually soakingly, the pavements having a greasy sheen to them.

'What do you suggest we do next?' I asked as we left the side lane and turned into the main road.

Patrick was silent for a moment or two and then said, 'As we're all too aware, there's no actual evidence yet that would point to Harmsworth having been murdered. There are no real leads with regard to the Gray inquiry either – I checked up on that while you were in the shower earlier. No one yet questioned saw anyone suspicious near his house around that time and none of the forensic evidence has so far been useful. No fingerprints, DNA samples other than Gray's, nothing useful at all. I think we're looking for a pro for that killing, who wore gloves and took other precautions. The same might even apply to Harmsworth's death, if he really was stabbed. It might be time to make something happen.'

And with that something did: a man came at us from an alleyway at the run, on us instantly to grab me around the neck to haul me back from whence he had come. I took him unawares by collapsing, deadweight, getting him off balance so that he almost fell. I curled up in a protective ball and other than a desultory kick in my general direction that landed on my left shin he abandoned me only to run straight into Patrick. I was just in time, jumping to my feet, to see what happened next – a knife flashing as the blade caught the light from a street lamp. It was wrung from his grasp and clattered to the ground. In the next second Patrick had gone headlong into the road, a foot slipping off the kerb. A car screamed to a standstill, stopping just short of him.

Footsteps pounded off into the distance.

Patrick was swearing inventively when I got to him, a passenger having got out of the car to assist him.

'You OK, mate?' he asked.

'Don't touch it!' Patrick said as the man moved towards the knife. 'Yes, thanks, I'm fine.' I saw his teeth gleam as he grinned fiercely. 'Just dented pride.'

★ ★ ★

131

'No, that wasn't an attempted mugging,' Patrick agreed when we were having the inevitable debriefing in our room. 'And for the record I don't think it was anything to do with Hicks either – unless he's even more stupid than I thought.'

'Just a random attack by a crazy sort of person who goes in for such things?' I hazarded, rubbing my bruised shin. Patrick was, I knew, furious with himself for not having grabbed our attacker, especially as, lately, he has worked hard to get himself back to the same standard of fitness as he had when we worked for D12, our MI5 department.

'What do you think?'

'I think, no, it wasn't a random attack.'

We'd taken the knife to the nick and made a report before heading for our digs – quite a long walk, as the former was in the opposite direction; Patrick had insisted we needed the exercise. I had actually wondered if he was half-hoping that whoever it was would have a second attempt, but nothing had happened.

'In other words, then, it's another attack on the police, or those connected with them?'

'Based on shaky info,' I replied, 'that the new boy at the nick's a semi-retired army bod who must have been driving a desk for years so will be a pushover – literally. Whoever it was probably meant to kill or badly injure you, though.'

'Info?' Patrick murmured. 'There's a mole,

you mean?'

'I don't really know why I said that,' I admitted. 'Yes, unless Jo-Jo was warning you off or trying you out.'

'It doesn't ring true. He gains nothing by antagonizing the local police. No, let's go back to what you said. If it's correct, it means that an individual inside, or connected to, the nick, is giving someone else information.'

'Civilian staff, friends, relations: just a few hundred suspects then.'

'Let's pray there's some fingerprints or DNA on the knife.'

'I *think* he was wearing leather gloves.'

'We may have our murderer. Or had.' Patrick groaned. 'God, if only I'd not let the bastard go.'

'Look at it from the point of view of your not being tucked snugly inside a mortuary chiller cabinet right now.'

The chill, or rather frost, proved to be in Woodhill police station as it had got round that one of MI5's one-time finest operatives had failed to apprehend someone who, after all, had behaved no worse than an armed mugger. I concluded that none of the critics, Hicks included, had ever suffered the attentions of such a person, least of all when accompanied by a female whose safety would be given priority. This female had accompanied the maligned one to work the following morning: it was time I put in an appearance.

'I thought you were bloody-well armed,' was Hicks's remark when we came face to face with him – too neatly for it to be a co-incidence – in a corridor.

'Would you have had me shoot him in the back?' Patrick demanded to know. 'Not to mention all the resulting publicity. And, by the way, I want you to apologize to Erin Melrose before the day's out for quite ruthlessly being prepared to drag her name through your own personal stinking midden.'

With a curl of the lip Hicks walked away.

'Please remember what Greenway said,' I pleaded.

Silence.

'I'm serious,' I continued. 'Erin might not know anything about it yet. If Greenway's as good as you say he is, he'll have a quiet word with her, or has done so already. We don't need a full-blown war here right now or the consequences might be disastrous. Divide and rule and all that.'

'As usual, my dear, you're right,' he muttered.

He knows it infuriates me to be thus spoken to.

Superintendent Fred Knightly, who apparently wanted to see us, was in his office, reading a newspaper. When he saw us appear in the open doorway he thrust it into a

134

drawer of his desk and switched to brisk efficiency. He looked older than he had in pictures in the local paper and for some reason I took an immediate dislike to him.

'D'you read anything serious into the attack or was it just a random mugging attempt by a drug addict?' he enquired by way of a greeting.

'A random mugging attempt by an armed drug addict not being a serious crime in your eyes?' Patrick said in amazement. 'Superintendent, if I'd been an ordinary member of the public and not someone trained in self-defence, Ingrid likewise, you'd probably have a another murder case on your hands right now. But to answer your question: yes, it could well have a bearing on other inquiries, John Gray's for one.'

'We're still awaiting the initial results of tests on the knife,' Knightly said. 'But as you know, DNA testing will take longer. I understand you're suspicious of the findings of the inquest on DCI Derek Harmsworth and have a list of names of possible suspects that Gray compiled.'

'That's right, and Sergeant Paul Boles has given a statement to me to the effect that he thought Harmsworth tried to tell him in his dying moments that he'd been stabbed.'

'Boles is bloody useless, frankly.'

'Someone thought him good enough to be promoted to sergeant.'

'Before my time here,' Knightly said darkly. His heavily lidded eyes came to rest on me. 'It's unusual, you know, for men to have their wives along.'

'Sometimes we swap,' I retorted. 'Some days I do the talking and sleuthing and have *him* along. Most of the time, though, we work together. Thank your lucky stars it's his turn today or I might just have given you a real piece of my mind and you'd have happily joined that tabloid crap in the drawer.'

He sort of gibbered before managing to get out, 'No – no offence, Miss Langley, just stating fact.' He uttered a strained falsetto laugh. 'The force is changing all the time – every day, in fact. For the better, I'm sure. I just wanted to ask your opinions of the affair. Well, shall we not waste time and get on with it, eh?'

Outside, Patrick turned a pained expression on me but could not keep up the pretence and rocked with mostly silent laughter. It was unfortunate then to run head on into someone for the second time – only Greenway this time. He stared straight through us.

'I'd better go off and do something truly heroic,' Patrick said under his breath. 'Meanwhile it had better be coffee – no, not there,' he added as I turned right to follow a direction sign to the canteen. 'Somewhere where you can drink the bloody stuff.'

Seven

We concentrated for the rest of that morning on activities not at all heroic, just plain hard work: doing as Michael Greenway had ordered, trying to trace the six remaining names on Inspector Gray's list. Postponing looking for Peter Forbes, the one whose house no longer existed, we headed for Romford in search of Ungumba Natolla, only to be told by an openly hostile father – and I was thanking everything holy that Patrick was with me at this particular high-rise block of flats – that he had just started a life sentence for murder, having been in custody for three months. This same sink estate was also the address of Clem and Ernie Brocklebank, who I had just noticed were mystifyingly listed as one entry; but there was no answer when we rang the bell. Patrick hammered on the door with his fist as well, in case it was not working, but there was still no response.

'Remind me who else there is,' Patrick requested as we were driving away.

I consulted the list. 'Zak Bradley, last known address in Tower Hamlets; Anthony

Babbington-Jones, whose last whereabouts was Guildford, and another one who used aliases – might be calling himself Francis Applejohn or John Appleton – and was of no fixed address.'

'Any murderers among them?'

'Anthony Babbington-Jones was sent down for being a con man who got high on drink and drugs one night and battered to death someone who had just rumbled him. The others seem to have been career criminals who Harmsworth caught after painstaking detective work.'

'Any knife artists?'

'Yes, Ungumba Natolla, but we now know we can discount him. The Brocklebanks sound nasty: Harmsworth managed to get them to court for a gangland murder, but then several witnesses refused to testify or changed their stories. Gray's made a note that the pair are probably responsible for other killings. They've done time for GBH and violent robbery.'

'I reckon the Met can be asked to look for Bradley, ditto Surrey police with Babbington-Jones. That leaves Forbes, the Brocklebanks, who sound the right grade of hoodlums to murder a copper, and the bloke with no fixed address. Now, though, lunch.'

This was a working one, in the canteen, while we questioned people in order to try to find witnesses to Harmsworth's last hours. We spoke to the staff there and then progressed to the civilian clerks, probationers – anyone to whom he might have mentioned a sudden change of plan. Those who could actually remember that night of the third of April – and there were only a handful – had nothing useful to tell us. We found the constable to whom the DCI and Boles had spoken in the park after Giddings's murder and another who had accompanied him to question a suspect in an unrelated case the day before he'd died, but they could shed no light on anything either.

'Nothing,' I said round about two thirty. I had a thumping headache. 'Shall we go back to the bridge and see if there are any houses nearby where people might have seen something?'

'It did happen in the early hours of the morning,' Patrick said dubiously. 'But let's go anyway – I could do with some fresh air.'

A preliminary report on the knife with which we had been attacked indicated that there were no actual fingerprints, but the entire weapon, a flick knife, was very smeary, as though it had been wiped with a greasy cloth. Minute deposits in the mechanism might – *might* – be blood and further tests would be carried out. We were asked if either of us had been scratched by the blade, to which we answered in the negative.

'Everything's so green and beautiful,' I said as we got out of the car, having parked it in the same place as we had on our first visit, in a small lay-by at one end of the bridge. I found myself yearning for the wide-open spaces at home.

Patrick took a deep breath. 'I'm getting really bloody-minded about this business. But if we don't get a good lead soon and are able to present Greenway with proper evidence then...' He left the rest unsaid.

'Have you phoned Brinkley yet?'

'No, like cheese, I've left it for a bit to ripen.'

I gazed about, the unceasing roar of the traffic below us somehow reminding me how impossible it can be to re-create the past: the world grinding on uncaring.

'There's a big house just up there on the hill,' I said, shading my eyes against the glare of the sun. 'It seems to be the only one from which there could be any kind of vantage point of this road.'

'A big upper-crust house,' Patrick said thoughtfully, taking a look for himself. 'Perhaps if we tug our forelocks they'll give us a cup of tea.'

It always amuses me, Patrick's total obliviousness to the fact that he comes across as pretty upper crust himself.

He was right about the house, Buckton Manor, though; a butler answered the door. 'I shall ask her ladyship if it's convenient,' he said, asking us to wait in the hall.

A Lutyens house, no less, every last inch of the place straight out of *Country Life* magazine.

'This lady isn't going to be the right person to ask about possible dodgy goings-on down on the road below her home,' I whispered.

Just then the butler returned and, after a longish walk along a panelled gallery lined with paintings, mostly portraits, ushered us into a light, bright room with views over a terrace and immaculate garden. A thin, elderly woman sat reading by a log fire.

'Lieutenant-Colonel Gillard, I understand,' she said in an amazingly strong voice for her frail-looking frame, 'from the Serious and Organized Crime Agency. How fascinating!' She waved away Patrick's proffered ID card. 'Do sit down. What can I do for you? Tea first, though? Yes, tea, please, Hurst – for three. And a few pastries.'

We sat on a settee that would have accommodated six.

'I hope you're not overwarm in here,' she went on. 'I feel the cold rather and as the house is listed as well as being ferociously draughty we can't have proper double glazing fitted.' Her gaze came to rest on me, 'My dear, I feel sure I know you from somewhere.'

It turned out that she had read most of my books.

'Your ladyship...' Patrick began.

'Oh, call me Thora, do. Hurst gets a bit carried away by it all and by the time some poor souls get to see me they're practically

141

curtseying, men and all. It puts up a barrier immediately.'

Patrick explained the reason for our presence.

'I clearly recollect the night,' said Thora. 'I was woken by sirens and even up here the flashing blue lights flickered on my bedroom ceiling. But prior to that I confess I heard nothing.'

'Perhaps a member of your staff did?' Patrick suggested. 'Or His Lordship?'

She laughed. 'Oh, you heard me say "we" just now, didn't you? I meant me and my staff and helpers. No, Manfred won't have heard anything. The silly man went down with his racing yacht and a clutch of girl-friends somewhere off Bermuda thirty-five years ago. Apparently the whole lot were roaring drunk at the time, so they probably never even noticed.'

Hurst appeared with a tray.

'That night there was the accident down on the bridge when a policeman was killed,' his employer said to him, 'did you hear any-thing before the police and ambulances arrived?'

'As you know, madam, my room's at the back,' said Hurst. 'No, nothing but the usual owls.'

He made it sound as though the owls were there specifically to annoy him.

Patrick said, 'There were no other noctur-nal sounds that you might have questioned?

Nothing suspicious at all?'

Hurst shook his head. 'No, sir, nothing like that. But I'm quite a heavy sleeper.'

When the butler had left the room Thora said, 'It would appear that you think what happened might not have been a straightforward accident?'

'It might not have been,' Patrick agreed.

'Only I'm aware that a lorry went through those railings a couple of days prior to that, which is a coincidence. It occurs to me that...' She broke off, looking embarrassed. 'No, it's not my place to offer theories.'

'Please do,' Patrick said earnestly. 'We need all the theories we can get.'

A faint flush had tinted the pallid cheeks. 'I was going to say that if there was any malicious intent, the hole in the railings was a perfect place to stage what would look like another accident. Someone would only have to be aware that a certain person, a policeman, would be travelling along that stretch of road in the early hours and then could run out and wave them down, pretending there was an emergency of some kind...' She stopped speaking again, shyly smiling.

'That is exactly how it could have been done,' Patrick said quietly, staring into space as he thought about it.

Thora said, 'I suggest you talk to the gardener. Well, he's sort of a gardener. You have to stand over him all the time or he digs out all the wrong things and prunes the roses to the ground. He's a bit of a reprobate, really – someone told me he used to be a poacher – and Hurst thinks I ought to get rid of him; but he does other jobs as well – chops wood and sees to the fires. He'll turn his hand to most things, really – as long as there's money in it for him.'

'Where can we find him?'

'Well, you might have to look for him as I'm not sure whether he's finished clearing out the old greenhouse. I'm hoping to have it restored. In the summer he lives in the old potting shed in the walled garden – that's where the greenhouse is. It's quite large and there's a stove in there and a room above where the under-gardeners lived donkeys' years ago. Where he lives in the winter months is anyone's guess, but he still walks the boundaries just before dark and keeps an eye out for trespassers. I don't like to ask about his arrangements – he's an independent sort of man but loyal in an odd way and it makes me feel safer having someone keeping an eye on the place. If anyone heard anything that night, it would be Danny – but, obviously, only if he was here.'

Smoke was drifting slowly out of the tall chimney pot on the lean-to potting shed. It was situated just inside the double gates of the walled garden, this now down to grass, a few fruit trees and a vegetable patch, which was freshly dug and raked.

Although our approach was not noisy, we

had been detected, a scarecrow-like figure appearing in the doorway of the greenhouse, again lean-to, next to the potting shed. A shovelful of broken glass was dropped into a dustbin with a crash and he stood still, staring at our approach.

Patrick nudged me, a silent request that I should make the introductions and do most of the talking. He knows I have good results with people, and animals, that can be described as fairly harmless semi-feral. My first thought on beholding the man more closely, however, was that if he had not been human or animal, he would have been in the category of something that I would have been told, as a child, to take back immediately and put where I had found it.

'Oh yes,' said this short, swarthy and none-too-clean individual in bored fashion when I had explained our presence. 'Well, you're wasting your time; there was no one lurking about 'ere. I see to it.'

'Did you look over towards the road at all on the day of the accident?' I asked. 'Would you have been able to see if anyone was hanging about from up here?'

'Only if it was light and when the leaves aren't on the trees. But no, I didn't see anyone or anything down there. I don't have time to stop and gawp around. Besides, it all happened in the early hours of the morning, didn't it?'

'So you weren't living here then?'

145

'No, it weren't warm enough.'

'It was, though, wasn't it? – unseasonally hot, with thunderstorms.'

'I told you: I weren't here.'

'Where do you live when you're not here?'

'Mind your own bleedin' business.'

Patrick had wandered away for a short distance – remaining close enough to provide assistance if the need arose – and was looking at the greenhouse, or what was left of it, with interest.

Abandoning that question for now I said, 'The lady of the house told us that you walk the boundaries before dark. Did you do it on that night?'

'I can't remember – probably.'

'And you saw nothing then?'

The man shrugged. 'Can't say as I did.' He turned to move away.

'I've not finished yet,' I said. 'Or would you prefer to carry on this conversation down at Woodhill nick?'

'I saw and heard nothing!' he shouted in my face.

'We'll take a walk down to the southern boundary,' Patrick called across to me. And to the gardener, 'It's all right, we'll find our own way.'

'I was hoping you'd back me up there,' I said stiffly when we were out of earshot.

'It doesn't always do to lean too hard on people right at the beginning. Why didn't you insist on an answer to the question about where he lived?'

I thought about it for a moment or two and then said, 'Because I was worried that he'd get really aggressive.'

'And shove you over and there's a lot of broken glass lying about. Yes, exactly. So he's someone to keep an eye on then. That greenhouse is made of teak, by the way.'

We exited the walled garden through a narrow gate on the far side and immediately found ourselves in an overgrown semi-wooded area obviously used as the site for bonfires and compost heaps. There was a large pile of wood – broken off branches of trees and so forth that looked as though they had been torn off in winter gales. We followed a path of sorts that wound between the trees, going downhill, the sound of traffic on the motorway getting louder. It did not take long to reach the limit of the property, a brick wall in dire need of repair.

'Thora probably has no idea it's this bad,' Patrick said musingly, gazing at a broken-down section. 'Anyone with a mind to could get in through here – or out.' He looked around quickly. 'Please stay in this area and trample about noisily. I'm going back to have a quick look at Danny's living quarters.'

'Be careful,' I urged. 'He's awash with grudges and I'm sure there's a GBH or two in there somewhere.'

He went from sight, leaving me to walk along by the wall, careful not to trip over dislodged bricks, scuffing my feet though the grass and humming softly. It seemed to me that it reflected exactly our efforts so far on the investigations: plodding around on the edges, making noises. Perhaps my own perceptions were flawed and I had made a mistake in persuading Patrick to change tack. Perhaps the oracle should have stayed at home and carried on writing fiction.

We have known each other for almost always, or at least from schooldays, the evening when Patrick arrived to help me with my physics homework. The difference between our ages had been like a chasm up until then and I had only just noticed the new head boy and his somewhat aloof manner, mostly, ye gods, because he had had the temerity to tell me off for taking a short cut across the main hall, forbidden to lowly third-formers. Looking back, even now, I cannot recollect even the trace of a smile on his face as he issued the reprimand. My dad giving me the news several days later of his impending arrival – the two fathers were friends – had initiated a mood of gloom and when Patrick had walked through the kitchen door he hadn't been smiling then either. In short, he had sat and simmered, the unsaid message being that as girls were always lousy at physics, what was the point anyway?

Something most odd had happened to me at that point. I had drawn a neat line under the words 'Specific Gravity' while somehow undergoing a headlong plunge into woman-hood. Here was the man I wanted for ever and ever. But he was not of the kind to be won by flaunting my nascent bosom beneath his nose, then little more than ribs with embellishments. No, there was far more to Patrick Justin Gillard than that.

We soon discovered that we could make one another laugh and after that evening we became involved not with physics but chemistry. All that summer we went for long walks on Dartmoor – both families lived in Plymouth in those days – with the dogs, picnicked, rode our bikes. My parents were delighted with our friendship, for, after all, Patrick had no bad reputation of any kind, his main interests being singing in the choir and going fishing in the Tamar. Then, one afternoon, we had laughed until we cried, hugging one another in the hot summer sun-shine. A delicious feeling had gone though me as I had felt his lithe body move beneath the thin material of his shirt. For the first time we had kissed deeply, up until then having greeted one another with just pecks on the cheek. One moment we had been children and the next as close as two people can become. Intense pleasure had come as a huge surprise and for the rest of the holidays we had escaped to the Moor and wrung every moment of it from our young bodies.

We knew we were doing wrong, of course; opinions on such matters were different then and we had both been strictly brought up. I have never forgotten the day not so long afterwards when Patrick had a crisis of conscience and proposed to me and my reply had been that, yes, one day I would, but at the moment I was only fifteen. He had attained a shade of paleness that, up until then, I had thought humanly impossible. But he had repeated the offer, come hell, horsewhips and jail, and I had accepted, on condition that we waited several years and said nothing to our families until we became engaged. After that we had forgone the intimacy: I simply had not had the nerve to approach the doctor for the Pill, as he was another family friend and neither Patrick nor I had wanted a baby as a result of what we increasingly thought of as 'furtive sex in a damp ditch'. It was not easy – in fact I can remember it being hellishly difficult – but gave our relationship a depth and power that it has never lost.

After a few minutes of strolling slowly along by the wall I began to fret; I always do. Telling myself sternly that Patrick was more than a match for any once and future poacher, grudges or no, I turned and started to walk back the way I had come. Then my eye was drawn to a pile of bricks built up like a cairn but well away from the wall itself, half-hidden by a clump of hawthorn bushes. I went over to it.

It immediately became clear that what I

was looking at were items of clothing hastily screwed up together, the bricks piled over them in an effort to conceal. What appeared to be the end of one leg of a pair of jeans stuck out from the bottom, a fold of pale cloth that might be part of a grey sweatshirt was visible from higher up the pile and near the top peeped out a section of cuff. All the fabric was wet, that on the ground muddy, and the cuff material, probably part of the sweatshirt, was blotchy with pale-pink staining. Was it blood almost washed out by rain?

I hurried back to my starting point by the broken-down section of wall. I had not really expected Patrick to be back already and he was not. I did not think he would come back by the same route either: undercover soldiers never forget their training. Nevertheless I jumped out of my skin a couple of minutes later when he silently came up behind me through the gap in the wall and whispered, 'Boo!'

'Anything interesting?' I enquired in superior fashion, heart thumping.

'His hovel is as filthy as he is,' was the laconic reply.

'How did you get on the other side of the wall?'

'There are gaps everywhere.'

'I've found something.'

Patrick surveyed the heap. He bent down, sniffed it in several places and then said, 'There's a lot more bloody cloth inside here.

It's decomposing but doesn't smell rank enough to be from game animals. I think it's human – unless I'm losing my touch.'

Half an hour later Fred Knightly himself was present while Scenes of Crime personnel took photographs and then carefully dismantled the pile of bricks. As I had predicted, the Super did not share our suspicions about the find; in fact, he left shortly afterwards. Patrick, meanwhile, with a constable as back-up, was questioning Danny in the potting shed. I had volunteered to escort Knightly and those with him to the discovery, found myself ignored by all and sundry and was in time, on returning to the walled garden, to see Danny being frogmarched in the direction of an area car.

'He denied knowing anything about the clothing, which is obviously a lie as we already know he patrols the grounds, and then gave me a mouthful of abuse,' Patrick reported. 'And now I'm a policeman and not allowed to threaten, or even start, to wring suspects' necks, I've had him taken to the nick for formal questioning. I suppose we'd better tell Her Ladyship that he's helping with enquiries.'

Patrick's wry comment had a bizarre sequel. Danny – or, correctly, Daniel Smith – continued to refuse to answer questions, tried to attack a constable in the interview room, ranted and raved and generally behaved extremely badly. This was not first-hand knowledge as far as Patrick and I were concerned, but information given to us by the duty desk sergeant when we called in at the nick late that afternoon to see if there were any preliminary findings on the items of clothing.

Fred Knightly appeared, looking peevish, obviously searching for someone. His gaze lighted on Patrick, who, even more obviously, was not the one he sought.

'A word,' he snapped across the reception area. 'My office.'

Patrick clicked his heels and followed at the double, the oracle trotting to keep up.

'It's just occurred to me that you must be used to interrogation methods, having worked for the security services,' the Super said, slamming the door behind us. 'And this little shit of a gardener is a problem that I could well do without. He's a well-known poacher of deer and game on the Essex farms and estates and has been involved with thefts of cattle and sheep. It has to be animal blood on the clothes and I can't be doing with all this rural, cowboy stuff right now, as far more important things are going on – as *you* well know. Is his name on the list Gray made that you keep banging on about?'

'No,' Patrick said.

'Question him. I don't care if he trips and bangs his nose on something or walks into a door before it's actually made a formal interview. Pin him for his latest foray into private property armed with snares or a shotgun, have him bailed and get rid of the bastard.'

I went into full preparation mode for Patrick making like a Cyberman and deleting Knightly, but it did not happen. He said nothing, merely gave me a sideways smile and we left the room.

'He's dangerous, mind,' Knightly shouted after us, perhaps with his conscience twinging. Perhaps, on the other hand, not.

I said nothing in the way of warnings as we made our way, my husband being perfectly capable of perceiving the dangers – several of them.

Smith had been brought back from the cell where he had been banished to cool off and was in one of the interview rooms, where, as a result of Knightly having trawled through those present in the canteen, two burly traffic cops were keeping Lady Thora Trillingford-Apsley's gardener company. Patrick sent them away.

'Don't bother to swear in front of Ingrid, old son,' he said in disinterested fashion. 'She knows all the naughty words and might even teach you a few. And you can forget throwing punches, as that won't get you anywhere either. Now, do we have a quiet little chat without tape recorders and all the boring stuff like that *first* or do I do as I've been ordered and beat you to a pulp to get some answers?'

Smith mouthed something obscene and then sat with his arms folded, staring into space, ignoring us.

'Fag?' Patrick enquired. He took a packet from his pocket and tossed it on the table.

Scowling, the man helped himself to one and I was astounded when Patrick did the same, produced a lighter from the same pocket and lit both. To my certain knowledge he has not smoked for over twenty years except for the very occasional small cigar. Perhaps it was because of the aroma emanating from the suspect – possibly ferrets.

Smith was staring at the lighter that had been put with the cigarette packet. 'Those are mine!' he bellowed.

Patrick blew out a plume of smoke towards the ceiling. 'So they are. I used to be in an undercover unit a bit like the SAS – went over all your stuff while you were back in the greenhouse and had an idea I'd be lumbered with interviewing you. So don't lie to me, because I don't need to beat you up. I can make you scream without leaving a mark on you. How long have you been working at your present job?'

Smith visibly decided to co-operate. 'A coupla years.'

'Quite a while then. Where d'you live when you're not sleeping over the potting shed?'

After a longish pause Smith muttered, 'I've

got a caravan.'

'Where is it?'

Another silence. Then: 'Behind the Blue Boar at Kingsbrook. I help out there too.'

'What's the name of the landlord?'

'Joe. Joe Masters.'

'And you shift casks and clear up – things like that in lieu of rent?'

'That's right.'

'I take it the bike in the potting shed's yours.'

'Well, I can't afford a bloody car, can I?'

'Those clothes under the pile of bricks – whose are they?'

'I don't know nothing about them.'

Patrick turned to me. 'Perhaps you'd better go and then you won't be upset when I get started on him.'

I started to rise.

'No!' Smith yelped.

'No?' Patrick echoed.

'I'll tell yer.'

I sat down again.

'They're mine. I helped butcher a deer, shoved 'em there and forgot about 'em.'

'When was this?'

'Last week.'

'Where was it shot?'

'On an estate on the other side of the forest. I was with some blokes. We gutted and skinned it and brought it back in some-one's van. I got blood all over meself so I chucked my gear out of sight until I could wash it. I forgot, that's all.'

'That stuff had been there for longer than a week.'

'Well, perhaps it was the week before then.'

'You're a liar.' Then, without warning, Patrick's hand shot out to grab Smith by the front of his dirty sweater, yanking him close. 'Those garments had been there for weeks and weeks and d'you know? – in my trade you get to know the smell of death as well as recognizing filthy little liars. Not just animal death either: the smell of murder. You must have had run-ins with DCI Derek Harmsworth in your criminal career. I think you were involved in killing him.' He flung the man back into his seat.

Smith, whose face had gone a strange putty colour beneath the grime, had dropped his cigarette and, eyeing Patrick all the while, slowly bent down to retrieve it. 'No,' he whispered. 'You're just guessing – trying to frame me.'

Speaking more quietly, Patrick said, 'You have only got until forensic testing proves that the blood on those clothes – and there's quite a lot of it – is human. This will happen within the next couple of hours. Tell the truth.' He gave his partly smoked cigarette a distasteful look and stubbed it out on a tin lid that passed for an ashtray.

'You and who else?' I said to Smith, breaking the silence. 'Who did you help push the car through the gap in the railings?'

Smith gaped at me and then stammered, 'You – you can't know about...' His mouth clamped shut.

'You're terrified of him, aren't you?' I went on. 'They're probably his clothes that he told you to get rid of and you've been meaning to burn them but it's been too wet.' All this was pure conjecture, straight off the top of my head, but Smith did not possess the kind of brain to organize a crime that must have had some complexity.

Eyes closed, he sat there, shaking his head as though he wished the whole world would go away.

'He'll let you take the rap,' I continued, hoping I sounded sympathetic. 'There he'll be, sitting at home, reading about the case in the papers and laughing all over his face. "I always knew he was a fool," he'll say to himself. "I made sure I lumbered him with my clothes."'

The silence seemed to go on for ever and then Smith whispered, 'I want a solicitor. I'm not saying another word until I've got one.'

I persevered. 'But you didn't actually kill the chief inspector yourself, did you? *He* did.'

Very slowly, Smith nodded. 'Yes,' he grunted.

'So you're going to get it all off your chest and make a statement?'

Again, he answered in the affirmative.

'I must tell you that if you change your mind as soon as we've gone we'll be recalled and have to go right back to square one.'

Smith did swear at me then, in effect saying that he bet I nagged my old man to death too.

As our code of practice demanded, we handed him over to the permanent staff at Woodhill, not at all sure about the likelihood of any useful outcome, and then went back to our digs.

Eight

One and a half hours later we were recalled
to Woodhill police station. A sense of fore-
boding – nothing to do with half a dozen or
so binge-stricken teenage girls screaming
and/or lying prone on the floor of the reception area – hit me as soon as we walked in.
Erin Melrose, who appeared to have been
waiting for us, came forward.

'They're all in the Super's office,' she said
in an undertone before shying like a horse as
someone vomited near her.

'What's happened?' I asked, likewise getting out of range.

She hesitated, then said, 'I'm not supposed
to say a word, but it's only fair to tell you that
Daniel Smith's hanged himself.'

With Knightly were Michael Greenway, a
middle-aged woman by the name of Greta
Cunningham, who was with Greenway in a
capacity that was not made clear, a man I
only knew as Keith, a custody officer, and,
oddly, DI Hicks. I did not find it surprising
that the latter had a superior smirk on his
face that he was, however, being careful only
to point in our direction.

Knightly gave us the news.

'This is appalling,' Patrick said before any-one else could speak. 'How did he do it?'

'With his belt,' Knightly answered.

'How, exactly?'

'Put the end through the buckle to make a loop. Then he must have stood on the bunk, tied the end to an overhead pipe that serves the toilet and then stepped off.'

'I thought belts and shoelaces were remov-ed from suspects before they were locked up.'

'Apparently his trousers kept falling down and as his brief was due here at any minute it was given back to him. It's not as though he was thought to be a suicide risk, for God's sake! And I'll ask the questions, if you don't mind!' Knightly went on, now shouting. 'What did you do to him? I did ask you to question him before he was formally inter-viewed but not to lean on him that hard.'

'All rather irregular, surely,' Greenway protested.

Knightly said, 'Look, if I stuck to all the rules and regulations for every smallest mis-demeanour that takes place on this patch, I'd never get home at night. Smith was a com-plete drop-out. He'd been in trouble with the law since he was five years old. God knows what was going through the man's mind – or what passed for one in his case – when he topped himself. All I know is that as a result of one of your lot pasting hell out of him the bugger's now dead!'

'No,' I said. 'Patrick didn't do anything of the kind.'

Grandiosely, to the room at large, Hicks said, 'I'm not surprised: the man has a reputation for violence and losing his temper.'

Greenway rounded on him. 'Who asked you?' he bellowed. 'Why are you here, for that matter? I thought you were supposed to be working on the Giddings case. Sod off!'

'You're SOCA – you can't order me around,' Hicks retorted.

'No, but that doesn't mean I have to be within the same square mile as someone who tried to stitch up one of my subordinates!'

I have heavily censored that last comment.

Hicks went.

Greenway met Knightly's questioning gaze. 'I suggest you don't concern yourself with the matter, Superintendent. I shall be reporting to *his* boss.'

Although rejoicing, I thought it best to behave as though these exchanges had not taken place and carried on with what I had been about to say. 'Although we no longer work for MI5, Patrick and I still behave professionally – which is why, in such situations, I always utilize the small tape recorder that I never quite got round to handing back. It was switched on in my bag when the Superintendent asked Patrick to question Smith and was also functioning through the entire interview with him. I deposited the tape with the sergeant on the desk as we left the building, asking him to put it somewhere safe. While I realize that it couldn't be presented in court as evidence, it at least helps to sort out the blame game and means we can begin to work together on this.'

Erin Melrose then knocked and entered with a report from the path lab. The blood on the clothing that I had found was human; DNA testing would take longer.

The tape was brought, I produced my little spies' recorder and we all listened to it, Knightly wriggling in quite gorgeous fashion and everyone else being very careful with their faces when his voice came over loud and clear telling Patrick that it did not matter if Smith met with a couple of small 'accidents'. Erin had stayed in the room, no one having asked her to leave, and was standing rather touchingly in Patrick's lee. For protection, I wondered, Knightly having bullied her too? If Greenway had told her about the libellous, if not downright disgraceful, photograph, she might feel a need for the victims of this to stick together.

'He really was about to cough, then,' Greenway said into the silence that followed the switching-off of the machine.

Patrick said, 'I wish to make a formal request for the exhumation and a second post mortem on Detective Chief Inspector Derek Harmsworth. His wife has given her verbal permission.'

'We don't know it's Harmsworth's blood,' Knightly said.

At least two of those present rolled their eyes heavenwards and it was left to me to state the obvious. 'We won't until we have a sample of his DNA with which to compare it. It's highly unlikely after all this time that Mrs Harmsworth will have things like his unwashed clothing or brushes and combs.'

'No,' he agreed a little sheepishly. 'I get your point. All right, yes. It's got to be done.'

I felt that other things ought to be discussed. 'And Smith?' I said. 'Did he commit suicide because he was about to confess to being an accessory to murder? Was he such a sensitive soul he would feel there was no other honourable way out? Was he so disgusted with himself that he could no longer face looking at his own reflection in the mirror? Or was he strung up by someone on the orders of the actual murderer who managed to get hold of the key to his cell?'

Everyone was looking at me, their eyes rather round.

'Murdered *here*?' said Greta Cunningham, making her debut in the proceedings. 'You're mad!'

'Ingrid, that's a truly staggering thought,' Greenway said. And to Knightly: 'Is the body still in situ?'

The Super was away with the birds. 'Er – er – yes, still in the cell, I think. Yes, that's right. He was taken down, of course. In an effort to

164

revive him. And – er – obviously, a doctor saw him and signed the death certificate. But there'll have to be a PM.'

'I suggest you get a pathologist and a Scenes of Crime bod in there – fast.'

'When was the last time a suspect in custody was murdered?' said Cunningham. 'Isn't their safety and that of the general public paramount?' She was still looking at me, askance. I had really ruined what was left of her day.

'I suggest we take a look at him,' Greenway said, acknowledging the question with a brief nod. Then he said, 'You're the IT wizard, Greta – why don't you go and look it up on the Internet?'

'It would be preferable to looking at a corpse,' the woman said stonily. 'Besides, that isn't what I'm here for.'

'Plenty of computers in the general office,' Knightly said helpfully. 'Erin, perhaps you'd show Miss Cunningham the way.'

We all prepared to leave the room, Greenway taking the deep breath of a man now unfettered from bureaucracy as he took from his document case a notebook and pen. I never saw the wizard again – why did I think that Greenway had been positively yearning to say 'wonkess'? – but Erin quietly reappeared a few minutes later as we entered the cell where Daniel Smith had died.

He had been laid out neatly on the bunk, covered by the thin official-issue blanket.

Greenway twitched the top of it aside.

'I take it no one heard anything at the time it was reckoned to have happened,' Patrick said as we all stared down into the suffused, distorted face.

'We've been inundated since quite early on this evening and it's been very noisy,' Knightly said defensively. 'Young drunks mostly, brought in for their own good. The result of two lunch-time hen parties, I've been given to understand.'

'No bruising on the face,' Greenway said musingly. Then, to the Super, 'He's been moved already and the whole area well and truly contaminated. Can we take a look at his hands?'

With no objection forthcoming the blanket was taken right off.

The knuckles of Smith's right hand were grazed and there was heavy bruising on both bare forearms.

'He took a swing at someone,' Patrick said, 'and clouted his hand on something solid like a wall when they ducked. Didn't he attack a constable when he was first brought in?'

'Find out who it was,' Knightly said to Erin, having noticed her presence.

'Peter Mason, sir,' she said. 'I was there. But Smith didn't hit himself on anything other than Peter's shoulder. He was restrained and then handcuffed before he could do anything else.'

Patrick said, 'Restrained with sufficient force to bruise his arms like that?'

She shook her head. 'No.'

'Look, I know all about loyalty to chums, but please answer honestly – we might have a murder inquiry here.'

'It's the absolute truth, sir. Mason got him in a headlock while I cuffed him.'

Patrick was looking more closely at the body. 'This livid mark just beneath his left ear can't have been caused by the belt, surely.' He stood upright. 'I think he was struck by the edge of someone's hand. I take it the poor sod's neck wasn't broken. So he must have been slowly strangled to death.'

The implications seemed to have just hit Knightly, who had gone very pale. 'We'd better get someone out to this caravan where he lived,' he mumbled.

'Does this unfortunate man's death open a can of worms, or is it new evidence?' Greenway murmured. He had accompanied us as we left the building, cleaners still busy with buckets and mops. He wrinkled his nose at the smell. 'You know, when I started as a trooper in the cavalry, we didn't make complete idiots of ourselves with booze like this. Drunk yes, but...' He gestured at the state of affairs speechlessly.

'I think the answer to your question might be both,' Patrick said. 'But the real answers will come after Harmsworth's exhumation.'

'How are you getting on with checking the

167

names on that list?'

'Two are in other forces' areas and I've requested a check be made, one was stated to be of no fixed address and we haven't traced him yet, another's back in prison, another's address has ceased to exist and the final two were out when we called. Not very successful so far, I'm afraid.'

Greenway departed without further comment.

Patrick said, 'As you know, once upon a time when we worked for MI5 our brief permitted certain out-of-hours activities. Partly for sheer nostalgia reasons I can feel one coming on tonight.'

'We do no longer work for MI5,' I agreed. 'But what have you in mind?'

'I'd like to gatecrash a certain private club that has illegal undertones.'

'Jo-Jo's?'

'Jo-Jo's.'

I knew he was in a good mood after getting agreement on the exhumation and said, 'Well, as I'm supposed to be your adviser, you'd better give your other reasons. Pretend I'm Greenway.'

Standing by the car he ticked off on his fingers: 'It's run by an Italian who's almost certainly the local godfather and who was Harmsworth's snout. Harmworth might not have realized quite how deeply the old snake's involved with pushing up the crime figures round here but, as we've already sur-

168

mised, he could have done and reasoned that his presence kept out far worse hoodlums. Also, Theodore du Norde is a member, even though he lives quite a way from here in west London and gives the impression of being a bit sneery about Woodhill. And thirdly, after asking a few polite questions in the club you and I were set upon by a knife-carrier who might be connected with the place, or it could have been another attack on the law. So I want to address all these little un-answered niggles by taking the place apart at the seams, with explosives if necessary.'

Deeming the last remark to be mere wish-ful thinking, I said, 'There are still a lot of "coulds" and "mights". What do you hope to achieve? – and I'm only asking this be-cause ten to one it won't be the kind of thing that can be used as evidence in anyone's trial.'

'Sometimes, as we've discovered before, you have to make things happen. And then people behave in a way that can be used as evidence.'

'They'll recognize us.'

'We'll be masked and I propose, unless circumstances change, to use my very good line in ex-IRA bad boys – with current lay in tow.'

'We'd have to have a convincing reason for what we were doing.'

'You're right.' He pondered. 'Yes, I know. Your brother has gone missing and was last seen in the place, in the bar, by one of the members – du Norde.'

I hummed disapprovingly, Marge Simpson-style at this and then said, 'It stinks. And I hate to be such a wet blanket but you shouldn't go armed. You're only permitted to carry a handgun for personal protection purposes. If our nocturnal activities are traced back to SOCA, I'm more than sure you'd be finished with them.'

'An Italian won't expect an Irishman to be useful with a knife.'

At a little before midnight we were in the narrow lane, almost medieval in its dirt and darkness, behind Jo-Jo's. We had eaten there earlier – and observing our present surroundings I was wishing we hadn't – kept our heads down, paid our bill in perfectly normal fashion and gone back to our digs to change. Matters at Jo-Jo's had not been normal, however, everyone for some reason being in a high state of jitters. A waiter had dropped a whole tray of clean glasses and bolted from sight leaving the mess to be swept up by someone else. The bar staff and waiters had whispered in huddles and of Jo-Jo himself there had been no sign. The fact that my meal had not been the one I had ordered, actually much more expensive, and we had not been charged the extra even though we had pointed out the mistake, spoke of chaos behind the scenes as well.

Perhaps something had really gone wrong and everyone was nervously awaiting the boss's arrival and subsequent wrath.

Helpfully, the lane was not a cul-de-sac, running parallel for most of its length, as might have been expected, to the one fronting the properties. The southern end, farthest away from the main road, ended up in what must have been the Shire's Yard of its name, a dismal area with another exit that appeared to serve as delivery access to the rear of shops; the other did a right turn and narrowed until it was no more than a footpath between terraces of Victorian houses that led to a side street.

We were dressed in dark clothing: navy-blue tracksuits, 'yachty' shoes with non-slip soles of a similar colour and black balaclavas, and right now, after our initial reconnoitre, were perched on a low wall, our backs to another higher one in the company of several large and malodorous refuse bins. It was dark and slightly foggy in a smoky way and although the rear entrance to the restaurant-cum-club was only about ten yards away I knew we were quite invisible to anyone who emerged from it unless they were carrying some kind of light.

Patrick gestured in the direction of where we had just explored, with the aid of his 'burglar's' torch – steps that led down into a basement – and whispered, 'That's probably regarded as the emergency exit of the club in the event of a police raid. The main entrance, a door with a very large gentleman keeping guard, is at the bottom of a wide staircase inside. I propose we get in this way.'

'I thought these places had to be inspected,' I muttered. 'The steps look lethal and there aren't any lights, not even down by the door.'

'I should imagine there's everything to gladden a fire-prevention officer's heart when the inspections are made, but things like lights, or rather the bulbs in them, are quietly removed afterwards. These folk don't want to make entry easy to outsiders.'

'The door looked solid enough.'

'It's just as well I brought my sonic screwdriver then,' said the avid *Doctor Who* fan.

The basement area was not completely dark, a weird sort of glow rising through the misty air from below ground level, presumably escaping through the blinds on the windows. I suddenly remembered that I had planned to write a novel encompassing everything Sherlockian, gloomy and bog-ridden. In the next moment my imagination had galloped away, forcing me to strangle at birth lurid ideas involving evil miasmas emanating from putrescent corpses in mires and, as Katie would say, 'all sorts of silly stuff like that'.

'What was going on in there earlier, d'you reckon?' I said in Patrick's ear. 'They were freaking out.'

'God knows. Perhaps a fridge has failed and everything in it's gone off.'

A church clock struck twelve and still Patrick sat motionless. I shifted my weight slightly: the wall was freezing cold through my trousers and getting harder by the minute. At last I could stand it no longer and said, 'What are you waiting for?'

'I rang Theodore du Norde pretending to be Jo-Jo and asked him to come over. I'm giving him time to get here, that's all.'

'Why, though?'

His teeth flashed white as he grinned at me. 'Just stirring things up a little.'

'You won't know if he's arrived from here,' I pointed out grumpily.

'There were several cars parked down in that yard. I reckon anyone who didn't want to be seen on the streets would park there. So if he does come this way, it suggests he's as dodgy as Maggie says.'

Another ten minutes went by, during which my rear end went quite numb.

Then, even above the traffic noise on the main road, I distinctly heard the sound of tyres crunching over the rough ground of the yard, parts of which were liberally scattered with dumped hardcore and broken bricks. A door slammed and a couple of minutes later a small hurrying figure appeared. We froze, for whoever it was carried a torch. But he was too involved with finding his way and we saw it was Jo-Jo as he went from view into the light emanating from the basement. There were a series of knocks at the door and we heard it open and close.

Patrick was listening, head cocked, a hand on my wrist. Another car was arriving. There was a lot of door-slamming, but only one person eventually materialized: the unmistakable, blundering, portly outline of du Norde, using a flash lamp with an almost flat battery. He was swearing under his breath as he struggled to see where he was going and then uttered an expletive out loud as he tripped and nearly fell over some projection or other. I waited, breathlessly, for him to go headlong down the steps, but he survived and after knocking in the same fashion – three quickly, a pause and then two more – was admitted.

'We go!' Patrick said.

We were off the wall and making our way towards the steps when I heard people coming at the run. I was grabbed, thankfully by my working partner, finding myself momentarily airborne and then, only a little scratched, in very close proximity to one of the rank and overgrown bushes that grew at the bases of the walls – inside it, to be precise. Seconds later several dark shapes ran past us, almost close enough to touch, actually brushing the foliage, and disappeared down the steps. There followed the hammering and smashing of wood as the door was broken down.

I spat out the leaf in my mouth.

From the building came a subterranean convulsion, a megaton upheaval of the terrified accompanied by shouting, screaming and the crash of overturned furniture. Several people tried to escape up the steps but were hauled back. We heard the sound of blows, more shouts, groans and then it went quieter as though the main activity had moved farther within. No, just one sound – that of prone bodies being dragged away.

'Oh, brother,' Patrick whispered and then had gone.

Over the years I have discovered, the hard way, that the safest place to be in situations like this is not hanging around nervously on the fringes but right behind him, if necessary passing the ordnance. Nothing like this was required to begin with as the two masked men standing just inside the shattered door who disagreed with Patrick's insistence on entry ceased to take further interest in the proceedings and we locked their unconscious selves in what turned out to be a storeroom. Then we stood quite motionless, listening.

I think it had occurred to us both that the raid might be a police one, in which case we had no choice but to silently retire. But police left on guard would have identified themselves – in fact, would probably have mistaken us for part of their own team from the way we were attired.

Whoever it was was turning the whole place over. At least, I thought, the restaurant was closed at this time of night, so the chance of members of the public being caught up and hurt in the violence was slim. Then we heard male voices: not speaking English.

The man in my life immediately binned his Irish nationality and strutted into the large, opulently furnished room that led off a short passageway in which we had paused, and surveyed what was going on. Everyone conscious – three were not – stared at him, as still as waxworks. Jo-Jo and his staff were lined up against one wall together with club members, including du Norde, and, facing them, several more masked individuals protectively clustered around another man, who was not masked. The latter – finely honed features, olive complexion, galactically expensive suit – gestured imperiously to one of his henchmen, who produced a flick knife and lunged in Patrick's direction.

Or, at least, he began to do these things, the weapon dropping to the carpet as another embedded itself in his upper arm. Patrick thoughtfully supplied the general anaesthetic of a chop across the neck before he retrieved it, scooped the other knife from the floor and went back to stand in exactly the same place as he had been before.

'What do you want?' asked the boss with a strong Italian accent. 'I have no quarrel with you.'

'You are threatening my good friend Jo-Jo,' Patrick said silkily, likewise, but with his voice pitched a little higher than normal. 'And it goes without saying that you are not welcome here. Leave.'

The other sneered. 'He can only afford to pay you a pittance. I offer you more. But first I must know who you are. Remove your mask.'

'Pittance!' shrieked Jo-Jo. 'You call 50k a year for doing next to nothing a pittance? He is not joining you. I will have you killed first!'

'Big words from a nobody,' said the intruder with a false chuckle. And to Patrick: 'Skill with a knife is rare in the UK.'

I supposed, afterwards, that he must have surreptitiously nudged the man standing nearest to him. There was an explosion of movement – although at the time it always seems that things like this happen in slow motion – a gun was produced and coming up to aim in our direction. Patrick and I both flung ourselves aside and a shot cracked out, very loud in the low-ceilinged room.

I left the Glock pistol where everyone could see it, in my right hand, and stood upright. The would-be sharp-shooter had gone over backwards as though an express train had hit him but was now sitting up, hugging his right leg, moaning.

Patrick said it, but personally I would have cut the crowing.

'We're not too bad with firearms either,' he drawled.

'This bastard is a liar and – and – will kill you when he knows who you are,' Jo-Jo babbled to him, pointing accusingly with a quivering forefinger. 'I give you half the protection money from the other restaurants on top of your retaining fee if you get rid of him and his murderers and stay with me!'

He certainly deserved a prize for thinking on his feet.

'What else will you give me?' Patrick said in a bored voice.

'A – a cut in the proceeds of the dog-racing scam.'

'I'm not interested in working-class crime,' he was loftily told.

'OK, a share of the drugs business, then. Please, I give you that if you help me – keep on helping me, I mean.'

'That sounds more like it.' Patrick gestured towards du Norde. 'But what about greasy fatso? Does he run things for you? – he looks as though his fingers are in all your pies.'

'No, he – he just gives me information about what rich Londoners have in their homes and I sell it to antiques thieves.'

'You stupid old *git!*' du Norde bawled.

'Well, you do!' Jo-Jo retorted furiously. 'And you cost me more than you bring in, you fat fool, with your expensive taste in things that you expect me to supply free of charge.'

'What else does he do for a living?' Patrick asked.

'The Holy Mother alone knows,' Jo-Jo replied with an elaborate shrug. 'Nothing, probably.'

I really thought for a moment that du Norde would spontaeously combust in his fury and we would have the equivalent of a very large chip-pan fire on our hands.

'And all these other people,' Patrick went on. 'Do they need my services too, under the auspices of your good self, of course?'

Jo-Jo gazed along the short row of his associates, an unhealthy and shifty-looking bunch, most dressed in shiny and ill-fitting business suits. 'Yes, I think they will all need your protection,' he said. 'They are all ... useful to me.'

Patrick handed me his mobile and took charge of the gun.

I had no need to dial any complicated numbers, or even 999, as it was an official phone and had been programmed to call a police hotline when I just pressed zero.

'You're all under arrest,' Patrick said, removing his mask, and to Jo-Jo, 'Nice try, Lorenzo.'

The paperwork took most of the rest of that night but the look on all their faces, especially du Norde's, was worth every minute.

Nine

While it was gratifying to learn that, by a complete fluke, we had netted a couple of serious criminals and several minor ones whom the Met, and other forces, had been trying to catch for a long time, the evening's work had done nothing to advance our own investigations. With one exception, that is: one of his waiters was immediately shopped by Jo-Jo as being the man who had attacked us in the town. Denounced as 'stupid' (he was) and having 'acted without orders, hoping to impress', this turned out to be the one who had dropped the tray of glasses. I can only think that Patrick had glanced in his direction and that, on top of the grapevine warning that had been received of trouble brewing from a rival gang, this had broken his nerve.

I am not sure if the restaurant owner had been hoping to make a good impression himself with the police by this happy willingness to co-operate and never actually found out, his premises having been emptied and boarded up the next day after Scenes of Crime personnel had finished their work. A quantity of drugs had been discovered and several weapons, plus some counterfeit £50 notes, in a safe in an office, and a computer had been taken away to see what information it contained. I gather that those arrested who were not actually wanted in connection with crimes locally were dealt out like cards to the various London police departments who wished them to help with their enquiries and, as far as we were concerned, they disappeared without trace. Quite simply, they were not our responsibility.

Theodore du Norde, on the other hand, was, but like the others he was whisked away, by the Arts and Antiques Squad, his name already on a list of suspects owing to someone having put two and two together after properties had been burgled not long after a visit from a certain interior designer.

Patrick had said nothing the previous night but was not pleased with me. 'You should have told me you were carrying the gun,' he said under his breath when we were leaving a slightly awkward debriefing late the following morning, during which he had lied through his teeth about his knowledge of my possession of it.

'It was a last-minute decision,' I told him. 'Jo-Jo bothered me – I thought him nastier than you did and had an idea he was behind the attack on us.'

'I don't care about your reasons. I wouldn't necessarily have asked you to leave it behind.

But I need to *know* about things like that – it affects how I plan and carry out the job, especially, like last night, when it's affected by circumstances beyond my control. You should know that after all this time.'

There was an awkward silence. Ye gods, here was the head boy all over again, but as before I was in the wrong – very much so this time. There should never be a breakdown in communication, not in this line of business.

'I'm sorry,' I said. 'I didn't think ahead – and that you might have to lie about it.'

He thawed. 'You're still a bloody fine shot.'

Because of bruising to one of his hands, his arms and other parts of his body, the pathologist's view was that Daniel Smith had been unconscious before being hanged, having first been overpowered with some violence in his cell. This verdict, only the preliminary findings, resulted in a visit from the Met's Complaints Department and Woodhill police station became embroiled in an internal inquiry. Patrick was interviewed, in Michael Greenway's presence, and I gather that the recording I had made was listened to again.

'No one's saying much, mostly because there's no evidence, but a bloke who works in the canteen hasn't reported for work since the murder,' Patrick said. 'Someone's out checking at his home address now.'

'What about the caravan where Daniel

Smith lived – do you know if anything of interest was found there?'

'Mostly half a ton of rubbish, dirt, bedbugs and lice, apparently. Scenes of Crime are probably using it as a training ground before the army are let loose with flame-throwers as it's a hazard to public health.'

'Shall we go back to trying to track the names on the list?' I suggested, knowing someone who would be first in the queue for a finger on that particular button.

But again we drew a blank; there was no one at home at the local addresses, no one seemed to know how to trace the people whose houses had been demolished, and there was no news from the other police departments who had been asked to trace the remainder.

'We must refocus, then,' Patrick murmured. 'Harmsworth's body is being exhumed tomorrow night with the second PM taking place the following afternoon. Professor Denyer, a Home Office pathologist, is doing it, apparently. Until then—'

I interrupted with, 'We could have twenty-four hours off. We've worked every day since starting here.'

'You had a day at the seaside,' he reminded me.

I blew a raspberry.

'Oh, that reminds me: I saw Paul Boles just now. He's back on the job.'

'I hope they don't make the poor man

183

attend the PM.'

'No, I am. I volunteered in case that idiot Knightly had precisely that in mind.'

Sometimes you can just look at a man and know what he really, really wants you to say next.

'Would you like me to come as well?' I asked lightly.

'If you want to,' he replied in equally off-hand fashion.

Inwardly, I was worried, and not about the PM. When we had been walking through one of the graffiti- and litter-ravaged underpasses on the estate I had seen a figure, fleetingly, who had crossed our line of vision where two tunnels merged. Patrick had been checking his mobile for text messages at the time so had not noticed her. I was almost positive it had been Erin Melrose. Not sure enough, however, to say something and possibly cause friction if Patrick mentioned it to her. For, after all, she had every right to be there and was possibly working on another case, the estate being the kind of place where quite a large proportion of those living there would be helping the police with their enquiries at some time or other.

I was quite sure, though, that if it had been Erin she should not have been there on her own.

I have attended several post mortems in the past, one in connection with research I was undertaking for a novel, others because of the job, or, rather, Patrick's job. This I knew would be different and, although such a procedure is hardly anything to look forward to, I was absolutely dreading it this time.

It was different, of course, because I felt that I knew this man. I had seen photographs of him taken in life, spoken to his wife and colleagues and spent part of every day since arriving in Essex trying to find out what had happened to him. And here he was – or, rather, here were his battered and decomposing remains – lying in a stainless-steel shallow tray awaiting another mauling.

Surprisingly, Michael Greenway had decided to attend as well and I found myself liking him even more as he had told Patrick that the reason for this was not that he was following his latest recruit's every move but that he somehow felt he owed it to the dead DCI to set the record straight. Despite the fact that Denyer's comments would be recorded, Greenway had asked me to take notes. I was grateful. It meant that, already trying not to look at the blackened and slimy body, the legs and one arm almost severed, a ghastly injury to the abdomen, I had something else upon which to focus my attention.

Professor Denyer was all ready to begin and had waited, slightly impatiently, while the two and a bit members of SOCA donned the necessary anti-contamination suits. He was a stout, fussy little man who, according to Greenway, had so many letters after his name you could play Scrabble with them.

Before any new evidence could be investigated Denyer went through the full routine, rattling off comments, as he worked to reopen the Y-shaped incision in the torso, removed the heart, lungs and other organs, closely examined them and then moved on to the intestines. He was very slow and painstaking and, like all people of his profession, appeared utterly oblivious, despite the extractor fans, of the appalling smell. I tried not to breathe at all and scribbled down everything he said in shorthand. All too soon I began to feel a bit faint, cold beads of sweat running down from my forehead and soaking into my face mask. I shifted my position a little and took a few deep, stinking breaths.

Denyer progressed to the brain, removing the already sawn-off top of the skull and taking out the contents, a move that caused Greenway to walk rapidly to the far corner of the room, turn his back on what was going on and lean on the wall with both hands. Patrick went over to him, but Greenway just mutely shook his head and nothing was said.

Denyer then went on to prod around in various parts of the cadaver, muttering to himself, and I began to feel that I was trapped in a time-warp, the only positive occurrence being Greenway recovering and returning to stand by the table.

'Remind me of the new evidence we have to go on,' Denyer ordered, at last, in his somewhat squeaky voice.

Greenway's eyes, the only visible part of his face above the mask and below the cap, swivelled in Patrick's direction, who nodded and said, 'Harmsworth's sergeant Paul Boles was first on the scene and saw that the DCI was still alive. He pointed to his neck, with his left hand, a finger moving in a stabbing motion. He then died. This piece of evidence did not come out at the time, for various reasons.'

'Pointed exactly where? – do you know?'

Yes, he did, for Boles had demonstrated and indicated a spot just below the left ear.

Denyer found the tiny wound in the putre-faction and opened up the whole neck to find out more. I wrote down everything he said, the clarity of my penmanship now in dire straits, and I even succeeded in asking the great man to spell the medical terms, which meant nothing to me. Arteries, veins, processes, sinews, muscles...

It is sufficient to record that Derek Harmsworth had been murdered, stabbed once with a long, thin-bladed knife.

The three of us then made it to the nearest pub, where, together with the men and for only the second time in my life, I downed a double whisky, neat.

Michael Greenway had got his colour

back. 'Right,' he said. 'We must not lose sight of our mission in this cobweb of events, which is, as you know, to investigate the deaths of various individuals and discover if there's an ongoing risk to police personnel. Partly due to the fact that the perpetrator of the attack on you both has been charged and it patently has no bearing on these other cases, I'm beginning to think that the man we're after has gone to ground and there isn't a risk *now*.'

Patrick looked dubious but said nothing.

'We now know that Harmsworth was murdered and it was made to look like an accident,' Greenway continued. 'He was investigating the Giddings killing before the case was handed over to what appears to be a newish branch of Special Branch because the murder victim was an MP. Why was that so slow to happen? Do either of you know?'

We did not.

He went on, 'Harmsworth could have been on the verge of making an arrest and the killer somehow knew he was on to him. DI John Gray was also murdered and although he had assisted Harmsworth on the Giddings case it really wasn't his pigeon, so I'm going to stick my neck out and agree with Woodhill CID that he was killed in a burglary that went wrong. Obviously the crime was committed by someone who wasn't your run-of-the-mill burglar, but it's reasonable to suggest that it was a spur-of-the-moment

188

copycat crime done in a panic.' Here Green-way rubbed his hands over his face tiredly. 'How does that sound so far?'

'And Daniel Smith?' I asked.

'Yes, I'd forgotten him for a moment. It seems that he really was an accessory to Harmsworth's murder and was about to cough. Knightly's on the hunt for someone who works in the canteen who hasn't been seen since Smith's death and could have kept his ears open to what people at Wood-hill were talking about. This person could be in the pay of whoever killed Harmsworth – and possibly, under orders, killed Smith himself.'

'Why suspect someone who might just have pulled a sickie, though?' I asked.

'Well, apparently this guy's nickname is the Nose, as he's always trying to listen to people's conversations and sticking said nose in where it's not wanted.'

'Money troubles?' I wondered aloud.

'I don't think anyone's got as far as asking that kind of question.'

Patrick said, 'Most of your theory hangs together, but I must point out that as far as the Giddings investigation goes the trail had gone stone cold. It seems inconceivable that a man of Harmsworth's experience and pro-fessionalism would keep a red-hot lead all to himself, without even making a note in the case file, and yet noise it abroad in the can-teen before heading off into the sticks one night at a time when he would normally be at home in bed – without even telling his wife he was going to be late.'

I followed this up with, 'Your theory, condensed, points to only one killer plus a violent burglar. The former killed Giddings for reasons unknown and then Harmsworth because he'd found out the DCI was on to him. He then, with the help of his trusty mole at Woodhill, got rid of Smith, his accomplice, because he was about to confess.'

'Yes,' Greenway said. 'That's neatly put.'

'It means Gray's conviction that Harmsworth was finished off in revenge by someone he'd shoved in the slammer and the list he made of possibilities is a complete red herring.'

'A very well-intentioned red herring,' Greenway agreed, '– unless whoever killed Giddings is named on the list.'

'But what was the *motive*?' I argued. 'Most of the men on that list are history – they're old, poor, ill, just out of prison; most of them not remotely connected to the social circles in which Giddings moved. Sorry, but I think Giddings's killer will be found in, or on the edge of, his own circles.'

'It could have been a contract killing,' Patrick offered, 'and still carried out by one of the men on the list.'

'Come on!' I protested. 'Hit men for MPs are not going to be the old, ill, poor, etc. folk on the list either. They're professionals, ex-services, and so forth, who have gone wrong.'

'People like me, if I'd gone wrong, you mean.'

'Frankly, yes,' I told him.

There were a few seconds of thoughtful silence, which I utilized for a little prayer of thanks that he had not. Some of the things he has done, though, sort of in the line of duty...

'What had Giddings *done* to deserve a ghastly death like that?' I persisted. 'Hicks is convinced it was a mugger, but what mugger, high on drink, drugs, you name it, would disembowel his victim, cut off his head and chuck it in a litter bin? It's crazy. We pointed a finger at du Norde because he had a motive – he still might be in the frame. Giddings despised him. He'd stopped his allowance. He probably belittled him in front of others. That's just the kind of motive those investigating the crime should be after.'

'Let's go back to the main line of thought for a moment,' Patrick said, '– about the possibility of a further risk to police personnel. I personally think there's every risk while this character remains uncaught.'

Greenway mused for a while. Then he said, 'OK, I'll go along with that even though my instincts tell me otherwise. As I said just now, I think he'll lie low and not risk himself in further action now he's possibly lost his source of information, and hope everyone goes away.'

Patrick spoke earnestly. 'So what do we do now? Or rather, Michael, what do you want Ingrid and me to do?'

Again the SOCA man was lost in his thoughts. 'Go and find the bastard,' he said all at once. 'Knightly's bloody useless.'

We went back to the list, really to clear it from the line of inquiry. Working into the evening, partly at the nick, we first succeeded in finding out that Peter Forbes, the one whose home had been demolished to make way for new development, had been rehoused by the local authority, the compensation, he himself told us when we immediately went to see him, having been insufficient to buy anywhere else. He was now living in sheltered accommodation, was eighty-one years old and riddled with arthritis. Although this career criminal had been one of Derek Harmsworth's worst ongoing headaches in his time, we rather felt that, as he could hardly walk, was a little confused and could not even remember who Harmsworth was, he was out of the picture as far as the DCI's recent demise was concerned.

Patrick then sent fairly, as he put it, 'shitty' emails to the police departments making enquiries for us about another three to get some action and just over an hour later had replies. Zak Bradley, like Ungumba Natolla, was back in prison; Anthony Babbington-Jones had inherited a lot of money and a title from his father and was busy on the estate in Wales, and Francis Andrew Applejohn was now a born-again Christian helping at a mission in Nigeria.

'That leaves Kevin Beardshaw, whom we've already interviewed but who, although apparently seriously ill, hasn't been eliminated from the case, and the Brocklebank brothers,' Patrick said with a sigh. 'I'm in no mood to mess around with this any longer – if the Brocklebanks are neither in nor answering the door this time, I'm going to break in.'

'It's pretty late,' I pointed out, not fancying that particular estate at night.

'Good – all the better to surprise them.'

Fortunately, the mood of patience exhausted manifested itself in body language and the kind of eagle stare under the inevitable orange-coloured street lighting that kept any would-be troublemakers at a safe distance. They were present: in the shadows at each end of the underpasses, in stair wells, rustling through the litter and dead leaves beneath the occasional bank of sickly and vandalized shrubs. It might have been my imagination, or echoes off the endless concrete structures, but it seemed that the light sound of the footsteps of watchers were all around us, like the relentless padding of the paws of wolves.

'So be it,' Patrick said under his breath

when, for the third time, there was no response to his ringing the doorbell of the second-floor flat, the batteries of which were probably dead, and banging on the door with his knuckles. He flashed his burglar's torch over the door frame. 'Interesting. This bears all the marks of having been forced before – by the police, it's safe to assume.'

Less than a minute later both locks had yielded to skeleton keys and, with a hefty push, for it was ill-fitting, the door swung open. All was dark within, the dingy illumination provided by the series of lights along the walkway where we stood, some of which were not working, not being powerful enough to penetrate. There was sufficient light, however, for me to see that Patrick's gun was now in his hand as he leaned within to click down a nearby light switch before jumping back to one side.

Nothing happened: either there was no bulb in the light or the power was off.

'I've always adored playing murder in the dark,' Patrick muttered. 'Flash lamp please, and as we only have one with us, do stay out here for a moment.'

Back in the MI5 days I had received instruction in the techniques used for entering darkened spaces with or without a torch. I was not very good at it, ending up by falling over my own feet, the furniture or any soldier or marine lying in wait, usually armed with a wet sponge in lieu of anything

194

more dangerous. It was not thrown and I will not mention the area they invariably went for, especially if one was female, although I did learn to wear very robust knickers.

I stood to one side of the doorway, seeing the occasional flash as the light jumped about in the way I had never mastered, a combination of examining the interior, dazzling any opposition and at the same time staying alive. It requires far faster reflexes than mine and the ability to move like a cat – shaming, really, when one remembers the lack of Patrick's own right foot.

Seconds later there was a flash and a thunderous bang and smoke and fragments of God alone knew what blasted past me out of the doorway.

I suppose I froze to the spot for a moment and must have stared stupidly at the thick smoke that continued to billow out, hardly believing it, but then got down on my hands and knees and went in. Smoke is always less dense nearer ground level. Immediately, I saw the light from the torch, but dimly through the murk. I reached it; it was lying in a corner of the hall. Using it, and coughing on the acrid fumes, I crawled into the nearest room that was in the opposite direction to where the smoke appeared to be emanating from, reckoning that that was where anyone might have been blown. Judging by the tiled floor it was the kitchen or bathroom.

I encountered a shoe, thankfully with a foot still in it and a leg attached, and, only able to feel because the smoke was getting thicker by the moment, groped upwards. There was a heart-stopping moment when there seemed to be just space beyond the knee, until I realized that the leg I was touching was bent under the other. My hand encountered the gun and I shoved it into my pocket. Now I could see nothing at all, could not breathe, but somehow swivelled Patrick around on the floor, his head having been jammed against a cupboard, got him under both armpits and began to drag him out backwards. To do this I had to abandon the flash lamp and knew that if I lost by bearings now we were both finished.

He was horribly limp: I could feel his head lolling.

Dear God, was the man's neck broken?

I still sometimes have nightmares of endlessly being in a smoke-filled maze trying to get Patrick out. That was what it was like: I kept reversing into walls and slipping on detritus on the floor. Then, finally, my back hit the edge of the front door hard. I cannot recollect reaching the outside, only lying on the ground coughing as though my lungs would turn inside out. The next thing that I was aware of was having an oxygen mask placed on my face and gazing at a concerned fireman. He sat me up.

There was no need to ask the question, for

the answer was sitting right next to me, also being administered oxygen, holding my hand.

It had been a sophisticated booby trap and Patrick, trained to watch out for wires and other similar devices, had not expected infra-red sensors in what he had been treating as a domestic setting. By a miracle the contrivance had slightly misfired, the full force of the blast having gone upwards, bringing down part of the ceiling. But it had still been sufficient to propel him backwards into the kitchen, where he had stunned himself on a cupboard. The consequences were a few very minor burns on his left hand and face, a bump on the back of his head, utterly ruined clothes and that, like me, he was suffering from smoke-inhalation.

But before discovering these things we had to spend the rest of the night in hospital and were only released the next morning after promising that we would rest for another twenty-four hours. The GP whose home we were temporarily sharing chivvied the pair of us to bed when we arrived at the house, dosed us with pills that we dared not enquire too deeply about, and we slept the dreams of angels until nightfall – whereupon she cooked us a light meal.

I suppose our brains resurfaced at round about that point to take stock of the fact that we now had two cast-iron suspects for

197

Harmsworth's murder, but either because of shock, or the pills, discussed nothing about it, falling into bed again as soon as we had eaten.

It was daylight when I woke and Patrick was in the shower. He was not supposed to get water on his burns but is one of those people who would rather hurt a bit and be clean than the other way round. (Females should heap rose petals in gratitude upon such men.) When he came back into the bedroom he gave me a rueful smile and then came over and added a top-ranking kiss.

'Thanks for getting me out.' He sat down on the bed. 'God, I wonder if the doc has some headache pills.'

'I have.' I said. 'Who called the fire brigade?'

'The woman next door. The chief fire officer told me that she and her son actually dragged the pair of us away from the smoke. We must go back and thank them – and to ask a few questions about their neighbours. I seem to remember a large black lady furiously telling me about the "trash we have right on our doorstep", but whether she was referring to dumped rubbish or people I'm not sure.'

It turned out to be both and Esme was delighted to tell us all about it, having embraced us both with huge enthusiasm, thankful that we were recovering. A lump came into my throat, the way her gaze kept straying to the flowers we had brought. In her life, obviously, there was very little of such things, a reminder of what Vera Harmsworth had said about her husband – that he had cherished every second of beauty: a sunset, a bird, a flower.

Ten

While Esme put the kettle on – she insisted on making us tea – we went next door where the Fire Brigade's Arson Investigation Department's team had just arrived. They had, we were informed, done some preliminary work the day before after Scenes of Crime personnel had finished but had decided to return the next morning when their expert on explosive devices was back on duty after a spell of leave. It was this man, ex-army Bomb Squad, who told Patrick exactly how lucky he had been. They were deep in technicalities within the still smoke-reeking flat when the local police came on the scene in the shape of DS Paul Boles.

'Brocklebank,' he said thoughtfully, when I had brought him up to date on recent events. 'Yes, but it'll be Clem we're after, not Ernie. Ernie's dead.'

'But he was on John Gray's list,' I said.

'I guess John didn't actually have time to check the records too closely but just lifted out as many useful names from the boss's own files as he could find. No, Ernie's dead all right – he was killed in a gang fight about six months ago. It might have been when the

200

DI had a long spell of leave to go to New Zealand. Come to think of it, I don't think we ever got anyone for Ernie's death.'

'Were the brothers close? I mean, it could be a motive for his hatred of Harmsworth if he thought the police hadn't bothered themselves too much to find his killer.'

Boles shrugged. 'It's a bit rich, though, isn't it? – when you've lived the life those two have. They should both be inside right now serving life sentences after the things they've done. We know what they've done but proving it and finding witnesses who'll testify against them...' After a pause he added, 'I can't remember the boss being too upset when someone pumped Ernie full of lead one dark night, mind.'

Patrick emerged and warmly shook Boles's hand. 'What do you know about Clem and Ernie Brocklebank?' he asked.

'We were just talking about it,' I said. 'Ernie's dead.'

Boles said, 'Clem was always the clever one. Ernie was a bit thick but could be relied upon to roll up when required with a pickaxe handle and wearing his big boots. Clem was the one with the firearms.'

'Did he ever use a knife?' Patrick enquired in an offhand tone.

'He bragged that he could kill anyone, anyhow, in his younger days. I wasn't here then but the boss was.'

'Would Clem have any *particular* reason for

201

wanting to murder Harmsworth?'

I was glad that Patrick was adopting a feather-light touch, not even looking at the sergeant as he spoke, apparently giving all his attention to the peeling paint on a window frame.

'Not that I know of,' answered Boles stolidly, 'unless he's gone off his rocker.'

'And killed two policemen plus tried to blow up anyone who entered his flat. Yes, that would figure. You know, Sergeant, what makes me really angry about this is that it could have been just some poor sod from the council who was investigating why no one's paid any rent on this place since God knows when.'

I remembered then how I had thought I had seen Erin Melrose here. What if she had tried to get into this flat?

'So he's got a bolt hole somewhere,' Patrick was saying to Boles. 'Any ideas on that one?'

'No,' Boles replied. 'He's kept his head down recently.' After a slightly awkward pause he added, 'I – er – actually need you to make a short statement about what happened last night, if you don't mind.'

'The paperwork – the paperwork,' Patrick groaned but with a grin. 'Yes, sorry. I should have done that first thing. Tell you what: come next door and have a cup of tea with Esme and you can soak up all she wants to say as well.'

'He's a dirty nobody up to no good,' said Esme, presiding regally over two teapots, an assortment of colourful mugs and a plate piled high with biscuits. 'And a crook,' she added, flourishing a teaspoon before whirling it around in the pots.

'You *know* he was up to no good?' Patrick said.

'When he's here he throws bags of rubbish outside instead of putting it down the chutes. And I've even seen him chuck it over into the area below. Once a television set, when he was drunk. He could have killed someone, but I dared not say anything after he called me a black cow one day when I complained about the rubbish. I'm frightened of him and I don't have a man here to help me with things like that now – he left years ago and good riddance.'

Standing nervously by the door of the room was Esme's son, Evian, tongue-tied by the presence of so many upholders of the law, even though two of them had just thanked him profusely for his prompt action the night before last. I rather felt that young Evian might have had his collar felt by the police for much less noble deeds, but was soon to be proved wrong.

'There's always folk knocking on my door asking if I know where this Brocklebank is,' Esme said. 'Housing people, other policeman, men from the electricity and gas. And

I have to say no, I haven't seen him for months except when he sometimes sneaks home at night. I hear the door close. It does not fit properly and has to be pushed hard. I hear him go away again and that is all. Only rats sneak about in the dark and have good people looking for them. Yes, he's a crook all right.'

This pronouncement was followed by the serving of the tea and Esme became even more delighted with Patrick when he took two biscuits.

'Have you any idea at all where he might be living?' he asked her.

'Rough,' she replied. 'For surely a man like that would not have another home.'

'Did you notice other people coming to see him when he did live here?'

'Hundreds of people live here, man.'

'Yes, but you'd notice comings and goings next door, wouldn't you? – because of the dodgy front door,' Patrick wheedled.

Esme gave him an old-fashioned look. 'I'm not one of those curtain-peeping people, you know.'

'No, but you're a law-abiding lady who hates to have unpleasant neighbours who give the place a bad name.'

Mother and son exchanged somewhat nervous sideways looks and then Esme said, 'No, I haven't seen other folk go in there.'

I think none of us had missed that glance. Smiling disarmingly, Patrick said, 'Did he by any chance try to involve your son in criminal activities?' He turned his gaze upon Evian – perhaps thinking that there was the germ of an idea in that young man's mind that he would depart – whereupon he remained riveted to the spot.

Mother and son gave each other another worried look.

'This was bound to come out,' she snapped. 'Well, shall I tell him or will you?' And when no response appeared to be readily forthcoming, she bellowed in stentorian tones, 'You answer now or even though you helped to save this man's life he will take you down to the nick and give you hell!'

Evian looked wretched as we all stared at him and then said to the floor, 'There was this other bloke – and him and the bloke next door, Clem, was talking outside one day when they saw me coming along. Clem says, all sarky like, "Here's a bright young bloke who'll help us out." I really thought he was taking the mick, but then he said I'd get twenty quid if I'd take a parcel to a bloke in Woodhill. I had an idea it was drugs and they wanted someone who hadn't shown their face around there before as the Drugs Squad was watching the place.'

'He did it,' said Esme in disgust. 'But not again, I'll tell you, after the talking-to I gave him when he came back with his wretched twenty-pound note.'

'What did the man he was talking to outside look like?' Boles wanted to know, taking out his notebook.

'He was a real mess,' said Evian, 'like a man who sleeps in his clothes and never combs his hair. But not someone from round here. I've never been there but I reckon this guy lived somewhere out in the sticks. He stank in a strange sort of way – like animals.'

'Did Clem call him by name?'

'I don't think so – I can't really remember.'

Patrick said, 'I'm not going to take you down to the nick and give you hell, Evian, but I would like you to tell me about anything else you've done for this man. He's wanted in connection with a very serious crime.' He rose to his feet and went over to where the youth stood. 'And I shall want your word that you'll stay right away from people like him in future. Otherwise you will get into trouble with the police.'

Evian looked at him desperately. 'No one'll give me any other kind of job.'

'*I'll* find you something to do.' On an apparent afterthought he asked, 'D'you have mates here? Belong to a gang – that kind of thing?'

Evian shook his head. 'No, they do stupid things – just for the hell of it. The big boys steal cars and drive them round and round. I hate that, but it means I have to stay in most of the time. They call me names and throw stones because I won't go with them.'

'There's nothing for good boys to do here,'

Esme lamented. 'The place we lived before had some grass where they could play football. There was even a little garden and we – me and my friends – put plants in for people to enjoy. We used to joke that we would grow vegetables there one day. Here everything has been destroyed.'

To Evian, Patrick said, 'Do these boys go to your school? Do they bully you at school?'

'I don't think any of them go to school.'

'OK, come and sit down and tell us everything you can remember about what Brocklebank and the other man said while you were with them.' To Boles he said, 'Sergeant, please do me a favour and see if you can get hold of a picture of Daniel Smith to show him.'

'That was it!' Evian exclaimed. 'Danny! That's what he called him!'

'He's a clever boy when he really, really tries,' Esme said proudly.

In actual fact, Evian could supply little further useful information although it was established, thankfully, that he had never been to Smith's caravan and had done mostly innocent errands for Brocklebank along the lines of buying him cigarettes, payment being a can of lager, although, strictly speaking, he was under age for both. Patrick and I get very angry about shops that sell cigarettes to children and there was a short detour on the way back to Woodhill when my husband delivered a severe verbal strafing to the establishment in question, getting back into the car with a contented smile on his face.

'You told Evian you'd find him something to do,' I reminded him. 'But surely he's still at school – or should be.'

'Yes, when he feels like turning up,' Patrick agreed. 'I'm not going to lose sight of this. I shall – with his mother's permission, of course – do something, and it'll have to be soon.'

Michael Greenway gazed at us soberly. 'Well, I'm bloody glad I'm not having to attend your funerals.'

'I should have carried out a better surveillance,' Patrick said.

'But for God's sake this isn't a terrorism case!' Greenway exclaimed. 'I'm sure the worst you were expecting was that he'd be waiting for you with a firearm or knife behind a door.'

'I was trained never to assume anything. But at least we now know to expect anything – which might save someone else's life.'

'In my view the case will be really sewn up when we get the DNA results on that clothing. If you're on the right track, they'll find it was Harmsworth's and there'll be traces of that of a person unknown, matey with a handiness in setting explosive devices: Brocklebank. D'you reckon any of his might have survived that blast?'

'I'm no expert on that,' Patrick replied, 'but probably. Sergeant Boles is working on that side of things.'

'Until Brocklebank's found there'll be a continued risk to police personnel. Any idea as to where he might be?'

'None,' Patrick said. 'But obviously, he's not at Smith's caravan.'

'Just about every other form of life on the planet was, according to what I was told. What does Central Records have to say about Brocklebank?'

'Hardly anything really useful. He's fifty-five years old, five feet nine inches tall and of stocky build. Sandy-coloured thinning hair, brown eyes, slightly pockmarked complexion. There's no record of his ever having had a permanent job. He originally came from the North-East and is not known to have any relatives in the South.'

'So did I. Tough as nails, then.' Greenway gave us an appraising glance. 'Where do you two hail from?'

'I was born in the West Country,' Patrick said. 'My father's a Devon man, my mother's Cornish. She was appalled to discover only very recently that her forebears were wreckers.'

So that's where he got it from.

'I'm a southern softie,' I said.

For some reason the men laughed.

'With this latest development I think you have fulfilled your brief on this case,' Green-

209

way went on to say. 'Would you like to hit home base until something else comes up?'

'But you told us to go and get the bastard,' Patrick countered.

'You have. We know exactly who he is now and it's just a matter of putting out a full description and photo of him. If the DNA tests throw up something else we'll have to go back to the drawing board.'

'I haven't actually got him in my *fist*,' Patrick pointed out softly.

'SOCA don't have to get involved like that,' he was told.

'With respect—'

Greenway interrupted with, 'Richard Daws told me you had a way with words – while the expression on your face said something else, usually the opposite. He said you always argue. Give me one good reason why I should listen to you.'

'Because you're a good leader and value the opinions of those working for you.'

'OK, you're flattering me, but I do value your opinion so I'll buy it.'

'We already know the reason why I should go after him. You need someone with experience of special operations. He's far more of a risk to police personnel than to me, now we know what he's capable of. He doesn't know my face – not unless he's been carrying out some kind of surveillance of his own. I shall go undercover and take myself off to the kind of places where he might be known.'

'I hope this isn't a revenge thing.'

'No, it isn't.'

Greenway pondered for a few moments and then said, 'I know that Ingrid used to partner you in MI5 days, but not this time, not now. If you go, she spends time at home, or somewhere else that's at a safe distance, on the end of a phone should you need help.'

'Ingrid is of far more help to me when we work together than you could possibly imagine.'

'That's the deal. I can't risk anything happening to her. Take it or leave it.'

'I'd rather like a few days at home,' I said wistfully, having an idea that the Jo-Jo's business, as far as I was concerned, had unnerved him. 'To see the children, spend time in the garden, hear the cuckoos.'

Patrick and I have our codewords, 'cuckoo' being one of them. Somewhat ridiculously, it can mean absolutely anything and relies heavily on who's doing the talking and who's listening. He knew exactly what I meant.

'OK,' he said.

'You have one week,' Greenway declared.

Despite my indication to Patrick that I had no intention of sticking rigidly to the directive, I did have a sense that some kind of full stop had occurred, the news that Hicks had made an arrest in connection with the Giddings murder adding to the feeling. He had, we were told shortly after talking to

211

Greenway, turned over a squat and found the MP's wedding ring – it was engraved and had been identified by his wife – in a bundle of possessions belonging to a drug addict who hung about the area and who had been previously imprisoned for violent muggings. This individual had been duly hunted down and arrested and, when questioned, his story of having found the ring in the park where Giddings was murdered had, understandably, not been believed. He could give no reason for not having sold it other than saying it was a good ring, and, like Gollum, had snivelled that it was precious to him. 'So why wasn't it on your finger instead of being hidden in an old knapsack under floorboards?' his interviewers had gone on to enquire. There had been no answer forthcoming to this, the man being too far gone on drugs, or drink, and not fit, just then, to be questioned further. Nevertheless, after another interview during which he had refused to speak at all, he had been charged with murder.

'One of those piece-of-cake results that Hicks no doubt goes in for,' Patrick commented crisply. 'Still, it's nothing to do with me – the jury'll have to decide.'

'He told me he was convinced a drop-out had killed Giddings,' I said.

'Special Branch, or whatever-the-hell category Brinkley's outfit falls into, isn't supposed to be *primarily* tuned in to drop-outs – they're called in to examine any possible hanky-panky in the higher tiers of society. I shall send John a congratulatory text message.'

This, I could see, was going to run and run.

I said, 'I didn't know Giddings's wedding ring was missing.'

'Nor did I. Still, I suppose something so small is easily overlooked in such a blood-bath.' Patrick looked up from searching for some paperwork in his briefcase. 'What will you do?'

'As I told Greenway, go home – today,' I replied. 'Just for a short while to make sure everything's as it should be and the children are all right.'

'Good, that'll put my mind at rest too.'

'And then I'll have heard from you and we'll go from there.'

'That suits me fine.'

But when Patrick rang me at Lydtor during the evening of the following day and I had told him that all was well at home, he said, 'I've been thinking about what Greenway said. Look, neither of us is getting any younger and if something happened and we were badly injured, or even killed, it would be appalling for the kids and even worse for Mum and Dad, because they'd have to cope with the aftermath. I really think you should stay out of this one – I'm going to get myself into some pretty nasty places to look for this character and not going to carry a mobile, as it gives the game away if you're searched. I do promise, though, to get in contact should I need help of the kind that the police can't provide. Is that all right?'

I told him it was. He sounded stressed so, right now, what else could I do?

I had already decided on the line of enquiry I would undertake and saw no reason to deviate from it just because we weren't going in like elephants two by two. But, first of all, I had to put my mind at rest on another matter: Erin Melrose.

My difficulty was that I had to stay away from Woodhill police station in order to avoid bumping into anyone who might mention seeing me to Michael Greenway. My conscience was not bothering me as far as he was concerned, for I had indeed gone home to check on the domestic state of affairs. The problem was that I was not sure, even now, where his base was situated and had rather got the impression that senior SOCA people cruised the policing scene a bit like surfing the Net, preferring a fluid style of working. All this meant that, in order to speak to Erin, I would have to lurk near the nick and not look remotely like Ingrid Langley.

I was quite sure of one thing, though: the customized Range Rover would go back to Essex with me, even if I had to leave it in the leafy drive at our digs and walk and use public transport everywhere. The expediency of it plus the emergency equipment that it carries far outweighed any risk that Greenway might spot it among the lime trees, should he even venture into that part of Woodhill, causing him to pull the plug on Patrick's assignment immediately.

My concerns about Erin if she was disobeying orders and investigating John Gray's list were twofold: first, that she would be injured should she succeed in finding Clem Brocklebank and endeavour to arrest him herself; and second, that she might inadvertently cause havoc by waltzing into whatever Patrick was doing, putting the pair of them at risk. At least I had the woman's mobile number, gleaned from his official phone. This had been placed in his briefcase for me to take home for safe keeping, together with the Glock pistol in its shoulder holster. I thought separating himself from the latter sheer madness and had no intention of leaving these items behind either.

Erin was still in the land of the living and in the Woodhill area, agreeing to meet 'someone with information about Harmsworth's killer' in a coffee bar opposite the nick. This was a sticky, grubby sort of place, the kind of establishment that the well-dressed and somewhat fastidious Greenway would not have been seen dead in. I did not want her to spread it around that I had contacted her before we could speak in private so had not phoned her mobile but called the main desk, and she had phoned me back.

'Good God, it's you! I hardly recognized you in that get-up!' she exclaimed when she saw me.

'Perhaps you'd like to sit down and cease trumpeting,' I suggested, probably too coldly.

She sat. 'What's all this about then?'

'Would you like some tea?' I asked to make amends for snapping at her.

'Yes, thanks.'

'Milk?'

'Please.'

'Something to eat?'

'No, thanks.'

I went to the counter to fetch it for her.

'What on earth are you dressed like that for?' she wanted to know when I got back, wrinkling her nose.

'I'm disobeying orders.'

'And where's Patrick?'

'That's why I want to talk to you. He's gone after Clem Brocklebank and we're worried that you're doing exactly the same.'

She coloured. 'I'm not working on anything in connection with that.'

'I'm sorry but I think you are. You have a copy of John Gray's list and I saw you at the estate in Romford where Brocklebank lives on and off. Erin, you must have heard how Patrick and I were involved when an explosive device went off at the flat. He's a very dangerous man and Michael Greenway has given Patrick just a week to find him.'

'Us plods aren't too stupid to be able to do the same, you know,' she said furiously.

I was determined to keep calm and said, 'It's nothing to do with cleverness or stupidity or anything like that. Patrick volunteered to look for him because of his special-forces training. He's planning on going to such low-life places he's asked me to stay out of it and Greenway has forbidden my involvement completely. I just don't want you getting hurt.'

Erin appeared to go into a deep sulk, head down, her face hidden, stirring her tea so that all I could see was her wonderful long, red hair. But she was not sulking.

'I have been doing some poking around, going through the list,' she admitted all at once, looking up and staring at me with her slightly prominent green eyes. 'I really suspected Kevin Beardshaw for a while, as he's a devious bastard and was heard to say to someone in a pub that he hated Derek Harmsworth's guts. But that booby trap clinched it – that's Brocklebank. I'd already done quite a lot of work on him. He's not what you think he is.'

'In what way?'

'He lives on more than one level.'

'Please tell me what you've learned.'

She went back to her thoughtful stirring.

'Please, Erin – a hell of a lot depends on this.'

'I know – and I'm getting really close to him.'

'Look, I'm not the kind of sanctimonious cow to tell you it's your duty to—'

'I should think not!' she exclaimed. 'Because it isn't – it's none of your business. This is my case and I'm doing it for Derek and John. Just because the Home Secretary's latest fantastic initiative SOCA's been brought in—'

'I don't care a monkey's about SOCA.' I hissed, for we were, of necessity, speaking quietly. 'All I know is that my husband's somewhere out there on the streets armed with only his wits and, possibly, a knife. He's doing it to try to prevent people like you ending up as just commemorative plaques on street corners. Erin, you can't go after this man on your own!'

'No, I'll call in other people before I arrest him,' she said after an alarming hesitation.

'And if he finds you first?'

'Are you doing this to give you ideas for your bloody books?' she snapped.

'God, I should hope not!' I retorted angrily.

Erin drank up her tea and then grabbed her bag. 'I've got this far...' she said as she rose to go.

'Look, you give me no choice but to tell Michael Greenway what's going on. I don't want to have to do that.'

'It doesn't matter if you do. I shall stay out

of everyone's reach.'

'Erin, that's stupid!'

But she was on her way out. Then she turned and said, 'Patrick won't come to harm. Brocklebank's not living on the streets – he never has been.'

I must have sat there, staring at nothing for a couple of minutes, aware only that I had failed.

Eleven

It was no use trying to follow her, Erin was too canny a woman not to notice. It was just about the only thing that gave me a little comfort in this ghastly mess – the fact that Patrick had told me she was streetwise. Therefore she would not be easily outwitted.

I was torn between contacting Greenway – by doing what I was doing I was going against his orders anyway – thus getting Erin into career-threatening trouble, and going to find Patrick. I did not really care what the SOCA man would think of me, other than that it reflected badly on the other side of the partnership, but hesitated to blow the whistle on what was obviously a very promising young CID officer who could probably well take care of herself.

Shit.

Before this latest development I had planned to try to find out more about Brocklebank's background, perhaps contact the police in the North-East and establish some kind of starting point from where to begin looking for him. Now I had to give priority to what Erin had told me.

No, the only person I could ask about all this was Patrick.

And the only way I could find him was to search and, if necessary, raise every kind of hell in squats, on waste ground, under railway arches and motorway flyovers – anywhere where the homeless and dregs of society tried to stay warm and alive. I was haunted by the possibility that Erin was quite wrong about Brocklebank and that he would indeed be located in places like that. In this case driving around in the car sounding the horn, not to mention being myself, was right off the agenda, as it would bust Patrick's cover wide open.

I was pleased with Erin's reaction to my appearance, for I had bought wisely at Oxfam, purchasing a gruesome collection of non-matching garments: red cotton trousers too short in the leg for me, a man's purple sweatshirt far too large, a green anorak, black socks and a pair of scuffed trainers. I had donned this lot back at the digs, removed all my make-up, back-combed my hair until it was full of tangles and stuck up as though I was undergoing a severe electric shock and left, assuring the aghast landlady on the way out that I'd been roped in to help at a charity stunt. Fearing that her nerve would go completely and she would ask us to depart altogether, I had left further embellishments until I was in a small park – not the one where Jason Giddings had been murdered – where I had rubbed soil into my hands and face and anointed myself liberally with the squidginess from a rotting onion I had rummaged through rubbish for in an alleyway by a greengrocer's shop, hence Erin's wrinkled nose. It is no good pretending to be down and out and at the same time smelling of toothpaste or the body spray you used that morning. Unlike Patrick in our working-undercover days, I have always drawn the line at decomposing potatoes, which smell utterly, retchingly, disgusting but keep other people at a distance.

No, Erin, I do not do this kind of thing to get ideas for my bloody books.

Another difference between me and never-do-anything-by-halves Gillard was that I had my mobile phone – switched off – and some cash in a body belt strapped next to my skin around my waist and the Glock in its shoulder harness. This latter addition might have been unwise, but I had no intention of prolonging the search after twenty-four hours. When that period of time had expired and nothing had been achieved, I would contact Greenway. But was that too long a time and by my actions was I putting Erin in danger? In the end there was nothing I could do but push all reservations to the back of my mind and just get on with it.

I had no problem in encountering the socially disadvantaged and started off by calling at a row of 'homes' constructed out of large cardboard boxes situated deep beneath a motorway flyover. Where sun and rain still meant something, at the edges of this vast and complicated structure, a Dali-style hell-hole with traffic thundering and thumping above, there were actually small paddocks with ponies in them. I turned my back on these, reluctantly, and penetrated further into the dry gloom where weather never reached, carefully picking my way through and around litter, used needles, dead rats and other things that I did not care to examine too closely. Then I came to the boxes, which had just been visible from afar. At least I knew that the man I sought would not be actually living in one; he would be mobile, man-hunting.

During the next ten minutes or so I was threatened with violence, shouted at, spat at and offered a sandwich that had only had one bite taken out of it. No one had seen a tall stranger, dark-haired but going grey, who might or might not be calling himself Paddy. The sandwich man, to whom I managed to slip a five-pound note when no one else was looking, told me where the squat was that Hicks and co. had raided, looking for Giddings's killer, and I headed for that next.

It turned out to be a once-imposing, large, detached Victorian house due for redevelopment into flats on the opposite side of Wood-hill. By this time it was early evening, the sky heavily overcast and beginning to drizzle with rain, but there was sufficient light for me to see that the windows were freshly boarded up, fences mended, new padlocks put on the repaired doors and that no squatter could now get in. I walked right around the perimeter to make sure – there were high brick boundary walls at the rear and sides with narrow access lanes at the foot of them which presumably at one time had led to other parts of the property – but the entire premises was now securely sealed.

Through increasingly heavy rain I walked back into the town, sat down in the recessed doorway of a defunct shop – it stank of urine – and pondered. It occurred to me with a pang of alarm that Patrick might not be in Woodhill at all. It was utterly feasible that he had had an amazing lead and taken himself off to the Kyles of Bute.

I remembered then that I was close to waste ground I had previously noticed that bordered the railway line where the tracks ran along on an embankment beneath which there were archways. I had spotted what could have been the signs of vagrant human activity: smoke rising from small fires, the glint of glass from discarded bottles. It seemed sensible to search there before it got quite dark. Wearily I got to my feet. No, first I had to have something to eat. Clutching some loose change I had in my anorak pocket I made for a mobile snack bar that always seemed to be parked near the entrance to the station car park.

It was one of those set-ups where the spoon for stirring really was on a piece of string. Having faith in my immune system, I settled for a large mug of tea – you had to pay a fifty-pence deposit on the mug – an equally generously sized sticky bun, and wandered away for a short distance to consume them.

There is something in me that meant I was quite enjoying slumming it – just roaming around what had probably been an old railway siding wolfing down sweet, soft bread and swigging tea. No one was bothered if I licked my fingers, or even burped. No one watched, no one cared. It was a weird kind of freedom. There was the sound of several police sirens in the distance but that did not affect me either.

I took back the mug, pocketed my fifty-pence piece and, deciding on a slight change of plan, strolled back into the town centre. On reflection, the waste ground I had spotted was farther away than I had thought, in the London direction.

For an hour or so I walked, and loitered around, questioned two *Big Issue* sellers and anyone who seemed to live mostly on the streets, and in doing so succeeded in covering most of the centre of Woodhill. No one had seen a man who matched Patrick's description.

The church clock struck eleven and I told myself that I would never be able to live with myself if I failed to look for him on the waste ground by the railway line and that turned out to be where he was and something happened to Erin.

Then I saw a dumpy old bag lady coming towards me, hurrying. She turned through the gates of the church, threw down everything she was carrying and flopped on to the steps. I could hear her gasping for breath.

'Are you all right?' I asked, going up to her.

She seemed not to hear me for a moment, holding her side as though in pain. Then she peered up at me. 'I 'aven't – seen you before,' she panted.

'No, I'm new round here. Are you ill?'

'The Bill always – make me feel sick.'

I sat down on the steps. 'Can I get you a hot drink?'

'No. But there's a bottle – in there.'

In the dim light I had seen the jerk of her head in the direction of one of her collection of carrier bags and duly rummaged.

'Thanks – 'ave some,' she invited when she had downed what must have been around half a pint of something or other – I could not see what, but it was in a small whisky bottle that the label appeared to have fallen off.

'No, I'm fine,' I told her. 'Where are the Bill then?'

'Down on the old goose field. They're

rounding up everyone they can catch and taking 'em there. People like me, travellers, the homeless – you name it. A lad told me it's about that MP what was done in. They've already got someone at the nick an' now are lookin' for 'is accomplice, God rot 'em. I wasn't all that near but I ran this way, I can tell ya.'

'But they won't be looking for someone like you.'

'No, but that must still mean you get questioned as to who you've seen, where you've bin and wot you know and they won't be nice about it. You stay right away, dearie.'

'Where is this goose field place? – so I don't go there by mistake.'

'Down by the railway line along the London Road past where the cattle market used to be. There's a fillin' station there now. Lots goes on down there, especially in the tunnel sort of arches. Don't never go near the place, dearie, not even when the cops ain't there and yer dyin'.'

I thanked her and, with the same caution as before, gave her some money. Her almost grovelling gratitude haunted me for a long time afterwards.

Hicks, I thought, as I started to run. Hicks doing a clean sweep among the vulnerable and possibly mentally ill in an effort to add a few nuts and bolts to his case against the man he was already holding. I supposed, grudgingly, there was every chance that

Brinkley's subordinate sincerely thought he had the right man who, for all I knew, really had knifed Jason Giddings to death. And while I could not imagine for one moment Michael Greenway telling Hicks what Patrick was doing, my real fear was that he did know now. There are few secrets in a nick. Might Hicks use the opportunity to kick around 'a violent vagrant' who 'resisted arrest'?

As the directions had suggested, it really was downhill all the way and I soon reached what I knew to be the London Road, no longer the turnpike of its early days but a three-lane carriageway in both directions. The filling station was actually on the corner on the far side and the only way for pedestrians to reach it was through underpasses. I ran on, thrusting aside a drunk who tottered at me from the shadows by the entrance. Then I skidded to a standstill, bawled 'Patrick?' at him and got a gap-toothed snarl in response.

'Two crowns but no bridgework, thank God!' I yelled at him and tore on, leaving him tripping over the bottoms of his frayed jeans in my wake.

It was farther than I had thought and I was forced back to a walk until I got my breath back. Ye gods, I could still hear police sirens. There was a walkway and a cycle path and, again, I ran for what seemed to be miles.

It was the same place we had flashed past

in the car some days previously and, true to my recollections, it covered several acres. Dropping back to a walk and observing from a distance, I could see that there was a fence of sorts, a chain-link affair that was collapsing under the weight of bindweed and the fallen branches of the trees that were growing against it. The area over by the embankment was brightly illuminated by the headlights of parked vehicles and, as I watched, the lights from a passing train. A patrol car, blue light flashing, was parked by what had once been the official entrance to the area – a one-time goods yard? – and a uniformed constable patrolled nearby. I turned smartly around before he noticed me.

Adjacent to the waste ground was what looked like a council depot of some kind, the gates of which stood wide open. I went in and then around the side of a building – no security lights, thank everything holy – and then could make out in the gloom a row of large vehicles which turned out to be dust-carts. I walked as silently as possible over to them and down the narrow gap between the end one and another building, a shed. The boundary fence here was little better than the one that fronted the road and it was easy to step through one of the gaps. Standing in the heavy shadow of the vehicle nearest to me, I paused to watch what was happening.

Some fifty yards away people moved to and

fro, their shadows thrown this way and that by the lights from different vehicles, radios chattered, someone coughed repeatedly. Nothing other than this sort of thing occurred for the next five minutes or so and I began to wonder how I would be able to cross the open space before me without being spotted.

In the end I began to make my way along by the fence, still in the gloom by the shed, in the direction of the railway embankment. There were at least a dozen archways beneath it, some seemingly with doors on, others without. All present activity appeared to be going on in three roughly in the centre. Still in comparative darkness I walked towards the railway as far as I could go before encountering piles of fly-tipped rubbish.

I was now about fifty yards from the first vehicle, an unmarked car of some kind which, unlike most of the others, was parked without lights. Bending low and keeping as close as possible to the stonework rearing high above me, I headed for it, hoping it was shielding me from any surveillance.

As I got closer I could hear voices. Crouching down by the car I peeped around it, saw that a van was parked very close to it and transferred myself to its larger, safer shelter. Then, alarmingly, it rocked slightly. Someone was inside it. Keeping the bulk of the vehicle between me and Hicks's – or whoever's – little circus, I slithered along and swiftly risked a rapid glance into the pas-senger-side window. The cab was empty.

Moving quickly I opened the door and got in but did not slam it shut. From what I could remember of these suspects', carriers for the use of, as Patrick referred to them, there was a spy window so the inhabitants in the back could be checked up on without opening the rear doors. There was, and I peered through it.

All was pitch-dark inside.

I tapped sofly on the glass and then jump-ed back, startled, as a face loomed at me. It was not Patrick but a black man. He was crying and began beating on the small re-inforced pane of glass and the partition with both hands. Frantically, I made shushing motions, a finger to my lips. He must have been able to see me for he ceased abruptly.

The realization that only the most irre-sponsible person on earth would release him went through my mind in the split second after I noticed that the van's keys were still in the ignition. No, but that did not mean never. I would find out what was going on first. I somehow mimed at him to wait and then slid out. An abject howl came from within. Someone who needed to be helped rather than easily manipulated into confes-sing to being an accessory to murder?

It was time for drastic action before the circus hit the road for home. I homed in on a rotund bobby whom I did not recognize as anyone borrowed from Woodhill, raced towards him with a few bloodcurdling screams for good measure and hurled myself at him.

'You've got my man, you bastard!' I shrieked, pounding with both fists on his ample front adorned with its array of radio, badges, buttons and other bits and bobs. 'You give him back to me – right now!'

I found myself lifted off my feet in an embrace from the rear.

'Here's another one, Sarge!' bawled someone right in my ear.

'Put it in with the rest,' a woman's voice called.

I spat at my first target, to miss, as I was lugged, kicking and struggling, over to one of the archways, which was obviously being used as a holding pen. There, a rickety barrier of wood was pulled open and I was projected within to land on my knees on something soft – actually, a someone. Arms flailed, a fist connected with the side of my head and I went right down.

Luckily, my face landed on a greasy garment of some kind, rather than the earth floor, but it was a small mercy, for the smell was enough to make anyone vomit and I almost did. Stand up or die seemed to be the choice, before the feet kicking at me did real damage.

'Pack it in!' I bawled, having achieved getting to my feet, my hand resoundingly slapping a whiskery face.

The lights from the facing vehicles were dazzling, but despite that I could see that my companions, around seven of them, were all bigger than me, and almost certainly male.

'Anyone here called Paddy?' I shouted in some desperation.

No one was.

'Anyone here *seen* Paddy?'

No one had.

They were closing in on me.

They did not expect it and I fought my way through them, using every trick that Patrick has taught me and not caring one jot that they were undernourished, some of them ill, but all of them with some kind of sexual harassment in mind. Then, back over by the barrier, I turned to face them.

They seemed to have changed their minds, a couple on the ground.

A uniformed sergeant, probably the one whose voice I had heard, was standing on the other side of the barrier, smiling nastily.

'Whoops,' she said with a careless laugh. 'We put you in with the blokes by mistake.'

I pulled a face at her that makes Justin shriek in glorious dread, turned, kicked where it really mattered someone who had had second thoughts, and looked back to see that she was walking away. Then I saw that crammed into the corner by the wall was an elderly man. He made a sort of whimpering noise when he saw me looking at him.

'It's all right,' I told him. 'I'm quite safe

normally.'

'I'm in a little alcove here. You have it – you'll be out of their way here. This is just – just – awful,' he continued in a whisper when we had changed places. 'I hope they didn't hurt you.'

'No, I'm all right, thank you. Do you know who the black man in the van is?'

'He calls himself Hippo for some reason. He's not safe at all, I'm afraid, and after he made a real nuisance of himself they put him in there out of the way.' He eyed me dubiously for a moment and then added, 'The trouble is, they've found out.'

'Who – the police? Found out what?'

He was silent for a moment and then said, 'That some of us were in the park the night that MP was murdered. There are seats near the entrance where we sit until the lady at the chippy across the road spots us. She's very kind and gives us chips and any fish that's been a bit overcooked.'

Keeping a weather eye on the assembled company I said, 'What's your name?'

'Tom.'

'I'm Ingrid.'

He seemed to come to a decision and said, 'You may wonder why we're not all being taken back to the police station. I wondered too, but it would appear that that's too complicated for this man. It's far quicker and easier to knock a few heads together somewhere like this than...' His voice tailed off and he shrugged miserably.

He had an educated voice, but I thought it better not to try to pry into his origins. 'Were you there – in the park?' I asked.

He nodded. 'At least four people who are here now were there that night. The man they've arrested was too, but poor Jamie's not in the real world and although he's been violent in the past when desperate for a fix he couldn't commit murder. Not in my opinion, anyway.'

'They found the murdered man's wedding ring among his possessions.'

'Oh dear, did they? And now they're looking for any accomplices. It does seem to me that whatever anyone says they'll be accused if something remotely like a case can be made against them. Personally, I'm not saying one word.' He gave me another nervous glance. 'Please don't say anything, but I always pretend to be simple when I'm picked up by the police.'

'But, if any of you have real evidence—'

He interrupted with, 'No one would believe what we saw ... if indeed we did see anything.'

'*Why* not?'

'Because most of us had been on the scrumpy that someone had got hold of. I'm not at all sure what I saw actually took place. Probably not. Scrumpy's like that. No, it was too bizarre for words. The scrumpy, that's what it was.'

'Try me,' I requested. 'See if I believe you.'

'You'll only think me a drunkard and an old fool.'

'Tom, just by talking to you I know that, while you may have terrible problems, you're neither of those things.'

While I spoke I was monitoring the company, but no one seemed to be planning any more expeditions in my direction. And where the *hell* was my (expletives deleted) husband?

'I saw a man who could have been him enter the park,' Tom began and then cringed back out of sight as the barrier across the entrance was thrust open, several constables plunged within and grabbed the first person their hands encountered. He was hauled off yelling and swearing.

'Who – *Giddings*?' I said.

'Was that his name – the MP? Yes. One can't be sure of course for it was still light and respectable people' – this with a certain irony in his tone – 'were still about. But there came this chap, city sort, briefcase, nice overcoat, through the park going in the direction of the north entrance. He wasn't strolling, or taking the air, as it used to be called, but obviously on an errand of some kind. There was a purpose to his walk.'

'What's at the other entrance? Is it just a residential area?'

'Yes, it's a little backwater really. There are a couple of corner shops of the old-fashioned sort, a newsagent's and one or two others in a side road.'

'Did you see him come back?'

The man averted his gaze and even in the dimness of where he stood I could see he was shaking.

'Please don't distress yourself,' I said.

'You asked me to tell you and I will. I didn't see him alive again but –' He broke off.

'You came upon the murder scene?' I enquired incredulously.

'It was quite a while later and the small group of us had had some chips when someone suggested that we could sleep in the park that night, as it has some good shelter in the bushes. That's if you don't get bothered by poofs or moved on by the police. I suppose we were wandering around in an aimless sort of way, still half canned and stupid when we saw – or at least I thought I saw, because no one else did – a ghost. It really frightened me, I can tell you, and I swore I would never touch cider again.'

'What made you think it was a ghost?'

'All white, bobbing about. In and out of the bushes. It was an alcohol-induced ghost, my dear. Be warned.'

'But—'

He silenced my protest with a movement of one hand. 'Then we came upon the blood. That *was* real.'

'How could you tell it was blood in the

dark?'

He gazed at me severely. 'There *are* lights in the park – not very good ones, but ... more than sufficient on this occasion. I was in the army, you know, and saw bad things. Blood looks black under the lights from orange street lamps. And you could smell...' Tom took a deep breath. 'Then someone saw entrails. God, it was ghastly. The others just ran.'

'And Jamie, the man the police arrested? Did he run off?'

'Er – no, I think he was still hanging around. I didn't see him later, though.'

'And then what happened?' I prompted.

'I realized I was standing by a litter bin and could see that there was a round thing in it. I struck a match and...'

I waited for him to resume.

'A head.' Tom's voice was barely audible. 'I struck another match to make sure and then removed myself from the place as fast as I could.'

'Are you sure it was the man you saw earlier?'

'No, not at all sure. Not with all the blood. The hair was different too. And there are thousands of men who work in the city and look like that.'

'Different in what sort of way?'

'I don't know, really. Sort of more stylish.'

I was about to ask more about the 'ghost' when another posse arrived, made straight

238

for me and bundled me outside. They took no chances, at least three of them frog-marching me into the adjacent archway. It was lit by what looked like camping lamps.

And there, in all his unwashed glory, stood Detective Chief Inspector Colin Robert Hicks.

'Christ, she stinks,' said one of my escorts, getting out of range.

'Is it a she?' Hicks enquired sarcastically.

'Don't know, guv, but the other blokes thought so.'

There were a few sniggers.

'It doesn't matter,' Hicks said.

I had made a point of slumping to the ground and from this new, lower, level I could see that around the walls were sitting, or lying, the previous candidates for ques-tioning. Most had bloody noses or split lips and one was a girl, sobbing as though she wanted to die.

'Take a good look,' said Hicks. 'It's called softening up, and that's what's going to hap-pen to you unless you talk to me really nicely.' He took a handful of my hair and jerked my head up so I had no choice but to look at him, but squinting and grimacing fiercely. 'Understand?' He frowned at me. 'Speak English?' Then he let go of my hair and slapped my face really hard.

Dizzy, I was wondering how long my cour-age would allow me to carry on like this in order to get sufficient evidence against this disgusting man to result in his being drummed out of the force, when a vehicle approached, the headlights beaming into the archway for a moment before swinging away. The car came to a halt.

'Who the fuck's this?' Hicks fumed, striding to the entrance. He spun round. 'Everyone block the entrance – kill the lamps. Someone turn the headlights of that van off.'

Like a sack of turnips I was heaved into a corner and it became very dark and quiet but for the girl who was still weeping. Then I heard someone returning. Whoever it was carried a small torch. Before I could do anything there was the sound of a blow and the crying abruptly ceased. He came over towards where I was in my corner, the beam searching.

I had already crouched like a coiled spring and launched myself, aiming for his shins. I misjudged in the dark, slightly stunning myself on a knee, but he went head over heels across the top of me most satisfactorily into the wall behind. Accompanied by an odd set of Christmas-tree lights and with chiming noises in my ears I ran for the entrance. There was no wooden barrier here, just a palisade of coppers with their backs to me. I got one of them around the throat, yanked him backwards at the same time kicking him hard behind the knees where the nerves are. Somehow evading clutching fingers I got through the gap and tore outside. No one had switched off the lights of the van, nor of any of the other vehicles either.

Range Rovers have a distinctive engine sound, actually a bit on the noisy side unless they are V8s. I would have remained in ignorance about the latter fact if the gorgeous man now getting out from behind the wheel had not, once upon a time, told me. He was dressed well too, in his best leather jacket and designer jeans.

Hicks was now right behind me but stopped when he saw the identity of the arrival.

'What the bloody hell do *you* want?' he shouted and then lunged forward and grabbed me by a wrist. 'Got a problem here with junkies running amok.' He had me in a hold that he might have thought was an armlock but was not.

'Please don't apologize,' Patrick said. 'I'm looking for Ingrid. DS Melrose told me that she might have gone undercover on the streets looking for a suspect.'

'I wasn't apologizing and I thought that's what you were doing.'

'No, first I took a mugshot of him around shops in the area and struck lucky.'

'Well, she's not here.'

I had been hardly listening to this exchange, working out what I was going to do, trying to remember every detail of the way I had been shown, practised: quite a difficult manoeuvre, come to think of it. With a bit of luck I would break Hicks's arm.

I heard myself grunt with effort, or it might have been a muffled roar of rage, applied all the science I knew and then Hicks was airborne. He thundered down on his back into the mud and stones and commenced to utter a sound not unlike a stuck pig.

Feeling really weak and wobbly now, I bent over, hands on knees, for some reason finding it hard to breathe and aware that Patrick was coming over to me. The rest of the audience seemed to have been turned to stone.

'I had an idea it was you when you came out of there like a burst water main,' he said under his breath, having peered into my face and offered a supporting hand.

'You need to talk to a man called Tom,' I panted.

But Tom, and all the rest of those not yet interrogated, had taken advantage of the lapse in security and bolted into the night.

Strictly speaking Patrick had no real authority to take charge but one-time lieutenant-colonels are programmed that way. Ignoring Hicks, who was on his feet by now wandering around aimlessly clutching his arm, Patrick delivered a memorable tirade to everyone else about the state of the unfortunates in the archway, called up medical help in the shape of ambulances, especially for the girl, who was still unconscious, and then, with a restraint that was an education to witness, arrested Hicks.

I too then melted away when no one was looking and took to the hills. Ingrid Langley was definitely not involved with this one.

Twelve

We said not a word: nothing useful could be gained by owning up to Michael Greenway that I had disobeyed his orders, never mind been present when Hicks was arrested. There was sufficient evidence against him already without anything I might say. But at a later date, perhaps...

I had arrived back at our digs before Patrick, obviously having walked, rammed all my outer clothing into a large plastic carrier bag to be binned, had a much-needed shower and hair-wash and fallen into bed, completely exhausted. I had only been vaguely aware of being joined in the warmth at some stage during what remained of the night but had surely dreamt the remark that, as I smelled of rotten onions, I was not being lusted after.

'They're looking for the woman who wrenched Hicks's shoulder and severely bruised his backside,' I was informed over breakfast. 'But only as a witness.'

'They won't find her,' I said, knowing that I was smiling like the Cheshire Cat. 'But we must find Tom.' I told Patrick what the man had said.

He grimaced. 'I don't like it when people start mithering on about things that go bump in the night – especially when you say he admitted he was the only one who saw it and the whole lot were sozzled.'

'He gave every impression of being an educated man,' I countered but suddenly remembering that Tom had thought what he had seen was as a result of the scrumpy. Basically, though, I believed him. 'He saw something white, or someone dressed in white.'

A piece of toast heavily loaded with butter and marmalade halfway to his mouth went back on to the plate and Patrick said, 'Ingrid, you don't go out to murder someone wearing some crazy outfit that means you're going to stand out like a neon sign!'

'So you're discounting everything he told me?'

'No, not at all. I think the group could well have happened upon the murder scene. He probably did see blood and guts and even the severed head in the litter bin.' Patrick saw that I was not happy with his rubbishing of my hard-won nocturnal efforts. 'Look, I'll make a note of it all and give it to whoever's replacing Hicks before we concentrate on the Harmworth case.'

'Does Brinkley know about his cherished underling?'

'Too right. I gave him the news just after

you did a runner – at a little after two this morning. And do you know what he said? He told me I ought to have accepted the offer of the job in the first place and then it wouldn't have happened!'

'Did you tell him about that photo Hicks tried to smear you with?'

'No. I've made an official complaint about that – but only because Erin Melrose was dragged into it.'

'As I said earlier, that's why I was out on the streets – looking for you, not Brocklebank. Erin told me she was really close to him and I'm worried that she'll get hurt.'

'And she obviously thought you yourself were at risk so that's why she rang me.'

'But you didn't have your mobile.'

'Yes, as I wasn't undercover I had my own and I'd already given her the number for use in emergencies. And now you've told me what she's up to I shall have to talk to her again. More coffee?'

I pushed my cup nearer. 'So what lead on Brocklebank did you get by going around the shops?'

He polished off the toast before replying. 'Well, as I said, I took a mugshot with me. Counter staff in a jeweller's in Woodhill High Street, of all places, thought it closely resembled a man who recently bought a gold chain and two rings and someone in the betting shop next to Woolworth's had an idea it might be a man who puts money on horses occasionally. He always pays with cash. Obviously this isn't someone who lives rough – far from it. He has a car and dresses as though he has money. We might be talking about nothing more than a lookalike, of course.'

'But a *jeweller's*. But Erin did say he wasn't what he seemed. Patrick, you must stop her persisting in her lone inquiry – just in case.'

'I can't, though, can I? I don't have the authority.'

'So, short of camping out in the betting shop...'

'I'll talk to Erin. Perhaps she'll agree to a joint effort.'

'She said she'd go out of circulation so she couldn't be contacted.'

'In that case she'd be in breach of regulations. You're not allowed to go private.'

But, as the day progressed, that was exactly what Erin appeared to have done.

There was no question of keeping *this* development from higher authority: to have done so would have been wrong even though the DS was not our responsibility. At first Knightly would not accept that there was a problem, especially when it transpired that she had taken three days' leave in order to use up some holiday entitlement carried over from the previous year. Patrick had already contacted Greenway, leaving my name right out of it, and was tersely told to carry on with his mission of finding Brocklebank and ignore any glitches that the regular police might have. They could, he said, look after their own personnel.

'Sometimes he doesn't seem to get what I'm on about,' Patrick complained, having related this to me when we met, as arranged earlier, at a coffee bar on the edge of town.

'No, he's just not the kind of guy to over-rate the talents of female detective ser-geants,' I snorted. 'But I take it you'll keep an eye out for her.'

'Of course. Luckily, the girl has two dis-advantages in staying unnoticed: her height and the colour of her hair.'

'And she's stick-thin, so be on the lookout for young people of both sexes wearing veils, big woolly hats or turbans.'

He groaned, pondered silently for a few moments and then said, 'No, it's no good.'

'What isn't?'

'I simply can't be doing with you just on the end of a phone. We're a team and I reckon that, as it doesn't look now as if Brocklebank's going to be found in the filthiest sewers of society, I'm damned if I'm going to work alone. Frankly, today I've been stalling.' He grabbed his mobile.

He got what he wanted. How could Green-way refuse when faced with a threat of resig-nation?

Erin's name had not been mentioned during

Patrick's ultimatum; nevertheless we went straight out to look for her. It had already been established that she was not answering her mobile – actually switched off – nor the phone at home. This turned out to be a rented flat over a florist's shop in the centre of Woodhill and reminded me of the bolt hole I had found when I first left the nest. My beloved father had been in a nursing home suffering from a ghastly creeping disease that would eventually destroy him, my mother being adamant that she could not look after him and, eventually, not wanting a resentful teenager under her feet in the evenings either, my sister having escaped to live with an aunt two years previously. So, in effect, she got rid of all of us. She is still living in the same house and, as yet, I have never been back.

That wonderful scent of carnations, stocks and greenery of which I had used to take a deep breath as I went up the stairs was the same here; we had passed the back room where vases and vases of them were stored. The shop owner where I had lived had observed my appreciation one day and thereafter had always saved a few flowers for me – perhaps with broken stalks, or a couple of petals missing, or just oddments. I am sure she could have used them in wreaths and have always remembered her kindness.

There was no response to ringing the door bell.

'You're going in?' I said in surprise, seeing Patrick's burglar's keys in his hand.

'I actually think we have a duty to go in,' he replied. 'For after all, whatever the girl has said, for all we know she might be lying in here gravely ill.'

But Erin was not at home. Everything was very tidy, with nothing left lying around to give us a clue as to where she might have gone or what leads she might be following. Being very careful not to disturb anything, Patrick opened drawers in a computer desk in the living room while I examined similar storage space in the bedroom. We found nothing useful.

I wandered into the kitchen. There was hardly any food in the fridge but a shopping list was fixed under one of the magnets on the door listing the usual things, so presumably Erin intended to return home soon. When I went back into the living room Patrick was sorting through the contents of a letter rack on the desk.

'Just a couple of bills, some postcards from friends on holiday, photographs of ditto and some letters,' he reported. 'I don't think I need to read those.'

'That's a lovely house,' I commented upon seeing a photograph on a business heading.

'It's an old manor house that's been turned into an hotel and conference centre,' Patrick said. He went to put the letter back with the rest, but his eye was caught by the wording:

' "Dear Miss Melrose," ' he read out, ' "I regret to inform you that we have no suitable staff vacancies at present but with your superior qualifications in mind I am able to give you an undertaking that I shall put your name down on our records for when such a vacancy should arise. Yours sincerely, Jennifer Lister, Catering Manageress." What on earth is the girl doing?'

'A change of career?' I hazarded.

'Surely not.' He frowned. 'No, definitely not. When we were in the Green Man once she said she was a lousy cook.' He tapped the letter. 'This, my dear Watson, is a lead that we must regard as important. But there are a few other things to attend to first.'

The Blue Boar at Kingsbrook did not look as though it had had a lick of paint since the Wars of the Roses. I made a note to inform fellow scribes who wrote historical crime fiction of its unmodernized charms so that they could fall on the place and savour every detail of the grime-encrusted oaken beams, the worn church pews that leaned crookedly against the walls of the public bar in lieu of chairs and upon which so many initials had been carved it was a wonder they had not disintegrated, and the strange smell, a cross between wet dogs and something very dead somewhere beneath the floorboards.

'You are *not* having a pint here,' I told Patrick.

'It's lunch time,' he protested.

'The locals will have developed the necessary antibodies,' I said, eyeing the smeary glass tankards hanging on hooks above the bar. 'You haven't, and you'll be on the loo for a week.' Detecting that right now he was probably regretting having put his job on the line in order to have me along, I added, 'Oracles have never necessarily said what people wanted to hear. The last thing you need right now is a dose of the trots.'

Nostrils flaring, Patrick slammed his ID down on the bar. 'Joe Masters?' he demanded to know of the bored-looking individual standing behind it.

'That's me.' The man had hardly glanced at what was in front of him and gave little attention to the photograph that was now plonked next to it.

'Seen him in here? He was probably an associate of Daniel Smith.'

Masters shook his head. 'Nope.'

'Have a closer look,' he was encouraged, grittily. 'This was taken some years ago. He might look quite respectable now.'

Masters peered at the photo in the manner of someone whose reading glasses are elsewhere. 'Can't say as I've seen him.'

'How long had Smith been living in the caravan?'

'It's been in the paddock out the back for years and used to be rented by a farmer to house veg pickers. But it started to get a bit too scruffy and what with the health-and-safety bods breathing down my neck already, I decided to get rid of it. But this bloke Smith came along and asked if he could use it sometimes in exchange for doing odd jobs for me. He seemed a bit down on his luck, so I agreed. In fact I said he could have it – so as not to be responsible for it any more, like. But the dirty little bugger ended up living there for most of the winter, did precious little to help; in fact he left his rubbish everywhere and spent far too much time in here making a half last the whole evening. I'm glad he's gone and the caravan's going as soon as you lot have finished with it.'

'The man's been murdered,' Patrick said reproachfully.

'He looked the kind who would mix with murderers.'

'Did anyone ever ask for him? Did you notice him in conversation with anyone on a regular basis?'

'No, he stank too bad to have real friends,' was the bald reply.

'We'll take a look at the caravan.'

'Question,' I said when we were outside and walking around the side of the building towards the rear. 'Caravans are dreadfully cold and damp things to live in in the winter. It would have been far cosier to have stayed where he did his gardening job for Thora at Buckton Manor.'

'There's no beer there, though and, don't

forget, he only possessed a bike and cycling down to the local on dark nights from there wouldn't have been a joke. I reckon the nearest pub to that place is at least two and a half miles away.'

Men always notice things like exactly where the nearest pubs are, of course.

The ground at the rear of the pub was little better than its interior, the so-called paddock being merely an acre or so of weeds surrounded by a sagging post-and-wire fence, the gate to it flat on the ground a short distance away with grass growing through it. The area might have been a garden at one time, for we almost fell into a pond choked with water plants and there were two or three good trees.

The caravan, set just inside where the gate should have been and surrounded by a walkway of broken paving slabs, was not sealed off, an indication that all forensic testing really had been completed. It was, however, still cordoned off by police incident tape tied to the trees and had 'KEEP OUT' notices affixed to it. We stepped over the tape and approached Smith's last home. With flat tyres, and greenish-black with mould in places, it gave every impression of slowly and inexorably rotting into the mud.

'I don't know what we can learn from this,' Patrick muttered, yanking open the door.

I had a sudden and inexplicable stab of alarm and grabbed his arm before he could enter.

'What's wrong?' he asked.

'I'm not sure – but please don't just walk straight in,' I said.

'Look, SOCA have only just completed their stuff. People have been crawling all over it.'

'Sorry, it's either that I'm all jittery after what happened last time or –' I broke off and shrugged, feeling foolish.

'Or it's your cat's whiskers and there's been every opportunity for someone else to mess around with it,' he murmured and walked away for a short distance over to a pile of rubbish. Selecting a few bricks and a chunk of wood, he put them all in an old plastic fertilizer sack and tied up the top with a length of rope. Then, carrying it, he came back.

'Go right over there,' he told me, waving an arm back towards the building.

'Do be careful,' I pleaded.

Positioning himself carefully a practical distance away, Patrick commenced to swing the sack – actually quite heavy – backwards and forwards until it had sufficient momentum. Then, he released it, putting distance between himself and the caravan as soon as it had left his hand to go hurtling through the open doorway.

There was a loud crash and the floor of the caravan collapsed completely. Moments later there was a flash, an ear-splitting bang and a huge cloud of debris-laden smoke.

I had taken refuge in the entrance to the noisome Gents', dived farther in when the explosion occurred, met someone on his way out and shoved him inside again as things clattered down on to the corrugated-iron roof above our heads. When it petered out somewhat, we ventured outside. Patrick was just picking himself up from behind some low bushes and appeared unscathed, so I sent the man off for a fire extinguisher, as all that was left of the caravan was a raging bonfire and rolling clouds of acrid smoke.

Patrick came over. 'That's it,' he said in the quiet, flat voice he uses when he is very angry. 'From now on we're on a war footing with this bastard even if it means I go to prison for cutting his throat all over his own living-room carpet.'

'I have a horrible feeling that he's watching us,' I said.

Patrick shook his head. 'No, not in the sense that he's perched up a tree with a pair of binoculars snooping on us in particular. Like the set-up in the flat, anyone could have been injured in that booby trap – even the guys from the council who would have ended up coming to take the caravan away. No, this is a two-finger salute to the police.'

'But he didn't plant the thing before Scenes of Crime people arrived.'

'There was probably no opportunity, as it

would have been guarded as soon as Smith was murdered and I told them where he lived on and off.'

We had found somewhere to have a bite of lunch that was less of a potential health hazard than the Blue Boar, but it was only a café so Patrick had to settle for coffee with his BLT. He had come off the boil but I knew would now be deeply involved with strategy for the rest of our lunch break. I did not interrupt his thoughts.

'No, there's nothing for it but to bury our own identities and come up with something that'll put us in a position to be out and about, watching people but without arousing their suspicions,' he said at last, pensively stirring his coffee.

'Well, we've done fencing contractors,' I replied briskly, '– or at least you have – and hell's angels and Irish terrorist plus bimbo and down-and-outs. No, as far as *that* goes I am not living on the streets again. Sorry.'

Patrick brooded darkly. 'Looked at from another angle, what is this guy likely to want that we might be able to give him that will lure him out of his rat hole? We already know he sometimes bets on horses and enjoys spending money on himself – yes, the chains and rings were for him. That's if it is the same bloke, of course.' He found his mobile. 'I'll ask Paul Boles if he knows any more about him.'

I recollected that the DS had said Brocklebank had boasted that he could kill anyone, anyhow, in his younger days.

The signal was poor so Patrick went outside to make the call. 'No, he can't think of anything that might be of use right now,' he reported when he returned.

'Brocklebank used to brag a lot and must be feeling very full of himself right now,' I said. 'He's literally got away with murder and the police haven't a clue where to start looking for him. But there's no brother Ernie now he can tell what a big man he is. If he has a family, they might not have a clue what he gets up to in his other life, so he has to keep quiet about it to them too. What he needs is a chum he can yarn with, drink with, pose around in front of, fool himself into thinking he's recovered his lost youth – someone with form, someone *dangerous*.'

'I can do dangerous,' Patrick muttered.

Was the man kidding? He's positively lethal.

'He might have someone like that already,' Patrick observed.

'Do a better someone.'

'Where will you be in all this?'

'Your somewhat sleazy bag of a wife – what else?'

In the end I ditched the 'somewhat' and went for the whole bling thing, hitting the charity shop again for a couple of tight miniskirts and tops, high-heeled shoes, phoney gold chains and a teddy-style bra (freshly laundered, I was assured) that pushed up my modest bust until it threatened to escape from the aforementioned tops. Patrick's reaction was a sight to behold when we had a dress rehearsal and I had added full make-up, including false eyelashes, bright-red lipstick, and scragged back my hair into the tight ponytail that I believe is referred to as 'a Staines facelift'.

'Overdone?' I queried.

He tore his gaze from my bosom and found his voice. 'God, no. But I hardly know it's you.'

'Good. I got a chain bracelet and a medallion for you too.'

He donned his black jeans and matching shirt, leaving several of the top buttons undone, and by the time he had added the jewellery and an amazingly naff belt I have never been able to prise away from him that has a buckle decorated with a brass skull with red-glass eyes, the picture was almost complete. Flattening down his normally wavy and slightly unruly hair with gel – something he learned to do when taking part in a film not so long ago – and switching on a sullen scowl resulted in someone I hardly recognized either.

'This look is a bit dated, you know,' he said, looking at himself in the mirror.

'The ignorant lawless often are.'

Neither of us was saying the obvious: that

it was an extremely long shot. But we had Greenway on board and this was manifested when we went out as it was getting dark and bought a local evening paper.

'Woodhill police are concerned that big-time criminals are moving out of London into the wider surrounding area,' Patrick read aloud from the bottom of the front page as we stood beneath a lamp post. 'The Home Office has admitted that gangs from central Europe are arriving here and, in some cases, have forced established hood-lums from their "manors", a fact borne out by the recent spate of shootings and knife attacks in the East End. One such dis-possessed "godfather" is Vernon Studley, one of several aliases used by a man on the Metropolitan Police's 'most wanted' list. He is described as tall, dark-haired and of wiry build and a man answering this description was seen with several others shortly before a disturbance at a public house in Ilford a few days ago when three people were admitted to hospital with stab wounds. Off the record the police are saying that this man and his associates are trying to remove any local opposition with a view to moving in. There is no need for undue alarm but under no circumstances are members of the public to approach anyone of whom they are suspi-cious, but call the police.'

'Vernon Studley?' I said. 'I seem to have heard that name before.'

'One of the incumbents of our church at home in the seventeenth century, if I remember correctly. The name sort of' – his eyes went back to my chest – 'popped into my head. Most of this article is true – even the fracas in Ilford, which, of course, lends authenticity.'

'Someone may well call the police and we'll be arrested.'

'Greenway thought of that. But we'll escape and go to ground. Knightly knows about the ruse so the law will be slow to react. Poor ol' Fred's good at that.' He dropped the paper in a rubbish bin and, with a raffish leer, crooked an arm. 'Fancy a drink, babe?'

Despite the get-up we had no intention of flashing ourselves around and sidled into a pub in an old part of Woodhill, the kind of place that still had etched windows advertising stout and locally brewed beer, those companies no doubt long gone. A few people were playing darts in the public bar, a couple of others propped up the bar, but it was otherwise quiet. Subjected to a few sideways glances we found a table in a corner and Patrick went over to order our drinks.

I saw to my glee that one of the women playing darts was dressed very similarly to me. We exchanged the obligatory glares and I tried to guess who she was with – the short, fat one, the short, thin one or the taller, hairy man wearing cowboy boots and, yes, a medallion. The whole lot, I guessed, were market traders.

'Wot are you starin' at?' the woman shrieked at me all at once.

This was quite unwanted and shook me. Perhaps I had overdosed on the mascara and eyeshadow. 'Not *you*,' I retorted, as though she was blocking what would otherwise have been a perfectly stunning view.

Heaven preserve me, she came over. 'I know 'oo you are!' she hollered. 'You're that Sharon Bigtits wot Kev at the paper shop slung out of 'is place for messin' around wiv uvver blokes.' She drew herself up with a toss of her head. 'Kev's my bruvver, I'll 'ave you know.'

'It's your turn, Chantelle,' one of the men called across to her, his tone weary.

'I am not Sharon,' I said heavily. 'That's my man over there and if I messed around with other blokes he'd wring my neck. Now, go back to your bleedin' arrers.'

Pausing to take a mouthful from his brimming pint, Patrick came over. He gave my antagonist a dismissive glance, she opened her mouth to bandy more words and he bellowed 'Cool it!' at the pair of us, making us jump out of our skins.

Cut, I said to myself. Take One in the can. That was the trouble with being in films.

'*Low*-key,' Patrick admonished in a whisper as he seated himself.

262

'I didn't do anything,' I whispered back.

'Yes, you did. I know more about the language of womankind than you imagine.'

For the rest of that night we loafed about in pubs and clubs, spending a small fortune in crossing palms with silver to gain admittance to the latter, almost certainly drank too much and saw no one who remotely resembled the mugshot of Brocklebank. It was unrealistic to expect success on the first night, but we told ourselves that we had made our faces known and went back to our digs. There, half undressed, I was taken in a fervent embrace.

'It's either the photo or that bra,' Patrick said before lifting me up on to the edge of a chest of drawers and deftly removing it together with the other small garment. 'We've never done it like this before,' he went on, and then his mouth was on mine, my legs around his hips and I found myself penetrated with huge and urgent enthusiasm, paradise commencing.

Never let it be said that buying things in charity shops is boring.

For the next three nights we changed the type of venues we visited, going both up- and downmarket, but had no success in finding anyone who looked remotely like the man in the photograph.

'I saw you come in at two thirty this morning,' said our landlady as she brought in our breakfast on the day after this, her tone making any further comment unnecessary.

Patrick, who had a slight hangover, said, 'I'm with the Serious and—'

She interrupted with, 'Yes, I know you said you were with the police, but how can I believe that now? I made a point of staying up, actually, as my neighbour told me how you creep in in the early hours looking like the cast of *Eastenders*. She thinks you're up to no good and –' She broke off, probably on account of the gestures of peace Patrick was making with his hands and the beatific smile he was beaming in her direction. He produced his ID card.

'We're undercover, looking for someone,' he said. 'But please don't tell your neighbour, or anyone else for that matter.' He showed her the photo of Brocklebank. 'We're looking for him.'

'Well, that's a relief.' She picked up the photo, took it over to the window and studied it. 'I've a good memory for faces and I've seen someone who looks like this somewhere. But not recently, by any means.'

'Where?'

'I'm not sure. Yes, how stupid of me: he must have been one of my patients before I retired.'

'How long have you been retired?'

'About six years. Do you have a name for this man?'

'Brocklebank. But he may use others.'

'That would be difficult with a medical card. Although he might have said he'd lost it. Records weren't on computers in those days, you see.'

'We need to know where he's living now. Officially he has a council flat on an estate in Romford but hardly ever goes there. It would appear that he lives a double life.'

'I could ring around a few colleagues,' she offered.

'We're more than grateful for anything you could do to help.'

'Do we go for a change of plan, then?' I asked Patrick later. 'We've had no luck so far. We haven't even had any run-ins with local godfathers.'

'Well, don't forget Jo-Jo's still helping the police with their enquiries and he's probably number one round here. I suggest we give it one more night and if there are still no developments then have a rethink.'

'How about giving that country-manor hotel, or whatever it was, a try tonight? You said yourself it might be a lead and there's still no trace of Erin. Not only that – we've only two more days before Greenway's time limit runs out.'

Patrick agreed, admitting that finding the letter had slipped his mind.

Thirteen

The hotel was situated on the edge of a village near the northern boundary of Epping Forest. We had changed our attire and gone upmarket for the occasion, definitely leaving all the bling behind. Patrick was wearing a suit, his partner in a little black dress *sans* the exaggerated cleavage, which was, I gather, one distraction, or rather two, less for him. With our personal security in mind we had not used our own vehicle but hired one.

Before leaving, Patrick had left a message for Greenway telling him of our intentions and contacted Paul Boles. The DS had set our hearts racing with the information that monied criminals were sometimes, when not detained at Her Majesty's pleasure, to be found at this particular converted and extended sixteenth-century manor house, complete with its casino, conference suite, three heated swimming pools, tanning and fitness studios and woodland all-terrain bike-racing track.

'A lovely house ruined – it's going to be horribly brash,' I lamented as I swung the car into the driveway and glimpsed illuminated fountains and flickering neon signs through the trees that flanked the entrance.

'It sounds spot on to find our man then.'

'I take it one doesn't have to be a member, or anything like that.'

'No, the hotel's open to non-residents. I booked a table for dinner. We could even stay the night if they've a room and things get interesting.'

One of the neon signs, the one right above the entrance doors, was pink and included flashing silver stars that formed the words 'HAPPY BIRTHDAY ROXANNE'.

'Blue for a boy?' I muttered as we walked beneath it.

'I gather this place was originally built by a favourite of Henry the Eighth,' Patrick said.

'Probably always been tacky, then.'

He chuckled. 'Smile, babe, the security cameras are on yer' – and proceeded to swagger into a lounge bar, his face wearing what I can only call a ratty smirk. It occurred to me that with his hair smarmed down and loud tie, another of my charity-shop trophies, even his own mother, Elspeth, would not have recognized him.

The place went in for elaborate cocktails and I was duly and ceremoniously presented with an edifice of fruit, greenery and little parasols that presumably had a drink inside it somewhere. I noted that Patrick's whisky was a double, but he then, uncharacteristically, put a lot of water into it.

'Look at them,' he said, back against the bar, facing the room. 'All phoney and bloody miserable and wondering what to buy next to try to cheer themselves up.'

The large room, with a conservatory extension to one side which right now was housing the birthday party – raucous, a flock of balloons, girls all bursting out of their dresses – was decorated mostly in gold and crimson and had had any traces of olden days ruthlessly obliterated. The lighting was bright and harsh and, as Patrick had just intimated, most of the people in animated conversation in it – botoxed, breast-implanted, face-lifted, bronzed – looked unhappy. As my glance fell on her, one woman gulped down her drink of what looked like pink gin and tonic and smacked the empty glass down on the table in front of the man she was with. Without even looking at her he rose and darkly came over to the bar to get her another.

I grazed my way carefully into my own personal tropical jungle, taking my time. 'Are you going to show the photo of Brocklebank to the barman?' I enquired quietly.

Patrick took a sip of his drink. 'No, I think I've already seen him.'

'Where?'

'There's a notice board just inside the entrance with photos of senior members of staff and head chefs on it. He's the man at the top, the manager. He might even be the owner.'

'Are you *sure* it's him?'

'No, because everyone changes as they age and the picture we have is twenty years old, showing a man with thinning hair. This one's bald, or shaven-headed.'

'Tanned, fit-looking and not a wrinkle even though getting on for sixty?'

'That's right.'

'You've always been good at faces.' I looked at him and he gazed soberly back. 'This will have to be handled very carefully,'

'Yes, we have to prove it's Brocklebank – he's calling himself Rex King, by the way.'

'How tedious of him.'

'Oh, we're not talking about an educated man. We must prove it's him while bearing in mind that he's dangerous – who else could have planted that gizmo in his flat?'

'He used to boast that he could kill anyone, anyhow. Did you book the table in the name of Vernon Studley?'

I got a wolfish grin. 'Too right.'

'So we wait a while. If nothing happens, what then?'

'We stir things gently, what else?'

That probably meant start a small war.

At the arranged time – eight thirty – we went through into the restaurant – artificial palm trees, blue-plastic water cascades falling into plastic-lined ponds with plastic fish in them – which was very busy and where another party was in progress, a retirement one by the look of the ages of those attending. But it was no less noisy for that and in the middle of the main course a woman, loud- and foul-mouthed, obviously sloshed, celebrated herself right off her chair into an elaborate, and again artificial, floor-standing flower arrangement. Every which way, red knickers and all, she was resurrected, placed inert on a chair and discreetly lugged away by her male companion and members of staff, presumably to a taxi.

'Go on, you're not Ingrid Langley tonight,' Patrick said, eyes sparkling and perceiving that I was struggling to keep a straight face, adding lugubriously and none too quietly, 'After all, the old cow might be stone dead.'

So, regrettably, we both howled with laughter, thus earning the repugnance of the entire assembly. One member of the party was all ready to come over and remonstrate with us but was pulled back into his seat by his companions.

Good: we looked the part, then.

Exercising caution in case there was trouble, we ate lightly and sparingly – which was a shame, as the food was surprisingly good – and drank only water. Afterwards we were asked if we would like to have our coffee in the lounge. This turned out to be a smaller side room situated some distance down a corridor in the hotel sector that had a real log fire. We were the only occupiers.

The waiter had set the coffee things down on a table near the fire and I gravitated over to it while Patrick prowled around the room – something he always does when in strange surroundings but already suspicious because of the lack of others present. I poured the coffee and he wandered back.

'I could do with a fag,' he said. 'Left 'em at home.'

The obvious telling of lies is one of our warning codes. Had he spotted some covert surveillance?

'Go and buy some at the bar, then,' I snapped pretend-bad-temperedly.

He sprawled into an armchair. 'Nah, can't be bothered. Time I gave up.' His gaze fixed upon the coffee. 'Come on then, girl – two sugars.'

I duly spooned them in. He does not take sugar now, so this was a message to me that he had no intention of drinking it. Hairs stirring on the back of my neck, I therefore knew I must not drink mine either, but behaved normally, passing his across, sugaring and stirring mine for something to do. I knew Patrick was armed, but circumstances had changed. We no longer worked for MI5: there were different rules of engagement now and firearms could not be used unless the situation became really desperate.

A couple of minutes later the door opened and a man entered. He was bronzed, fit-looking, with not a wrinkle, and had the rapacious demeanour of a healthy pack of hyenas. If this was not Clem Brocklebank – despite the shaven head there was a very strong likeness to the picture we had deliberately left behind – then I would go home and knit dishcloths for the rest of my days.

'You're Studley?' he said, coming over to us.

Patrick, who was already on his feet, eyed the incomer up and down and delivered the necessary time-honoured response. 'Who's asking?'

The other smirked and held out a hand. 'Rex King. I own this place. This is one of my private sitting rooms.'

Patrick ignored the hand. 'Have we spat in an ashtray or something?'

'No, not at all. No, I read about you in the paper and I believe we have something in common.'

Again Patrick looked the man up and down, only incredulously this time. (He *was* once offered a part in a film.) 'Really?' he drawled. 'OK, you can join us,' he went on to say as King seated himself. He affected to notice me. 'This is my friend Sapphire.'

Sapphire simpered suitably.

'Aren't you going to drink your coffee?' King wanted to know.

'It's got a funny smell, as though someone's shat in it,' Patrick said.

'Shall I get you some more?'

'No, thanks. And I don't like being on

surveillance cameras while I'm drinking it.'

King shrugged. 'I understand you're hoping to gain a hold in this area.'

'What if I do?'

'You won't be able to do anything without my co-operation.'

'How's that?' Patrick asked, all innocence.

'I run things around here. Not obviously, and the cops don't have a clue about me, but what I say goes.'

'You talk like the soundtrack from an old B-movie,' he was told.

I thought that King was also taking a terrible risk. Was it as I thought and he was desperate to parade himself in the criminal underworld – was fed up with not being, as he put it, obvious?

The bonhomie started to slip away. 'I can't say that I've ever heard of you,' he said. 'And I thought I knew all the big names in this game.'

'You're still reading it from a script. That's because Vernon Studley's not my real name. It even said that in the local rag.'

'OK, I believe you. I can offer you a lot if you agree to certain conditions.'

'Call you sir, you mean?' Patrick said with a sneer.

King sat forward suddenly. 'Don't play around with me. People who do or who get in my way don't get very far. I don't involve others to tell tales either. I deal with things – personally.'

'That sounds like a threat.'

'Take it any way you like.'

Ye gods, they still sounded like an old Al Capone film.

'Your conditions then are what?' Patrick enquired heavily.

'How many can you call upon?'

'Any number. But I don't go around with a pile of hangers-on. That's messy and unprofessional.'

'No boys to watch your back?'

'No, I watch my own back – unless I'm actually on a job.'

'I watch his back,' I said.

King chuckled indulgently. 'OK, darlin'.' To Patrick he said, 'You put some of your men under my control when I ask for assistance.'

Patrick appeared to think about it. Then, 'Agreed,' he said reluctantly.

'I take a share of your proceeds if I'm going through a thin patch.'

'No. You're not living off me. No one lives off me. Besides, you've got this dump.'

'In return for which I give you a take when I get a good run of money.'

There was a short silence and then Patrick said, 'A bloke calling himself Jo-Jo offered me a similar deal quite recently. I arranged for the police to raid his place.'

'Jo-Jo!' King whooped. 'He was one of my errand boys – a nobody and turning into another nuisance. You did me a favour – unless he decides to bleat, of course. But I doubt it; he'll want to keep his head attached to his shoulders.'

'Whatever you say the cops aren't going to stay asleep for ever and any arrangement we make might only be short-term. No, I'd rather stay independent and go hungry – only I won't.'

King relaxed back in his chair. 'The cops who aren't asleep tend to have ... accidents.'

'Is that what you meant when you said you deal with things personally?'

'Yes.'

'I'm impressed,' Patrick whispered, and the other man's eyes glowed.

'Hear about a DCI whose car went off a motorway bridge earlier in the year?'

'No.'

'Name of Harmsworth. He was becoming a real nuisance, so I got rid of him.' King's hand went into his pocket and I saw Patrick go as taut as a bowstring. 'There you are. I brought it specially to show you. That's his watch. I always take little keepsakes.'

It lay there, in the palm of his hand, the wind-up watch from the RAC, the hands stopped at two thirty-five. Then King's fingers closed over it possessively.

'And his sidekick,' King continued, 'although he might not have been really on to me, I just got in the mood to take control of the local filth. I took the computer that time – thought there might be useful stuff on it.

One of my staff is a real geek with computers and hacked into it, but it was all rubbish – his holidays and plants and notes on growing veg and things like that.'

Patrick shrugged dismissively. 'I can only remember something about an MP meeting a messy end somewhere in the sticks out here. Was that you too?'

King laughed, genuinely amused. 'God, no. He was knocked off by a junkie desperate for a fix. Why would I want to kill one MP? – they're all a waste of space, so once started you'd have to take out the lot.'

'Well, you might have got in the mood to take control again,' Patrick said, the irony in his tone utterly lost on the other.

'No, it's got to be really *useful*. To me. My time's valuable. That's why I'm talking to you now, so I don't meet you one night when you're least expecting it to settle things in more unfriendly fashion. Be warned, though: I don't do things in obvious ways; I leave little souvenirs of my own as I move through life to teach people to stay away from me.'

'You're thinking about the future,' Patrick observed grimly. 'Say things like that and you won't have a future.'

I thought it about time that a girl like Sapphire would start to lose her nerve. 'Don't talk of killing,' I pleaded. 'Please settle things nicely.'

Predictably, they both totally ignored me. 'All the staff here are my trained bodyguards,' King said, not taking his eyes off Patrick for a moment, '– men and women. I only have to shout.'

'You're all talk and you'd be dead before you shouted,' Patrick said in a flat whisper.

'A man was found hanged in the nick a few days ago,' King said. 'Did you hear about that or don't you ever read the bloody papers or switch on the TV?'

'I heard about that,' Patrick acknowledged.

'He helped me with the Harmsworth job and was just about to tell the story to the cops.'

'You went in the nick and killed him?' was the astonished question.

'Not me, no. That would have been too risky. I had a snout who worked in the canteen. He fed me all the gossip, stuff he overheard them talking about. He was a good boy and badly needed money after losing on the horses. Funny, it was tips I gave him too. He was quite happy to string up a little rat for a bonus. His problem was that he kept asking me for more. Got a bit shirty about it. So he went for a little swim in the river. Pity, really; the bugger couldn't.'

Patrick stood up. 'No, I've decided that I'm not impressed after all. A cop's car goes off a bridge and you – some shitty little hotel-keeper – are the big mafioso who killed him and then got rid of his helpers. Crap. You're a liar.' Turning to me he said, 'Let's go home.'

King shot to his feet. In doing so he must have pressed a hidden alarm button, for the door burst open and four armed men ran in.

'It's your last chance!' King shouted. 'D'you want in under my control, or not at all?'

'Balls,' Patrick said. 'You're a complete amateur.'

I reckoned he had red-ragged the bull quite enough, gambled on King not wanting a full-blown shoot-out within the hearing of what were presumably ordinary members of the public and proceeded to scream the place down.

King rushed over to silence me; I endeavoured to kick him in the very last place he would want that to happen, but my skirt was too tight, so I only got him on one knee. I fled and we commenced to play dodgems, he limping, around the armchairs and sofas with which the room was lavishly provided. Out of the corner of my eye I could see that the men had moved in on Patrick with a view to bludgeoning him to the ground with their gun butts. A deadly ballet ensued during which he floored two of them but the others cornered him, only stopping short when they saw the knife in his hand and he sprang the blade. They backed off.

'Shoot the bastard!' King bellowed, lunging at me again.

I shied like a horse, spun round and clumped him across the throat in a fashion guaranteed to silence and then was knocked flat by someone in full flight in reverse who had decided to disobey his order and save his own skin instead. Someone else made a weird squawking noise – of terror, probably. Seconds later I was yanked to my feet. They did not appear to touch the ground until I was outside the door.

'Run!' Patrick said – quite unnecessarily, as it happened.

Pursuit was right behind us.

We tore down the corridor and very quickly found ourselves in the main foyer, where there were several people, including a rotund man who had just entered through the swing doors and now jigged this way and that attempting to bar our way.

'Hey, hey!' he bawled over our heads. 'Hey, Rex! D'you know this man's a cop?'

It was Theodore du Norde.

As innocent bystanders fled, he got his revenge, aiming a kick at Patrick when he had been overwhelmed by at least eight of them and lay on the floor. It took him on the side of the jaw and he became very still.

Except for a bouncer-type who had hold of me by one wrist, Sapphire had been overlooked. I twisted free and in a moment I shall remember with mixed emotions for the rest of my life slammed my fist right into the middle of du Norde's pudgy, grinning face. The impact of the blow tore right up my arm; agony in my hand came seconds later,

279

but I was avidly watching the way his nose had gushed crimson, all the way from his mouth to his chin.

Then someone must have hit me, for everything went black.

Fourteen

How sad, I thought, for us to die in a ditch, really or metaphorically, after all we had achieved together. What a shame that the reconstruction I planned to write of Derek Harmsworth's last days would remain an author's flight of fancy even though murder would probably be confirmed once the DNA results came in. His killer would get away. Brocklebank would sell up and leave the country, no one suspecting that a man in receipt of a couple of million pounds for a thriving hotel business was the local linchpin of serious and organized crime, just the kind of person SOCA had been set up to deal with.

I was shut up in some kind of darkened room, tied down to what was probably a bed, some tape across my mouth. Even though I was blindfold the cloth was not very tight and by looking down my nose and moving my head I could see a strip of light that seemed to be shining through underneath a door. My head and legs were the only parts of me I could move, but I kept quite still for a while as every time I did a wave of nausea swept over me and I was terrified of choking to death with my mouth covered should I vomit. My right hand was pure agony and felt swollen.

Where was Patrick? Was he here? Already dead? By not drawing his gun for fear of innocent people being wounded or killed he had risked his own life.

Some indefinable while later, perhaps minutes, perhaps hours, I tried wriggling downwards, finding that by pressing myself into the mattress my bonds – thickish rope – became quite loose. Then something gave way altogether, it all went very loose and, moments later, with what was left of the bindings under my chin, I was almost free.

Sitting on the end of the bed seconds later, forgetting, I nearly screamed with pain as I tried to remove the cloth from around my eyes with my right hand, so yanked it off with the other, on the verge of tears. Then I dealt with the tape over my mouth.

Groping, and not daring to fumble for light switches with my sound hand while keeping the other protectively close to me, I carefully explored my immediate surroundings. I was convinced that I was still in the hotel. The tiny strip of light shining underneath the door helped slightly; at least it prevented me from blundering into the larger items of furniture such as an armchair and the other bed in what was a twin-bedded room. No one was lying on it.

I came to a door – a bathroom? If so, and if this was indeed a hotel room, would a light come on automatically and an extractor fan start up if and when I opened it? Hesitating, I leaned against the wall feeling sick, muddle-headed and very weak, the whole of my right arm aching. Finally, desperate for a drink of water, I opened the door. No automatic light, no fan.

Mostly by feel, I ran the cold tap, almost dropped a glass beaker in my clumsy haste and then filled the basin and gratefully immersed my right hand. I was convinced I had broken some bones in it, but after a couple of minutes the pain subsided a little. I discovered that I could move my fingers and thumb without any horrible stabs of agony.

To call the police, or Greenway, had to be the next priority.

I went over to where I could just make out a window and carefully peered through a chink in the curtains. I saw that I was on the second or third floor of a modern extension that had to be situated at the rear of the older building, of which I could just see a corner. Below me was a car park – not the one where we had left our vehicle. There were hardly any cars in it, tall lamps starkly providing illumination and the whole area resembling the desolation around a derelict factory. King – Brocklebank – probably used the business for money-laundering and in that sense it was a factory.

The two opening windows were locked, so there was no point in further wasting time on them. I went to the door, tried the handle as a matter of course and, astoundingly, this was not locked, proof that whoever it was who could not tie knots had been in a hell of a hurry to leave.

I opened the door and a quick glance left and right down the lighted corridor outside told me two things: first, the time – it was one fifty in the morning; and second, that while the lifts were to the right, the stairs were in the other direction. I have a theory that crooks, being basically lazy – too lazy to earn an honest living anyway – always use the lift.

I pushed the door almost closed and retrieved my bag, which I had spotted on the chair. My mobile phone had gone, of course, as had the keys for the hired car; but my purse was still there, complete with money and credit cards. All I had to do was find a public phone. Did hotels still have such things?

Closing the door as silently as possible behind me, I made for the stairs. There was no sound but my feet on the carpeted floor and the distant hum of air-conditioning units. Still feeling dizzy and sick I found it impossible to walk in a straight line and kept hitting the walls. Hopefully, any hotel guest who saw me would think the lady drunk. I had absolutely no intention of throwing myself on the mercy of any strangers I met for fear of them being part of the whole crooked set-up. But I saw no one.

The stairs were reached through double doors, which seemed to be surprisingly heavy, but I leaned my whole weight on them and finally got through. I would now have to be exceedingly careful or would tumble down them and that would be that.

Somewhere below and in the distance a man screamed.

Such was the shock of the ghastly, raucous sound that, standing on the top step, my legs almost gave way. Desperately I clung on to the handrail for a few moments and then took a deep breath, hung the strap of my bag around my neck to leave both hands free, whispered a little prayer and started to go down.

There had been a sort of echo in the cry, as though it had emanated from an area with plain or bare walls. A storeroom on the ground floor or in the basement? A kitchen or laundry room?

I carried on going down, my feet reluctant to be placed securely on the treads, always wanting to slip over the edges. Under my breath, I swore at them – swore at everything to do with this cursed place, cursed it to hell.

The man screamed again, in desperate agony.

Somehow, forcing myself to stay focused on what I was doing when all I really wanted to do was cry and beat my fists on the walls, I reached the ground floor. The stairs carried on descending, but uncarpeted, and there were more double doors off to the right with a 'STAFF ONLY' notice on them. I pushed my way through and stood quite still, listening. There was not a sound, not even of distant voices. In a small side room were vacuum cleaners, laundry trolleys and a row of pegs with overalls hanging on them. I took one and slipped it on over my dress. Hardly a real disguise, but at least it stopped me feeling so shivery.

Then, exercising extreme caution, I peeped though the door that led into the public part of the hotel, immediately realizing that I was a matter of twenty yards from the private lounge to which we had been taken. The lights were dimmed now. Then a shadow came into view as someone approached from around a corner and I shot back through the door and into the cleaners' store. But no one came; whoever it was must have walked by and not come this way. I went back and looked again and the corridor was deserted. Then, gathering myself together, as it were, I went as quickly as I could to the door of the lounge. This was do-or-die stuff, literally, as for all I knew King might be in there with his entire contingent of henchman. I had a purpose – unless, that is, my judgement was as seriously impaired as my co-ordination.

Ready, if necessary, to endeavour to flee in the direction of the main entrance, I went straight in. All was in darkness, but I felt for, and found, light switches and flicked them down. The room was empty. I went over to the writing desk I had previously noticed at the opposite end of the room to where we had been sitting and, one-handed, started yanking out and raking through the drawers. The first few, side drawers, were empty, but the large top one contained papers, writing materials, a wad of money and several old newspapers with certain paragraphs marked with a highlighter pen. The other side yielded a cashmere sweater, a miniature bottle of whisky, two glasses and several boxes of cigars. Then I saw it, under my nose all the time: Patrick's knife lying on the gold-embossed red leather by an antique pen tray.

No Glock, though, my real objective.

No time to search any more.

As I went back, my legs still refusing to obey orders to the letter, and had reached the top of the uncarpeted stairs, the scream rang out again. I glanced at the knife in my hand, the blade hidden inside the silver handle, the work of an Italian craftsman, the object I had always hated, refused to touch, knowing what it had done. It features in all my nightmares and represents the part of Patrick that I have always refused to think about.

Not any more.

The vital need for caution and silence steadied me and I went slowly down, holding on tightly to the rail with my left hand, the knife, heavy, tactile, perfectly balanced in my right, the pain just about tolerable. A cold draught of air came up to meet me, bringing with it a smell of gas. Then I heard voices.

The stairs went down to a small and gloomy cellar-like area, the only light coming from somewhere off to the left. I peered around and saw a long straight corridor, doors off to both sides, all seemingly closed, a single bulb in the ceiling providing the illumination. Round to the right more stairs descended, these being stone and worn. A very faint light from below shone on the risers as they twisted down in a spiral out of sight.

Voices again.

I removed my shoes, something I realized I should have done before as I instantly felt I had better balance, abandoned my bag with them and began to go down. There were no handholds here, so all I could do was touch the wall for support. It was cold and clammy as though the stone was sweating. I was sweating too.

The stairs went down and down and as they did and the area opened out, the wall disappearing on the inner side, the light became brighter. Seeing a floor looming up below me, I crouched low to look in case someone spotted my feet but could only see more stone walls. I reached the bottom. There was a strong smell of gas here.

Ahead of me was what had obviously been the cellars of the old manor house. These did not appear to be particularly extensive, although the light I had seen shining up the stairs did not penetrate all that far and was actually coming through a window set high up in a wall and a door, which was ajar, around to my right. Aware that people were very close by, just on the other side of the door, I tiptoed up the stairs again for a short distance to see if I could lean over and look through the window. In real danger of losing my balance and toppling into the stairwell beneath, I did so.

A museum-piece of a Victorian kitchen lay before me, reduced to authentic sepia tint by the filthy and cobweb-laced glass through which I was observing it. A cast-iron range, tables, dressers, shelving, gas stoves, even pots and pans – everything dust-covered, it was all there. This otherwise domestic scene was marred by the fact that a group of men – I could recognize the one calling himself Rex King despite the dirty glass – were utilizing it as a torture chamber.

As I watched, someone threw most of the contents of a bucket of water over a man who was tied, naked to the waist, face up on to the largest kitchen table. Patrick jerked, shuddering, and then coughed and spluttered as he was given the rest of the pailful in the face. King then leant over him and I saw his lips move as he said something. He received a spat-out mouthful of water right between the eyes.

They burned Patrick again on the stomach with what looked like a glowing piece of metal and again he cried out.

With the same kind of murderous detachment that had taken me over when I had punched Theodore du Norde I darted down the stairs, into the room and swept my hand up all the ancient metal light switches on the wall just inside the door. Instant and utter blackness. Men raved and swore and crashed into things and, in the darkness, having planned my exact route – not a direct one by any means – I sprang the blade of the knife. Holding it in front of me, reasoning that anyone who got in my way would spit themselves on it, I went my circuitous route to the big table. The smell of gas was really strong in here.

There was one bad moment when I went full tilt into the side of a dresser, but the layout of the room was in my memory as clearly as a photograph and the next time I encountered a solid object it was the table. Left-handed, I succeeded in locating the first two ropes, which were secured around the table legs, and cut them – the knife was awesomely sharp – then someone groped for and grabbed my other arm and twisted it.

When the man she loves is being tortured

and someone who is directly or indirectly responsible then lays hands on *her* and hurts her badly, a woman really can stab whoever it is with a real desire to kill. I felt the blade grate between ribs and then the weapon was almost torn from my grasp as the man collapsed at my feet.

Ducking beneath the table, which I had been half-leaning against while all this was going on, I felt for and found the two remaining ropes and sliced them through. The floor was wet and slippery and I almost fell over as I stood up again. Thinking that I would have to assist Patrick in some way, I discovered that the table had been vacated in almost the same second that we collided face to face. It had to be him, as he had no shirt on. I ran my hand down his arm and pressed the knife into his hand.

'Remind me to buy you some flowers,' he said, kissing me quickly and slightly off course on one eye.

The lights came back on.

Patrick threw the heavy wooden table over on to its side with a crash. It must have landed on at least one set of toes, as there was a roar of pain and a nearby honcho went down like a skittle. Another hopped away on one leg before overbalancing and going headlong. That was all I could take in before I was hauled down behind one of the ancient freestanding gas cookers. Two shots banged off it and there was the loud hiss of gas, the reek of which was now quite sickening.

Jinking desperately, we dodged past another cooker, one of the jets of which was alight, the kitchen fork with which they had been burning Patrick glowing in the flames. In passing, Patrick succeeded not only in turning the gas up full blast but in tossing on an old cardboard box he scooped from the floor as well. Ages-dried, it blazed up.

We shot into the first opening in the wall that we came to, bullets whanging into the wall around our ears, decided against entering any of a row of walk-in larders which yawned darkly and malodorously before us and made for a door at the end of a short passageway. It was locked and bolted, but the key was on the inside. Patrick opened it, removed the key and locked it behind us and then we saw that before us was a long flight of stairs. Fuelled by will power alone I followed him up them, but we had to stop for a few moments halfway up, Patrick weak and gasping for breath. People started to shoulder-charge the door we had just come though. We climbed on and came to another door – this one was not locked – and emerged into fresh air. Several yards away a man appeared from the darkness.

'Going somewhere?' called Rex King, adding, 'I knew you'd come this way.'

He was alone and now approached us to lounge against the wall of a lean-to building of some kind that we had entered. It was open at one side, fronting on to a yard. He motioned with the gun in his hand that we were to stand to one side.

The door at the bottom of the stairs was still holding.

I started to obey the instruction while observing that Patrick had his right hand behind his back and a quite crazed look in his eyes. Another sideways glance told me he had begun to follow my move and then he side-stepped, and with that classic sideways sweep of his arm, threw the knife.

The gun clattered to the ground, the blade having gone into King's wrist and out through the other side.

Patrick went up to him, King gawping with shock.

'If I pull it out you'll probably bleed to death,' Patrick said. 'I'd actually rather have it back right now too.'

'You wouldn't,' King choked.

'I would,' Patrick whispered. 'For Derek Harmsworth, John Gray and everyone else you've murdered. What have you done with DS Erin Melrose?'

'Nothing,' the other protested. 'Who's she?'

Patrick took hold of the haft of the knife.

'God, I haven't touched her!' King howled. 'We – we just gave her a little tap on the head when we found her snooping around in my private apartment. She's in room number 89 – quite, quite all right.'

Patrick pulled out the knife and King, Brocklebank, the bastard, fainted.

'I didn't think it had punctured any major blood vessels,' Patrick muttered, gazing clinically at the wound.

From deep within the building there was a thunderous bang. The door behind us blew open and a shockwave like a volcanic eruption hit us. There was a revolting smell, like a burnt stockpot. We jumped to one side just in time as a huge dust cloud poured out. In it, judging by the sound as they landed on the ground, were fragments of glass.

I did not care if Brocklebank bled to death. 'Are you OK?' I asked Patrick, stupidly I knew, seeing, as he came over to me, the burns and the bruise on his jaw livid in the half-light. No, of course he wasn't OK, swaying on his feet and half off his head with pain.

'You're the one with the black eye,' he pointed out with the hint of a smile.

In MI5 days we got used to the hand-wringing and teeth-gnashing of policemen – especially our friend DCI James Carrick – following our efforts to apprehend lawbreakers, often, I agree, resulting in some collateral damage; but, strangely, Michael Greenway proved to be an exception. He did establish to his satisfaction, there and then, before he would even permit a medic, or anyone else, near Patrick, that a jubilant King had stressed to him that there was no one left in the hotel above the old cellar kitchen who could come to his aid and, potentially, have been killed in the explosion. Greenway also ascertained for himself that the accommodation section had indeed been well out of range of the subterranean blast, as Patrick insisted to him that it was, and I did not hold this mild ruthlessness against him: I could understand it. Nor did I mind – and the timing of all that followed was not Greenway's fault – when the SOCA man dashed off, upon learning of her incarceration, to release Fred Knightly's errant Detective Sergeant from her room 89 prison. He appeared with her, wanly on his arm, just as the press arrived, having broken through some kind of cordon; and before the more responsible sections of the media reported an accurate account, although not mentioning our names, Greenway was credited with having raided the place, 007-style, single-handed.

'But *how* did you manage to turn most of the gas taps on without them noticing?' I asked the real perpetrator.

It was quite a while later that night and Patrick had been dosed, his burns dressed and had found his jacket, shirt and tie, not bothering with the latter. And right now, fresh from making a statement, he was rewarding himself – and Greenway, who he had just spotted coming in – with a very large tot of exceedingly expensive single malt from the hotel bar. All guests had been evacuated and there were so many police and firefighters in the place it was like Harrods' January sale.

'There were only seven of his mobsters left upright by the time they got me down to the kitchen,' he replied, putting down the tumblers on a table and sprawling on a sofa. 'Of the first four who came into the room we were taken to I put two out of action for long enough, another ran off never to return and I managed to lop off one of the fingers of his chum, who I understand is in hospital having it sewn back on before being arrested.'

'Indeed,' said Greenway, seating himself. 'Cheers. The bastard owes us a few of these.'

All I had wanted was a glass of cold water. While awaiting Patrick's reappearance I had endeavoured to repair, one-handed, some of the personal ravages of the night's work in a ground-floor ladies' cloakroom, and then exerted huge charm on a young fireman, who went down and found my dust-covered shoes and bag for me. There had even been time for a short nap on a sofa in a lounge next to the bar.

'I came round on the stone stairs,' Patrick was saying. 'It's difficult to carry someone in a cramped place like that and one of them was going backwards holding my feet.'

Greenway bellowed with laughter, knowing what was coming.

'So a shove here and there and a bit of

yanking and overbalancing and suddenly everyone went down a lot quicker than they'd anticipated, me somehow on top with a fairly soft landing. By this time Brockle-bank –' Here he broke off and looked questioningly at Greenway.

'Yes, it's him all right,' Greenway said. 'Several scars, old bullet wounds, made identification easy.'

'Good. Anyway, Brocklebank was raging; I played dead after we'd all bowled down the stairs and the ones without concussion or broken ankles hauled me into the kitchen and left me on the floor, then had to listen to a tirade from him telling them how bloody useless they all were. It went on for quite a while and I started to crawl back towards the door, getting up on my knees to turn on, just a little, every gas tap I could find. There were several at the sides of the room on water boilers, an old copper and a row of hotplates. Brocklebank didn't really stop shouting. Then they realized I was getting away.'

'What did they want to know?' I asked. I am a writer; I could put flesh on the bones of his account, insert what he was omitting, see the mindless brutality, witness the kicking, hear the shouted obscenities.

'Whom I worked for, where I was based, what I knew, police tactics on serious crime – all that kind of thing. I didn't tell them and made a lot of noise hoping someone would hear me.'

'I did,' I said. I could still hear his screams.

'I'm all right,' he said, succeeding in giving me a big smile this time. 'Honest.'

I said, 'Several people witnessed that fracas just inside the entrance. What on earth were they told to prevent them from calling the police?'

'Someone did,' Greenway said. 'I understand this lady wasn't sure what to do, as they'd been assured that the hotel management had already dialled 999. A squad car arrived and the crew was told the whole incident had been dealt with, having been a private argument. Apparently, some chap not connected to the hotel was punched on the nose and there was blood everywhere, but no one seems to know who he was or where he's gone.'

I owned up.

'Du Norde!' Greenway exclaimed. 'Isn't he out on police bail?'

'He tried to warn Brocklebank about us,' I said.

Greenway had caught sight of my right hand, which by now was colouring up nicely. 'Get this man of yours to show you how to use your knuckles without wrecking yourself. Du Norde's obviously another maggot in this rotten apple, then.' He chuckled. 'I reckon we'll find him in the nearest A and E.'

'I stabbed a man in the kitchen too,' I said, feeling shaky again at the memory, '– in the

298

dark. He grabbed me when I was trying to cut the ropes tying Patrick to the table.'

Greenway surveyed me keenly. 'Have you made a statement?'

'No, so far no one seems to think I was involved to that extent.'

He said, 'There were three bodies in the cellar, two burned almost beyond recognition. But one seemed to have escaped the blast – it might have been because he was already lying on the floor – with a knife wound in the chest, and he's already been identified. His name was Ricky Blears. He'd been lying low since he escaped from a prison van eighteen months ago with the help of cronies, during which a prison officer was shot and killed. Blears had been sentenced to life for murdering his one-time girlfriend and her two children by pouring petrol through the letter box of their house and setting it alight. Shed no tears, Ingrid; he would have delighted in killing you too and up until you spoke it had been assumed he had died by the hand of one of Brocklebank's hoodlums as a result of mistaken identity in the dark. I think that, right now, it can be left like that.'

I suddenly realized that Erin Montrose was hovering nearby.

'I just wanted to thank you, sir,' she said shyly to Greenway after we had called her over.

'This is the man to thank,' he said, indicating Patrick. 'He blew the bloody place up and caught Brocklebank.'

'*Erin* caught Brocklebank,' Patrick corrected. 'But ask her how she did it tomorrow. Meanwhile, I suggest you take her home.'

Greenway did not appear to mind being given these orders.

Erin, it transpired, had tramped the streets, pored over records and worked long night hours in order to track down Brocklebank, but to no avail. Then, one evening, she had gone to the country hotel for a meal with her parents and, like Patrick, seen the photograph of the man calling himself Rex King. The board with staff details had apparently only been put up that week. In her view its existence demonstrated Brocklebank's utter stupidity and also his contempt for the police, and this, of course, made her eventual triumph all the sweeter. All she'd had to do at the time was prove her suspicions and for that she'd needed an excuse to go behind the scenes there – hence the job application. When she hadn't even got an interview, she'd made the mistake of using stealth but not telling colleagues her plans for fear of being prevented from carrying on. This, in a way, had been Knightly's fault for forbidding her to investigate.

I thought there was also truth in my own theory that, above all else, Brocklebank had desperately wanted admiration, especially from those he was trying to emulate, the serious career criminals. That he was now almost certainly a laughing stock in those quarters I know made Patrick's quite serious burns and the emergence of more bruises than he had anticipated a little more bearable.

'I hope Erin's not in trouble for going it alone,' I said to Patrick the next morning at our digs.

'Well, yes, she is,' he answered, 'for the simple reason that the whole thing could have ended in tears. If we hadn't found that letter, they might have been trawling for her body in the river as well of that of the bloke who worked in the nick's canteen and murdered Smith. Actually, I'm finding that one hard to swallow. Just because some guy's a nosy devil and a snout for a crook it doesn't mean he's necessarily going to commit murder for a few extra oncers. I'd put money on him somehow having sneaked *Brocklebank* into the nick, who then did the dirty deed.'

Months later, during Brocklebank's trial and under cross-examination, he admitted to the killing.

With suspected structural damage to parts of the old building the country-manor hotel remained closed. A cache of weapons had been found in Brocklebank's private apartments, and, in a safe, a considerable number of counterfeit fifty-pound notes. Thrown into a cupboard in the same room Scenes of Crime officers had come upon a collection of grim 'mementoes', possessions of his murder victims. Brocklebank had shown us Derek Harmsworth's watch, which he had put back there, and together with several other items there was John Gray's computer, smashed, a name bracelet that had belonged to the man who had worked in the canteen and whose body was soon found jammed on a weir, even an elephant-hair bracelet that was eventually traced back to Daniel Smith. This was not the first time Patrick and I have come across this keeping of trophies and, whatever psychologists call it these days, in my view those who practise it are criminally insane. Another thing to come out in Brocklebank's trial was that he used to sometimes go to the cupboard and caress and talk to the things that were hidden there. He said that they reminded him how clever and important he was.

Mad? Yes, raving mad.

Fifteen

A week later, after we had both 'got our breath back', as Patrick put it, at home and spent time with the children, we returned to Woodhill, as we felt it was important to visit Vera Harmsworth. At this stage it was not possible to return her husband's watch as it was a court exhibit, but at least we could show her a photograph of it and promise eventual restitution. We would not mention the hoard of other possessions of murder victims or the find of the clothing that had been dumped by Daniel Smith in the garden where he had worked at Buckton Manor, the bloodstains on which DNA testing had proved to be the DCI's.

Although aware that Mrs Harmsworth would learn these more distressing details when the case came to court, we also kept to ourselves the circumstances of his death. Brocklebank had confessed to the killing and was taunting those questioning him with his skill in outwitting the police, bragging how he had told Jo-Jo to lure 'the old fool' to his restaurant early one evening with promises of information. It had been simple, he bragged, to get him into a back room, overpower him and force a lot of whisky down his throat. He had then been rendered unconscious and a few hours later been driven in his own car by Brocklebank to the bridge over the motorway, where he had killed the DCI with a single stab to the neck in a manner that he had thought would remain undetected. In doing so he had bungled it slightly and been covered in blood when the knife had punctured a vein. Then, with Daniel Smith's help – he and Brocklebank went back many years, apparently, but Smith remained in ignorance of the other's new identity – he had pushed the car through the gap in the railings.

It was eventually discovered that Brocklebank had lived a double life for almost ten years and had not even told his brother how he had been squirrelling money away from various ventures, mostly illegal, but also from buying and selling property and dealing in stocks and shares. It transpired that he had then gone on to win a stake in the hotel playing poker and subsequently had gradually bought out the other stakeholders, most of whom, one imagines, saw the cut of Brocklebank's jib and were glad to take the cash and run before they became enmired in questionable dealings.

On the way to Woodhill we met Michael Greenway in London for lunch. As we might have predicted, this proved to be not a sushi restaurant, or somewhere serving miniscule works of edible art, but a pub off Wardour Street where what was on offer was home-made, the choices being steak-and-kidney pie or chicken-and-ham pie, both with heaps of freshly cooked vegetables and gallons of gravy. Patrick also can tuck into this kind of fare even when the temperature is eighty in the shade, which it was, but at least they did children's portions.

'My treat,' said Greenway expansively, going on to say, before we could thank him, 'Fred Knightly's retiring – did you know that?'

We said we did not.

'I think they call it plea-bargaining in the States,' he said with a laugh. 'OK, I'll sod off for good if you don't take me to the cleaners for my sheer ineptitude and bad practice.'

'Good,' Patrick commented.

'Are you mended?' he was asked.

'The burns have almost healed.'

'Have another week off. No, don't argue; I don't use people badly and I never have.'

I said, 'Any more news on the Giddings investigation? – although I know it's not really your case.'

'Brinkley's lot are still going ahead with the guy they've charged. He's not a well man, though; drugs have caught up with him. He's in hospital – might not even make it to the dock.'

'Better and better for John, then,' Patrick said. 'Case closed all nice and neat.'

'You really can't stand him, can you?'

'The feeling would appear to be mutual, but we used to get on fine. Starting to have his hair blow-dried seems to have affected what goes on inside his head. At one time he'd never have tolerated someone like Hicks working for him.'

'Who's soon facing a disciplinary inquiry, and that's all I know. But the man's finished in the police – especially after the business of the photo. I can't think Brinkley's going to love you any more for that.'

'I want to know what happened to Erin Melrose,' I said.

Greenway grinned. 'She got the kind of carpeting from on high that's both a reprimand and a commendation for good work. It wouldn't have looked too good in the media either, would it, if it had got out she'd been hauled over the coals? And...' Here, amazingly, he went a little pink. 'We're moving in together, actually.'

We offered them both our best wishes.

'I got a rocket from my mother,' Patrick went on to say. 'She wanted to know how I'd managed to get myself pictured on the front of the gutter press without my shirt and looking as mazed as though I'd come straight from an orgy. It took a bit of explaining.'

Fortunately, the burns had not been visible in the photograph and Patrick had had no desire to tell her of torture.

* * *

306

It was quite late by the time we had been to see Vera Harmsworth, stayed for a cup of tea, undertaken a little shopping and then, at my suggestion, attended a concert given in Woodhill Town Hall.

'Peckish?' I enquired of Patrick afterwards as we went back through the twilight to the car park.

'That means you're hungry,' he replied.

'I didn't have half a bullock for lunch.'

'What do you fancy?'

'I know where there's a fish-and-chip shop.'

It was, as Tom – the man I had met during Hicks's round-up of vagrants – had told me, almost right opposite the entrance to the park where Jason Giddings had been murdered.

'We can sit over there,' I said when we had bought a fish supper to share, gesturing to where several seats were situated, just inside the park gates.

'It's not exactly salubrious,' he demurred.

I snorted, 'Considering the places where men are prepared to drink beer, some of which are so insanitary, so *insalubrious*, both in matters of—'

'OK,' he butted in, 'there's no need to pontificate all over me. The park it is.' He added, darkly, 'I might just sell you to the highest bidder.'

I did not laugh and we crossed the road, eating chips.

We soon saw that, following the park's recent notoriety, the authorities seemed to have made a real effort to improve it. Flower beds were freshly planted and a whole corner had been redesigned with new trees and shrubs. A sign warned that a warden now patrolled regularly, while another notice announced the setting up of a Friends of West Woodhill Park Association, with a view to improving the facilities and providing a children's play area.

It was still very warm; people, young families, strolled – proof that progress was already being made. As the light gradually faded, they began to file past us in the direction of the gateway.

'Why have you brought me here, Ingrid?' Patrick asked, screwing up the fish-and-chip paper and tossing it into a nearby waste bin.

'You know why,' I answered quietly: 'to try to find Tom.'

'People like that won't come here now.'

I rounded on him. 'People like *what*? He's timid and getting on in years and has nowhere to go. Obviously, something awful's happened to him to mean that he can't even start to sort himself out. I want to talk to him. We might even be able to help him.' Into the silence that followed I said, 'Sorry, that's the second time I've bitten your head off this evening.'

'Don't apologize. I think Greenway was right insofar as we both need another week off. I shouldn't be railroading your concerns about Tom or turning my face away from the fact that a dying junkie is being dragged through the courts for a murder he probably didn't commit.'

'But Tom could have imagined the ghost-like figure.'

'Yes, he could. Scrumpy tastes wonderful but is really easy to get dead drunk on. I stopped drinking it years ago, even though they practically give the stuff away around Hinton Littlemoor.'

This is the village in Somerset where Patrick's parents live: his father is rector there.

'But let's really think about it without the distractions we've had lately,' Patrick continued. 'What *could* the man have seen? A white figure that seemed to bob about. Someone in ski gear? No, that's usually brightly coloured. Some kind of plastic mack? A white leather biker's outfit?'

An idea sort of blazed into my mind. 'An anti-contamination suit?' I said.

In the gathering gloom our eyes met.

'The sort Scenes of Crime personnel wear?' Patrick whispered. 'The things you have to put on when you watch a post mortem? Bloody hell!'

'Honor Giddings is a pathologist,' I reminded him.

He waggled a finger at me. 'So are thousands of other people. And that kind of protective clothing can be bought anywhere.'

'It's too early for Tom and the others to turn up,' I replied, quite determined this was not going to be head-bite number three. 'Shall we have a quick look at the murder scene?'

'If you like.'

There was nothing to see: this section of the park had been completely reorganized, the dell with its dreary Victorian-style shrubbery where the body had been found completely swept away. At present the whole area was little more than a building site, but there were, to my mind, very promising piles of attractive rocks and coloured gravel waiting to be incorporated into a new design.

'This might be the bin Giddings's head was found in,' I said.

'No, it's not,' Patrick replied. 'I came here with Erin. It's that one over there. And the one where his wallet was found, minus the money but still holding his credit cards and driving licence, is right on the other, southern, side of the park.'

'So one assumes his killer went that way and disposed of the things he, or she, didn't want as they passed it. According to Tom, the man who he thought might be Giddings went very purposefully in a northerly direction towards a small gate that leads out to a residential area where there are a few shops.'

I remembered something else. 'Tom himself didn't think it was Giddings's head anyway, as the hair looked different from the man he'd seen earlier. As he said, there are any number of men around this area during the early evening wearing smart overcoats and carrying briefcases. They're all coming home from working in the City.'

'Had he been for a haircut?'

'You genius!' I said. 'Follow me.'

We went back towards the gateway and then turned sharp left on to a wide walkway that disappeared through the twilight into a copse. As Tom had told me, there were a few lamps. These were beginning to switch themselves on, attracting moths. I was glad Patrick was with me as, despite the fact that work was beginning on improving this place, it still had a dark, brooding atmosphere. Perhaps, on the other hand, this was no more than the figment of an author's overactive imagination.

We seemed to walk rather a long way, seeing no one, the hum of traffic on the main road behind us becoming muted so we could hear leaves on the branches above our heads rustling in the breeze. Then, ahead, we saw a group of lights which formed a pool of illumination by a gateway. Going through the rusting wrought-iron gates, we found ourselves in a quiet street lined with terraced Edwardian houses. Fifty yards or so away to the left, where there was a junction with another road, was a group of small shops. Even from where we stood we could see that one was a barber's.

'Can't be open at this time of night,' Patrick muttered.

This proved to be perfectly true, but someone was within – a man slapping emulsion paint on the walls. Patrick tapped politely on the door, placing his ID card against the glass so it was visible from within. He got a dismissive look in return. 'Police!' he then shouted, causing a few nearby windows to tremble. 'Open the door!'

'All right, all right,' grumbled the man, letting us in with alacrity. 'No need to bring the house down.'

'We won't waste your time,' he was assured, the introductions having been made. 'Are you the proprietor?'

'Yes, I am,' the man replied. 'Ken Dailey. This was my granddad's business – been in the family all this time.'

Patrick gazed about the interior. 'It's very smart,' he commented – no empty remark as indeed it was immaculate. 'You probably know that Jason Giddings, an MP, was murdered nearby recently. Was he a client of yours?'

'Yes, he was, poor chap.'

'Did you cut his hair on the evening he was killed?'

Dailey pondered. 'Not personally. It was a Friday, wasn't it? We have a late opening on Fridays for those customers who don't want to waste Saturdays having their hair cut. There are quite a lot of them. There's three of us working flat out then.'

'So one of the others could have done his hair?'

'It's possible. I mean, we're all good at what we do – I only employ the right people and the blokes don't tend to pick and choose; they're only too keen to get it done and go home for their dinner. There are a few, mind, who have a favourite operative. Mostly the old gents. They look forward to it, a chance for a chat – lonely old souls, likely.'

'Have Woodhill police or any other police department interviewed you?'

Dailey shook his head.

'Did you contact them to report that Giddings might have been here?'

'No, because it didn't really cross my mind that he had! You should come in here on a Friday evening. It's manic!'

Patrick put a hand on the other's arm. 'Look, this is absolutely vital. Would you please contact your employees and ask them.'

'What, now?'

'This is a murder inquiry,' Patrick responded gravely.

'I thought you'd arrested somebody already.'

'It might be the wrong somebody.'

'One question before you phone,' I said. 'Please don't be offended, but was there any particular reason – other than the late opening – why an MP would walk quite a long way across a park after he'd got off a train, take a taxi to the Green Man and then go all the way back again afterwards just to have his hair cut *here?* There are a couple of up-market gents' hairdressers in Woodhill High Street.'

'Oh, it was because of something that happened quite a while ago. He was cycling to get fit around the country lanes near his house – getting it in the neck from his doc, apparently, about being overweight. He fell off and bashed his head – blood everywhere. I just happened to be close by, taking the dog for a walk, and phoned for an ambulance. A lady brought out a blanket from a nearby cottage and we covered him up. We didn't know if he'd fractured his skull, you see, so didn't dare touch his head other than gently trying to staunch the bleeding with some kitchen paper. Then, when he'd been taken off to Romford hospital, I took his bike home and told his wife. That's all. Anyone would have done the same. He'd asked my name and where I lived and a week or so later he came in the shop with a couple of bottles of bubbly and said he'd have his hair done here from then on. I think he enjoyed the walk through the park, but if it was raining he'd get a taxi.'

'This was all on a very regular basis?' Patrick enquired.

'Every three or four weeks. He hated his

hair starting to look untidy.'

'Say what you like,' I whispered to Patrick when Dailey had disappeared to somewhere in the back of the shop to phone, 'but Honor Giddings must have known he was planning to get his hair cut before going home. *That* was why he was late.'

'What – and she popped out, ostensibly to look for him, ambushed him on his way across the park, indulged in a bloodbath and then went calmly home and entertained people to dinner? That's straight out of a crime novel.'

'Shall we carry on and find Tom?' I suggested smoothly. 'Then it might be a good idea to talk to Fiona, Honor's sister.'

'Honor loathes her.'

'Quite.'

'Hit the jackpot first time,' Ken Dailey called a minute or so later, his head around a door. 'Bob cut his hair. D'you want to talk to him?'

Patrick did so but learned little more – only that the MP had been one of Bob's clients some time after the normal closing time of six. When pressed to try to remember more exactly, the man could only say that he thought it might have been at around seven but could not be sure as they had been so busy. Giddings had not wanted a taxi, commenting that the fresh air and exercise would do him good if he walked across the park, but he would get one from the Green Man to take him home.

'I've asked him to call in at the nick and make a short statement,' Patrick said when he rejoined us. He then thanked Dailey and we left.

While this conversation had been taking place I had leafed back through my notebook and now paused under a street lamp to get my facts right before speaking. 'A taxi driver dropped Giddings at the Green Man at five forty-five. That means that if he didn't get to the barber's until sevenish, he must have gone in the pub for a drink, or three, before crossing the park. We've just done it and it's about a fifteen-minute walk, perhaps twenty from the pub. But Honor said she expected him between six and six thirty. I reckon that would have been his normal, non-haircut-day time. Dinner parties are usually timed at something like arrival at seven thirty for eight, so if he hadn't been waylaid he would have still got home in time to have a quick wash and brush-up and change – that is, provided he got a taxi fairly quickly.'

'You're wooing me on this theory,' Patrick murmured.

By the time we got back to the main entrance of the park there were indeed a few hunched figures on the seat farthest away from the lights, but opposite to the fish-and-chip shop. I placed a hand on Patrick's arm to signal to him that I wanted to go on alone.

'Is Tom here?' I asked the group of four quietly as I approached.

'Tom who?' grunted a man.

'I don't know his surname. We met when the police were rounding people up recently. I want to thank him for helping me.'

'And what the 'ell were you doin' gettin' trapped by the filth then, lady?' This was spoken in tones of utter disgust and disbelief.

'I was living rough to look for my husband, who I thought was doing the same thing.'

Another figure shuffled out of the darkness. 'Yes, it is Ingrid,' he said. 'But I only know from your voice.'

I said, 'I want you to know that the policemen who was in charge of rounding you all up that night was arrested.'

'Yes, I heard someone turned up,' Tom said. 'We'd all made ourselves scarce.'

'He was arrested by that man over there. He's my husband and we're trying to ensure that the right person goes on trial for killing the MP. Tom, will you talk to him – tell him what you told me?'

'I – I can't.'

'Look, he was in the army too. He'll understand and you can talk to him man to man. I'll go away.'

'You *tell* her where to go!' shouted the man who had first spoken. 'We don't need you to go crawling to the filth.'

Tom painfully drew himself up to his modest height. 'I shall decide what I do, thank you, Lanny.'

'Pathetic old git!' the other jumped up to bawl in his face, 'with your fancy talk and posh airs!'

'It's called an education,' Tom retorted doggedly.

'Go on, then! Sod off! But take one step over there and ya don't come back. They're both filth and you'll be filth and we won't want ya!'

'In that case,' Tom sighed, 'I don't think I want you people either.' And he began to walk over to where Patrick stood, about thirty yards away.

Lanny moved to go after him.

I said, 'I've kicked you in the goolies once already. Don't make me do it again.'

I too walked away, knowing that I was as safe as houses.

'Well, I'm sunk now,' Tom was saying, half to himself, when I caught up with him. 'They only really tolerated me because I was the brains.' He glanced at me sideways. 'Not that I would want you to think I'm boasting.'

'Come and talk to Patrick,' I said.

'That was my father's name. Is your Patrick Irish too?'

'Only sometimes.'

I kept my word and sat on another seat out of earshot, aware that I was probably in for a long wait, old soldiers tending to witter on endlessly nothwithstanding. Half an hour later I was still there. The homeless men had drifted off, coarse laughter following a remark of Lanny's as he had leered in my direction.

And, of course, Tom was now our responsibility.

I need not have worried; there was no dilemma and the solution was nothing to do with the police, SOCA, or anything of that ilk. Patrick pulled strings: a phone call to a retired very senior officer in his own regiment, the one-time Devon and Dorsets, who was closely involved with a charity ensured that Tom could be taken to a hostel run by the charity and the Royal British Legion, there to be helped in every way possible. But he had had to give an undertaking that he would remain there for the present, as he might have to appear in court as a witness.

'I can't give you money,' Patrick told Tom as they got out of the car at an address near Tower Bridge, 'because if I do and the defence lawyers get to hear of it, they'll make it look as though I bribed you to tell a tall story. But you won't need cash – you'll be looked after.'

They went into the building, Tom by this time quite bemused and almost speechless with what was happening to him.

'I feel we've sort of filed him,' I said when

Patrick returned, '– used him and parcelled him off, pigeon-holed him.'

Patrick turned on the fan of the air-con to maximum in an effort to clear the car of reminders of our passenger and said, 'Right now that's exactly what he needs: to be able to switch off in a secure environment. He's lived on his wits for over fifteen years after coming out of prison – something to do with drink-driving, after which his wife threw him out and the house was repossessed – is at the end of his tether and almost broke down as he begged me to help him. He has lice, thinks he has some kind of VD and has been having severe pains in his chest. Next winter would have been the death of him. Anyway, thank God for those who are prepared to help ex-servicemen like Tom, for I'm damned if the Ministry of Defence does.'

There had been a choke of anger in his voice as he had uttered these last words.

'What was he able to tell you?'

'Nothing much more than he told you: a white figure bobbing about. But quite slim, so it could have been a woman.' He smiled at me in the semi-darkness. 'So how do we find Fiona? We don't even know her surname.'

'We can't ask Honor, as she'd realize we were checking on things.'

Patrick turned the key in the ignition. 'Woodhill nick must know the whereabouts of du Norde by now. Let's ask them.'

'He might tell his mother.'

'It's a risk we'll have to take. But I can't imagine she'll be on speaking terms with him after the trouble he's been in lately.'

But mud *was* thicker than water.

Sixteen

Du Norde, it emerged, was at home nursing a broken nose having been released, again, on police bail. There had been witnesses to his part in the attack on Patrick, in particular the woman who had phoned the police and her husband. Unfortunately in his case, it is not illegal to be an associate of a criminal, so any shady connection du Norde might have had with Brocklebank would have to be investigated. We also discovered on visiting Woodhill police station that Knightly had already departed on gardening leave – causing some chuckles, as he apparently lived in a fifth-floor flat – and a super had been sent in from the Met to sort everything out.

Patrick phoned du Norde, aware that any personal visit at this stage would make him open to accusations of police intimidation by someone who would relish making trouble. He made no mention of recent events, merely requesting the information. I could make no sense of the strange honking noises I could overhear on the other end of the line, but Patrick seemed to be coping with the tirade and said nothing but 'Thank you,' at the end of the call.

'He's going to bring charges of assault against you,' he said. 'As you probably noticed, I ignored that remark.'

'And Fiona?'

'One Fiona Kettering-Huxley. She lives at Sunbury-on-Thames and in no circumstances are we to call round tonight, as she and her husband Quentin are throwing a big bash, as it's their twenty-fifth wedding anniversary.'

'Perfect,' I said.

'Yes, that's what I thought. Let's party!'

'I can just see that great big booby sitting at home with his nose stuffed full of cotton wool, sulking because he's not been invited.'

'You know, you really are quite nasty sometimes,' Patrick reproved me. Then he barked with laughter.

We had an address, of sorts, but no directions and ended up by slowly driving past large houses with gardens that backed on to the river, looking for more lights and parked cars than might be normally expected. Ending up with three possibilities, we chose the *least* likely to call at and ask first on the grounds that it appeared to be a muted and tasteful affair – something told me that Fiona was neither – the other two having distant beat music. We did not intend, necessarily, to announce our presence for a while.

'The Kettering-Huxley's live at the green-

and-white house with the white Roller,' Patrick reported when he returned. 'Personally, I'd prefer to get myself into the do here – a string quartet thrown in for good measure.'

'They're probably disinfecting the doormat right now,' I told him.

'No, they weren't like that at all – charming, in fact.'

By this time it was quite late, just before eleven. There was just room to park one more car in front of the house, but we ended up beneath one of the trees that overhung it, a giant willow, its graceful branches enveloping the vehicle in splendid camouflage. At either side of the building there were gates in the same style as those at the entrance – wrought iron with gold-painted finials – all of which were open. The thumping music and the sound of voices flowed towards us on a light breeze, bringing with it that reedy, muddy, river smell.

Passing the white Rolls-Royce, we walked down the left-hand side of the house, the lights in every room we went by blazing, the beat getting ever louder, and emerged into the garden. Here the sound, muffled before by buildings and trees, really hit us. I could feel the ground jumping under my feet. And the group? Was it Ragin' Rats? Roast Hog and the Wombats? I had not the first clue.

On the lawn, the boundaries of which were impossible to determine, was a large marquee connected by a short covered walkway to a conservatory, dazzling strobe lights inside the tent throwing the shadows of the crowd within, some dancing, on to the canvas sides. Twenty or so other people, couples and a woman cuddling a bottle for company, swayed and jigged outside on the grass, which was strewn with burst balloons and the remains of party poppers. Quite a few souls were flopped on to seats, some asleep, or perhaps dead drunk.

'It's like a bloody battlefield,' Patrick observed, of necessity, loudly.

For our day in London we were quite respectably attired, the author, for once as she usually lives in trousers, in a summery floral dress. A waiter must have thought we fitted the scene, for he hurried forward with a tray with glasses of champagne, safely circumnavigating a couple who suddenly emerged from nowhere and who were seemingly not of this world at all. Purely in order to blend in with the proceedings we helped ourselves to a drink – purely.

'I'm starving,' I said, having to repeat myself, almost shouting, before Patrick heard what I was saying, the music having upped it to plane-crash decibel level.

'Woman, you've been eating your head off all day,' he bellowed in his best parade-ground voice.

Unsurprisingly, the waiter overheard. 'The buffet's indoors, madam,' he shouted. 'Please help yourselves – hardly anyone else has.'

'You're trying to embarrass me and raiding the nosh is not ethical,' I yelled to Patrick when we had strolled away for a short distance.

'Yes, but you should know me by now, and it's quite ethical to go indoors to search out the hostess in order to ask her a few questions,' he bawled back.

'What, and our bounden duty to fortify ourselves on the way so we're in top professional form when we find her?' I shrieked.

'You have it in one!' he roared, taking my arm and quick-marching me towards the house.

Wide French doors on the conservatory stood open and we went in without going too close to the entrance to the marquee as, at this stage, we did not really want anyone to see us. It was not my sort of conservatory at all, being carpeted and lavishly furnished. The lush-looking plants, including orchids, were made of silk. I found myself comparing it with the interior of Brocklebank's country-manor hotel and have a theory that only the bad or incurably lazy can't, or won't, nurture living plants, but this is probably quite, quite wrong.

We went through another set of French doors. The buffet was laid out on long tables in a room within, more waiting staff hovering hopefully. The spread was truly awesome: cold meats, whole salmon, lobsters on beds of ice and other seafood, every kind of salad, cornucopias that had hardly been touched. A man and woman, who had just replenished their glasses from a large bowl that contained what looked like punch, gave us haughty looks and went outside.

'Is Mrs Kettering-Huxley indoors, do you know?' Patrick asked the room at large, having closed the inside doors after them to make some kind of conversation possible.

'She's probably in the marquee,' someone answered. 'Something to eat, sir?'

'Thank you,' Patrick said absently. 'You wouldn't happen to know if Mrs Kettering-Huxley's sister's here too? – Mrs Honor Giddings?'

They did not.

At which point the doors he had just closed sort of fell open again and a woman tottered in, bringing a huge blast of Ragin' Rats, or whatever, with her.

'Fiona, *darling*!' Patrick crowed, rushing forward to steady her before she fell flat on her face.

The woman – fair, fat, fifty and remarkably like her sister in facial features – stared at him and then, after a pause, slurred, 'I'm looking for Quentin. But you're not him, are you? He's uglier than you' – she struggled to focus her gaze – 'much uglier.'

I went forward and shut the doors again. Ye gods, it was turning into one of those farces performed in village halls.

'Oh, for God's sake have something to eat!' Fiona cried, gazing about. 'It's all spoiling and although I'm bloody rich I can't bear it when good food goes to waste. It's Adrian's fault. The idiot brought what he referred to as recreational goodies with him and now just about everyone's spiffed, spliffed, splatted – I don't know what the hell it's called – snorting this and smoking that and no one's eating.' She put both arms around Patrick's neck and gazed up into his eyes. 'I do like a drink, you lovely man, but I don't do drugs and I'm going to chuck Adrian in the river when I find him. Get me some bubbly, there's a good boy.'

Patrick glanced around swiftly and then steered our hostess through a doorway into what turned out to be a dining room. Lowering her reverently on to a Chesterfield, he gave her the drink that I had just obtained from one of the serving staff, causing a few smiles as I popped a tiny vol au vent into my mouth at the same time. It seemed important to get some food inside Fiona too before she passed out completely – and this was not just cold-bloodedly wanting her to stay awake so she could be questioned. I was feeling sorry for her – her special night ruined by the odious Adrian and her undeserving guests.

In the end I fetched supper for all three of us, giving Fiona things she could manage with her fingers, and for a few minutes she did not say anything, hungrily eating. Out-side, the music thumped on.

'God, I feel better for that,' Fiona said at last. 'Who did you say you were?' she asked Patrick, squinting at him.

He told her, exactly.

'But...'

'Sorry,' Patrick said, 'but I've never been particularly conventional.'

She gave him a rather lecherous smile. 'You can come and be unconventional all over me – any time.'

'And Ingrid's my assistant,' Patrick went on.

Yes, I did appreciate that he could hardly wrong-foot the woman at this stage by say-ing that I was his one and only that he had recently well and truly rogered on a chest of drawers.

'So what does the Serious and Whatsit Whatsit Agency want with me?' she asked, baffled.

'We're not satisfied that the person Wood-hill police have charged with Jason Gid-dings's murder is the right man.'

'And...?'

'We're exploring new lines of enquiry and thought you might be able to clarify a few things about the family.'

'Nest of bloody vipers, you mean. God, what a brood. Is there any more bubbly?'

'I'll get you some in a minute,' Patrick promised. 'I understand you don't get on with your sister.'

'I never have. But we rubbed along until she played around with a medical colleague and Cedric divorced her. Cedric was an architect, a lovely man – a real gentleman. He was gutted. Oh, God, I do still feel weird after all.'

'But we gathered from his son that the reason for the break-up was another woman in *his* life.'

'Well, Theo would say that, wouldn't he?' Fiona snapped. 'The bloody mummy's-boy creep. Not my words – Cedric's. No, as usual, Theo lied.' She swayed a little. 'For God's sake get me another drink – it'll do me good.'

Patrick nodded to me and I played the waitress again.

'Jason couldn't stand Theo either,' Fiona was saying when I got back. She thanked me for the drink and then, with a heavy wink, said, 'I bet your boss-man can't keep his hands off you, eh?'

I refrained from calling her a lewd old cow on the grounds that she was three-quarters canned and we had business to do, merely smiling politely.

'After he got over Mummy marrying again Theo seemed to think Jason was his meal ticket for life,' Fiona rambled on, spilling some of the drink over her Frank Usher sequins. 'Honor never says – not that we communicate, but ... Do you know, I went

330

round to see if I could do anything to help when Jason was murdered; I really thought it was a good opportunity to bury the hatchet and be sisterly and all that crap, and she showed me the door. Seemed to think I'd only turned up so I would get my picture in the papers!'

'What doesn't Honor say?' Patrick enquired.

'What?'

'You started to say, "Honor never says – not that we communicate...".'

'Oh.' Fiona thought hard. 'Yes – I know. About Theo. I think he's in trouble with the law. He has funny peculiar friends. Knocked around at a club place in Woodhill that always seemed to be full of men in shades whispering in corners. Quentin took me there once – never again.'

'Did you like Jason?' Patrick wanted to know.

'He was AC–DC, wasn't he? Or, at least in his youth. No, I didn't like him – bit of a toady, if you ask me – and if the truth were known Honor didn't either. She once said to me when we were teenagers that if you want to get to the top you have to make sacrifices. As it happened, Jason was the best she could snare. The silly woman should have realized he was real bargain-basement stuff before she tied the knot. He would always have been a shitty little back-bencher.'

'Do you happen to know whom she had

331

the affair with?'

'Yes, but there's not a lot of point in my telling you, as he was killed two years ago in a car crash. She has a thing about medics – used to collect them like stamps before and, come to think of it, after she met Cedric. He was the odd one out, from that point of view.'

'Is there a chance she didn't stop collecting after she married Jason?'

'Leopards don't change their spots, do they?'

'In your certain knowledge?' I asked.

Fiona was still having trouble focusing her eyes. 'Are you allowed to ask questions?' she said waspishly.

'Yes,' I told her. She was more like her sister than she knew.

'I have no knowledge of anything. But a friend told me recently she was having it away with someone on the quiet. She said she didn't know who it was and it was only gossip on a grapevine.' Fiona swayed again. 'Look, get me some coffee, would you? I need some badly.'

But when I got back from this latest errand she was fast asleep on the Chesterfield, Patrick having just prevented her from pitching on to the floor. We turned her over so she would not choke if she vomited and left, going through the house and exiting through the front door.

'No,' Patrick said as we were getting into

332

the car. 'I think I should tell someone where she is and what kind of state she's in.'

'If you can find someone sober enough to understand a word you're saying.'

We went back. All was much as before except that those still vertical were progressing indoors, presumably for something to eat. Moving between them, we went into the marquee. It was a rather splendid affair, the interior lined with draped silky fabric, chandeliers hanging from the 'ceiling', massed flowers.

Patrick went straight over to the hi-fi system, failed to find the off button and yanked out some leads.

Silence.

'That's better,' he said. 'I'm looking for Quentin.'

'You've found him,' said a tall, slim man wearing a bright-red waistcoat. He disentangled himself from a scantily dressed and seemingly sleepwalking maiden, who promptly folded up like an ironing board on to the floor and stayed there. 'Who the hell are you?'

There were a couple of other phrases added to these short sentences that I have not included.

Patrick tied a complicated knot in the leads he was holding and pulled it tight before answering. 'Passers-by. We came to tell you that some blokes are trying to break into the cars.'

The predictable consternation broke out and everyone but the girl on the floor and a youth sprawled over a chair ran out, shouting the news. Quentin Kettering-Huxley went to go too, but Patrick detained him with a hand on his arm.

'One moment, please.'

'Let go of me!'

Patrick produced his ID. 'You didn't really want to talk to the law in front of everyone, did you?'

For this he got another torrent of obscenities.

'The more you swear at me the more awkward I'll get, and if I become really annoyed you might just find yourself down at the police station,' Patrick told him. 'We've been talking to your wife in connection with the Jason Giddings murder investigation. I came to tell you that she's had far too much to drink and is now unconscious on the Chesterfield in your dining room.' He smiled like a shark, adding, 'And I've just decided that I'd like to ask you a few questions too.'

Consuming an excess of alcohol reveals a person's true character. On the few occasions in my younger days when I over-indulged I got a bit out of hand, laughing and crying, whereas my velvet-hand-in-iron-glove husband, who has not *quite* retired from such lapses, becomes truly maudlin and soppy. This man had had a lot to drink and standing before us, swaying very slightly, his mouth pressed into a hard thin line, white with anger, he did not present a pleasant picture.

'You can fuck off, *cop!*' he spat, wrenched himself free and hurried from the tent.

Patrick went over to the youth, who was showing signs of life, and said, 'Are you Adrian?'

'God, no, he's a right bastard,' said the other weakly but sounding really hurt, peering up at him groggily through a mop of blond hair.

'I'm sorry. Tell me: do you know what Quentin does for a living?'

'Of course. He's a surgeon – gastro-enterologist or something like that.'

'This is getting quite, quite fascinating,' I commented as we were making for the car through the crowd of predictably puzzled party-goers.

'I appreciate that your imagination's running amok with the thought that it's Quentin who Honor's having an affair with and one or the other of them killed her husband, but there are plenty of other medics in the sea, you know.'

'It's the sort of super-bitch thing she'd do,' I countered.

'I thought you'd come to the conclusion that she wasn't too bad after all.'

'No, I'd just decided she wasn't going to be the stinking red herring in my next novel.'

'That's promotion,' Patrick sighed. 'Any

ideas, then, how to go about proving all this?'

Patrick was buttonholed by a large man wearing a tartan suit. 'Say, where did you say these guys were?' Like nearly everyone else he was swaying on his feet, a phenomenon that was beginning to make me feel seasick.

'You probably scared them off,' Patrick said soothingly.

'Well, we sure didn't scare off Quentin – but he's high-tailed it away in his limo.'

'Which way did he go?'

An arm waved. 'That way, out of town.'

Patrick grabbed a stray hand and wrung it. 'God bless America, sir. Now, do go and carry on having a good time.'

'Gosh, thanks.'

We discovered at a later date that he was a senior diplomat with the Canadian Embassy.

'Shall I drive?' I offered.

'You usually say that when you want to go somewhere I might not.'

'I reckon he's panicked and gone to The Chantry.'

Patrick pulled a wry face. 'Ingrid, that really is a shot in the dark. But if you're right, is he the kind of man to do that?'

'No, not normally, but his judgement's affected by alcohol and you're bloody scary.'

'I'll drive,' he decided.

Seventeen

Kettering-Huxley had been clearly unfit to drive and I expected at any moment to see flashing blue lights ahead at the scene of an accident involving his car. But nothing like that occurred and a little over an hour later, after a fast journey on comparatively clear roads – it was farther than I had thought – we approached the village of Beech Hanger. Patrick cut the headlights as we neared the Giddings residence and parked in a lay-by some fifty yards from the end of the drive.

'I reckon we're only about ten minutes behind him,' he observed. 'That's if he's here.'

'We forgot to book somewhere to stay,' I said.

'It won't be the first time we've slept in the car.'

The sky was lightly overcast, the moon nowhere to be seen but clearly in a phase that meant that the sky was not wholly dark. The trunks of the group of birches just inside the gateway of The Chantry stood out like white poles and we paused among them for a few moments in order to scan our surroundings. It was impossible to see any parked cars from here: the house was concealed by more trees. Moving over to the right to walk in the darker shadow beneath a hedge, we carried on. I stayed a short distance to the rear of the one-time special-services soldier: my role now was to follow and remain as silent and alert as possible, the latter mainly because he would sometimes stop without warning to listen and scent the air like an animal. Then we heard a car. It was slowing.

'Down!' Patrick whispered.

The twin beams of the headlights swung over our heads as we crouched low by the hedge and then picked out the ornate brick chimneys of the house as the car came over the slight rise at the entrance to the drive. The vehicle sped on and out of sight, and almost immediately the front of the house was lit up, presumably by security lights.

'Any idea who that might be?' Patrick said as we cautiously stood upright again. 'Impossible to tell what colour it was in this light – or get the reg. Was it a Clio?'

I said, 'There was a yellow Clio parked outside the apartments where du Norde lives.'

'But they're girlie cars.'

'And your point...?'

He chuckled softly and we moved off again.

Only a matter of a few yards farther on we had again to dive low as a car approached.

'God, it's Kettering-Huxley,' Patrick said.

'He must have used side roads, hoping not to be stopped and breathalyzed.'

We carried on along by the hedge and quickly came to where the trees and shrubs screened and sheltered the house. Bending low we went through and between them, pausing before emerging on to the gravelled area at the front.

It is difficult to walk on gravel without making any noise and we had no intention of doing so, if at all possible. Nor did we wish to cross the brightly illuminated open space before us. Backing a little into the greenery, Patrick then led off, again to the right, until we came to a boundary wall. With me still in his wake we followed it. The cover petered out into a fernery, but by this time we were just past the corner of the house, out of sight of the front windows.

By a quick flash of Patrick's little torch we saw that the gravel here, a narrow path, was more compacted than that at the front, with moss growing on it in places. Slowly and carefully we went on, the boundary wall a high blackness on one side, the house on the other. We came to a lighted window and bent low so as not to be seen. All within the house was silent – not even the muted sound of a radio or TV.

'Does Honor live here on her own now, do you know?' I whispered when we paused for a few seconds.

'No idea.'

No, I should not have broken his concentration. I bit my tongue hard, repressing a giggle – definitely one of my MI5 failings.

Then, unmistakably, somewhere inside the house a door slammed. Patrick stopped again, fractionally, and then went on. We came to a widening of the path which split into two, one branch going off sharply around to the left, the other, in another quick flash with the torch, seen to lead into a courtyard with outbuildings.

Cautiously rounding a large shrub of some kind, we saw before us a sunroom extension. It seemed to stretch along most of the rear of the building and was lit by several table lamps. No one appeared to be occupying it. Presumably there was a door to the garden, but it was not visible from where we were standing.

'Voices,' Patrick breathed, '– raised voices.'

I listened and could indeed hear a man shouting – but well inside the house, not in an adjacent room. He sounded ferociously angry. Was anyone indoors in actual danger? Did we have grounds to enter? Patrick moved off again and I rather took it that we had.

Openly, we approached the sunroom, immediately seeing that the doors to it did lead straight out into the garden but had been hidden from our view by long curtains. A quick glance through one of the windows showed that nobody was in sight. A flight of three steps led up to the sliding doors and, as it was now the early hours of the morning, surely, I thought, they would be locked.

They were, but this was not a modern construction and the lock was a simple affair. Patrick peered through the keyhole to see if the key had been left on the other side, but apparently not, and it was a matter of a few seconds' work with a strong wrist and his set of skeleton keys to open it. The door slid open easily without squeaking.

Parting the curtains we went in, closing the door behind us. We could now hear every word of what was being said, or rather yelled, but those involved were not in the next room but somewhere nearer the front of the house. We stood quite still, positioning ourselves one on each side of the door that led into the next room, a rapid peep revealing a square hall with a low, beamed ceiling and a carved wooden staircase. I guessed that this was part of the original, oldest part of the building.

'For the last time will you get out!' a male voice shouted, almost certainly Kettering-Huxley's. 'We don't need you here. You're a complete pain in the arse – always have been – and I couldn't care a bloody toss if you're hanged, drawn and quartered tomorrow. Sort out your own grubby dealings with small-time gangsters.'

'I just thought that if I could stay here for a few days the police might not—'

There was no mistaking those honking tones.

'Are you deaf? Go! Get out before I throw you out!'

'Quentin...'Honor's voice began.

'I know what you're going to say, Honor. Diddums has a broken nose. By his own admission a woman hit him. That lady must pack quite a punch. She deserves a medal and if I meet her one day I'll give her one.'

'She knocks around with the cop who interviewed me at home,' du Norde went on grimly. 'He rang me tonight and wanted to know where Fiona lives. That's—'

'And you told him, I suppose.'

The hooting went up an octave. 'Did I have a choice? You haven't met this man. He'd have come round again and taken me apart. But I did tell him that there was the party at your place tonight and he wasn't to intrude.'

There was a short silence and then Kettering-Huxley said, 'But, wait a minute. I have met him. That's who it must have been who gatecrashed. He'd been in the house and grilled Fiona.'

'So you drove all this way for what reason?' Honor asked coldly.

'Well, I suppose I panicked when he homed in to question me too. I decided you and I needed to talk.'

'Your judgement being razor-sharp on account of having drunk a skinful of booze. You're a damned fool to drive in this state.

342

Just think what would have happened if you'd been stopped by the police. Your reputation would have been in ruins and I shouldn't imagine Her Majesty would have wanted you to be her new surgeon then.'

'That's all you bloody well think of – climbing the social ladder.'

'Quentin.' Honor said warningly.

'Oh, so you're shacking up with him now,' du Norde piped up, and I realized that he had been drinking too.

'I am not shacking up with anyone, as you so revoltingly put it!' Honor shrieked. 'Do as he says and leave!'

'Is that it?' her son blared. 'He divorces Fiona, you both get married and you've swapped a no-hoper back-bencher for some-one who'll soon be toadying at court. That would figure.'

'Get out!' Honor screamed.

'And for all I know it was you who did Jason in. That would be your style of nasty temper too. I remember when you went for that cleaning woman with a knife once and cut her arm quite badly because she broke your favourite vase. It was all hushed up and she was given a hell of a lot of money to leave and keep quiet about it. So what was Jason doing to annoy you then? Or was he just in the way? God, the more I think about this the more it all fits.'

There was the sound of a scuffle.

'A real scandal?' du Norde carried on,

struggling to speak. 'An affair? Something a bit more sordid? Going back to one of his old boyfriends? Was that why he was in the park that night?'

More sounds of a struggle.

'You know, I've a good mind to go and and find that cop and tell him what—' Du Norde was forced to stop speaking again and there was a heavy thump.

I looked at Patrick questioningly. He nodded in agreement and we went into the house. It was not difficult to locate them and for a long moment neither of the men noticed our arrival. Honor had disappeared – I supposed out through another doorway in the room.

It seemed fairly obvious that Theodore du Norde had fallen backwards over a footstool as Kettering-Huxley had carried on man-handling him in an effort to physically eject him from the house. Du Norde, still lying flat on his back on the floor, took one look at us, scrabbled on to his knees and with a speed incredible for such a big, bulky man, crawled towards us.

'For God's sake help me,' he babbled. 'My mother's having one of her tempers and she's gone to –' He glanced over towards the door and uttered a loud wail.

'So she has,' Patrick whispered. Then, louder, 'Mrs Giddings, I strongly suggest you put down that knife.'

The woman appeared demented, her eyes

glassy, her teeth bared in a terrible rictus like a silent snarl. In her right hand was a large stainless-steel carving knife.

'Honor!' Kettering-Huxley shouted. 'What the hell's got into you?'

'Everything I plan for is ruined by idiots!' she screamed. 'My whole life has been ruined by idiots!'

'She gets like this sometimes,' du Norde moaned, scuttling on hands and knees to come and hide behind me. 'Oh, God, she'll kill me too!'

Honor advanced on the pair of us. 'In answer to your question, Theo,' she said in a low, dead voice, 'Jason *was* about to go and live with one of his boyfriends, a particularly slimy individual who runs a chain of betting shops and whom I understand is a criminal. I don't know in which particular sewer they met – I don't care – and I damned well fixed it that he wouldn't!'

'You said you fixed it with a contract man!' Kettering-Huxley said, staring at the knife, clearly appalled.

'Well, I didn't!' Honor screamed. 'I fixed him *myself*!' She had turned the knife so the blade was now pointing towards her stomach, holding it two-handed.

'Please calm down and give me the knife,' Patrick said.

But Honor curled over slightly, straightening her arms before plunging the blade towards her body.

Patrick leapt forward and grasped both her wrists. My vision greyed when the woman shrieked, thinking he had been too late, and for a never-ending moment the two remained locked, as it were, in counter-effort. Then Honor's legs gave way and with a dispairing cry she slumped to the floor. I still thought she had succeeded in seriously injuring herself and went to her.

'Get away from me, you bitch!' she yelled, getting to her feet, at which point any sympathy I had for her ran bone dry.

'You're under arrest,' Patrick told her. He handed the knife to me and I took it and held it by the blade, hardly hearing the rest of it.

'... to say anything, but it may harm your defence if you do not mention, when questioned, something which you later rely on in...'

'Oh thank you,' du Norde was burbling at me from the floor. 'Thank you, thank you.'

I really thought that, had I tossed him a dog biscuit, he would have eaten it.

Eighteen

Had she really meant to kill herself? Perhaps we would never know, but the rages that she was prone to, and vented on others, a trait that had only manifested itself in the past five years or so, were not in doubt – something that would emerge during her and Kettering-Huxley's trial. But no one would ever know what had possessed her that night to drive to the park, ostensibly to look for her husband, having fully prepared herself not with the tools of her trade but with that same kitchen knife, plus another smaller one, and butcher him. On her return to The Chantry the knives had been rinsed and placed in the dishwasher, the plastic anti-contamination suit, together with plastic bags she had worn over her shoes, screwed up tightly and burnt in a Swedish woodstove in the hall.

The two had already planned to do away with Giddings, with the help of a contract killer who would make it look like an accident. What had made Honor decide to kill him herself? It would transpire on the evidence of the housekeeper, Hilary, that her employer had been in a black mood all day.

Also, Honor had discovered only twenty-four hours previously, from Jason himself, that he intended to leave her. But nothing could be proved as to whether he had indeed meant to leave her for a man and this was strongly denied by his parliamentary colleagues, a couple of whom did, however, know that he intended to seek divorce from Honor. Had he found out about the affair with her brother-in-law? I could imagine a situation where a man, at the end of his tether because of spiteful rages and adultery, would retaliate by shouting all kinds of outlandish things.

Discovery of all this was in the future, though, and after following the area car conveying Honor Giddings to Woodhill police station, where we completed the formalities of handing her over, we left. By this time it was three in the morning.

'Just the hour to tell Brinkley, that renowned head of a branch of a branch, His Twigship, that we've solved his case for him,' Patrick said, having consulted his watch.

'You might be storing up trouble for yourself again,' I warned.

'The wise oracle speaketh,' he murmured, punching in numbers on his phone and obviously on a high. 'And the crazed fool heedeth her not and sinneth mightily. And lo, the heavens opened and bolts of fire were hurled upon him until just his boots, which smoketh and – Hello, John you old rogue.

That was quick. Expecting a call were you? ... Oh, just got to bed after a hellish night. Well, we both know how it is – never off the job...'

I strolled towards the car. As had previously occurred to me, this was going to run and run.

A few weeks later there was an article in the *Sunday Telegraph*'s supplement about a new project in Woodhill, at the Benfleet Centre. The gardens, which were far more historically important than I had realized, were now in the latter stages of being restored and, following publicity and work done by the Trust's education officer, new applications for the allotments were being received, including for the first time some from ethnic minorities. People had apparently also been inspired to grow their own food by watching television gardening programmes and there were so many keen would-be vegetable growers that it had been decided to use part of an old meadow, at present still down to grass, in a new scheme.

'That's Esme!' I exclaimed, seeing a photograph of some new allotment holders – ladies – posing with their forks and spades.

Patrick had just come into the living room and looked over my shoulder. 'So it is.'

'You had nothing to do with this – or did you?'

'No, nothing.'

'I don't suppose Evian will want to dig and rake.'

'He might be too tired. Sorry, it had slipped my mind. The first day I trawled around Woodhill with the mugshot of Brocklebank I got talking to the local vicar – there was always the chance that he'd seen him around the town. I asked him what was available for young people to do in the area and he told me that the diocese, together with various other organizations, was setting up a sports club, which was opening very shortly. I phoned Esme and asked if she wanted me to put Evian's name down and he was mad keen and shot off to see all his friends where they lived before to get them involved as well.'

'That's wonderful,' I said.

He followed my gaze. 'What are you looking at?'

'I've been wondering if we could move that chest of drawers somewhere more private.'